# BLOOD RED, WHITE AND BLUE

*A Selection of Titles by Kathleen Delaney*

*The Mary McGill and Millie Series*

PUREBRED DEAD *
CURTAINS FOR MISS PLYM *
BLOOD RED, WHITE AND BLUE *

*The Ellen McKenzie Series*

DYING FOR A CHANGE
GIVE FIRST PLACE TO MURDER
MURDER FOR DESSERT
MURDER HALF-BAKED
MURDER BY SYLLABUB

* *available from Severn House*

# BLOOD RED, WHITE AND BLUE

*A Mary McGill Dog Mystery*

## Kathleen Delaney

This first world edition published 2017
in Great Britain and the USA by
SEVERN HOUSE PUBLISHERS LTD of
19 Cedar Road, Sutton, Surrey, England, SM2 5DA.
Trade paperback edition first published
in Great Britain and the USA 2017 by
SEVERN HOUSE PUBLISHERS LTD

British Library Cataloguing in Publication Data
*A CIP catalogue record for this title is available from the British Library.*

ISBN-13: 978-0-7278-8689-7 (cased)
ISBN-13: 978-1-84751-809-5 (trade paper)
ISBN-13: 978-1-78010-873-5 (e-book)

*All Severn House titles are printed on acid-free paper.*

Severn House Publishers support the Forest Stewardship Council™ [FSC™],
the leading international forest certification organisation.
All our titles that are printed on FSC certified paper carry the FSC logo.

MIX
Paper from
responsible sources
FSC    FSC® C013056
www.fsc.org

Typeset by Palimpsest Book Production Ltd.,
Falkirk, Stirlingshire, Scotland.
Printed and bound in Great Britain by
TJ International, Padstow, Cornwall

# ONE

Mary McGill, her cocker spaniel Millie tight by her side, stood in the middle of the bandstand in Santa Louisa's city park and watched the last of the costumed dogs depart. It had been an exhausting and exasperating morning.

Judging the best canine costume for the Fourth of July dog parade had turned out to be a diplomatic nightmare. Even though there were different categories, there weren't enough to satisfy all the people who had turned their dogs, big and little, into Statues of Liberty, George Washington, Martha Washington or rebel soldiers. They'd pulled carts, been decked with blinking lights, had tri-cornered hats attached, and one poor dog represented the fife and drum corp. At least, Mary thought the thing attached to his mouth was a fife. It was certainly a drum that hung from his neck, banging his legs with each step. She'd thought for a moment that John Lagomasino, one of the other judges and part-owner of the Furry Friends Pet Shop, was going to jump over the judging table and remove it, but his partner, Glen Manning, stopped him just in time. John had to content himself with mumbling uncomplimentary things about the owner under his breath while crossing the dog off his list of possible prizewinners.

But it was over and the next events didn't start until four. Those were scheduled for the large regional park just outside of town. Fireworks would start at nine. In the meantime, she and Millie, her uncostumed black cocker spaniel, could go home. Lunch sounded good. So did a glass of iced tea. It was hot, even for July. She picked up Millie's water bowl, emptied it over the side of the pavilion and tucked it into her tote. 'Let's go,' she told the dog.

Millie seemed more than willing.

They cut across the park and crossed the street toward the shops that faced it. There were a number of people out walking in spite of the heat, several with their dogs, and Millie had spotted one she wanted to greet. Stub of a tail wagging, she headed for a German shepherd who sat beside a tall, gray-haired man staring intently in the window of Lowell's Jewelry. Mary would have walked on by but Millie had other ideas. She pulled Mary up to the window and touched noses with the shepherd.

Mary sighed. 'Good morning, Ranger,' she greeted the dog then smiled at the man. 'Nice to see you again, Mr Miller. I thought you and Ranger were on your way to Pismo beach.'

He smiled politely at her then looked impassively at the dogs, who were still nose to nose. 'We were, but I heard it's foggy and cold over there. Thought we'd stay and enjoy your lovely town for another couple of days.'

'I hope you like heat then. We're supposed to be over one hundred today.' She glanced in the shop window, curious as to what had caught Mr Miller's eye. A new necklace piece held the place of honor. 'How lovely. Jerry Lowell must have made that. He does make the most beautiful pieces. I've never understood how someone can take something as clunky as a gold ingot and turn it into something as delicate as that pendant.'

'It takes a lot of skill.' Mr Miller turned once again to stare at the beautiful filigree piece. 'That sapphire is an old one and the diamonds are rose-cut.' He glanced at Mary. 'That means they're old as well. Georgian. You don't see them very often. But the necklace they're set in is new. Very innovative and very well done.'

'Yes.' Mary glanced once more at the piece, wondering how he could tell the sapphire was old and what rose-cut meant, then looked down the street toward home, iced tea and air-conditioning. However, rushing off might seem rude. 'Are you coming to the fireworks? I think we're going to have a spectacular display this evening. The Grady Brothers are local but have a great reputation for their pyrotechnics. We're lucky to get them. I know they had offers of jobs from as far away as Washington State. This year they decided to stay home.'

Mr Miller frowned. 'I'd really like to but I'm not sure I want to leave Ranger alone in a motel room. He's not too fond of loud noises.'

'Why not take him to the Benningtons' vet clinic? Pat and

Karl Bennington are offering free board this evening to people who are worried about their dogs and the fireworks. So many run away if not someplace safe. Millie's going.' She glanced at her dog, who stood beside Ranger, evidently exchanging pleasantries. 'I have to be at High Bluff Park about four. I'm chairwoman of the committee responsible for putting on today's events and it's going to be too hot and crowded and noisy for her. She won't like being kenneled much but she'll be safe and so will my sofa pillows. Call them. See if they still have room. Tell them Ranger's a friend of Millie's.' She grinned. 'That should get you a spot.' She set her tote bag on the sidewalk, pulled a notepad out of her purse and jotted down the phone number. 'Ask for Pat.'

Mr Miller took the paper, pulled a wallet out of the inside pocket of his perfectly pressed chambray jacket and slipped it in. 'I'll do that. I've heard about the Grady brothers and I'd like to see the fireworks. Thanks.'

Mary took another look at the necklace, collected her tote and gathered up Millie's leash. 'I hope to see you there. Oh. Bring a chair or a blanket or something. It's going to be packed. And there will be food booths as well as wine and beer. Also lemonade and water. Every organization in town has a booth so you won't starve or go thirsty.'

With a brief wave, she and Millie started back down the sidewalk toward home and iced tea.

# TWO

The last chords of the '1812 Overture' rang out, cannons roared, the sky was bright with a fiery America flag and the crowd cheered. Another Fourth of July celebration had come to an end. Chairs were folded, babies put back in strollers, ice chests closed and people headed for their cars by the hundreds.

Mary gave a sigh of relief. It had gone off without a hitch. At least, not one she knew of. The Lions had won the annual softball game, the Sweet Adelines had kept the crowd entertained for some time and even old Mr Bentwood had participated in the square dancing. All in all, a successful day.

She walked, not without difficulty, through the departing crowd toward the podium and the two men packing up their sound equipment. They had more computers, speakers and music players than fireworks, she'd decided, but the show had been wonderful.

'Heath, I can't thank you and Gabe enough. That was the best fireworks show we've ever had.'

The tall, usually dour-looking man pushed back his sweat-stained cowboy hat and smiled a rare smile. 'It came off pretty good, if I do say so.'

'It was better than pretty good. Thank you so much.'

Another tall man, younger, with an infectious grin, joined them. 'One of the best we've done. I've been working on getting those cannons to line up with the big bursts and tonight it came off perfect. Glad you liked it.'

'It was spectacular.' Mary paused and looked at the mess of equipment then back at the men. 'I've got your check made out but it's locked in my car. I can go get it or I can bring it out to your place tomorrow.'

Heath Grady took off his hat, ran an arm over a sweaty brow and replaced it. His brother handed him a water bottle and he took a long drink. 'We'll be a while yet packing all this up, then the fireworks. If it's no trouble, tomorrow would be great.'

Gabe popped the top off a water bottle for himself and nodded. 'Can't get to the bank tonight anyway. Sure you don't mind? Or I can come into town – well, not tomorrow, maybe the next day . . .'

'I'll bring it out tomorrow midday sometime. Do you need any help? There are still people here, the cleanup crew, some others . . .' She was stopped by the vigorous shaking of two heads.

'We've done this more than a hundred times,' Heath said. 'We know what we're doing and where stuff goes. People would mean well but they'd just mess us up.'

Mary took that to mean her too. They were as anxious to get finished and home as she was.

She smiled. 'See you tomorrow.' The crowd had largely disappeared. Only a few stragglers were left, along with some of her volunteers who were folding up the last of the chairs and stacking tables that belonged to the parks and rec committee and loading them on a wheeled rack that would be stored in a room behind the stage. A paneled van liberally decorated with images of exploding fireworks had pulled up onto the grass ready to take all the Gradys' equipment. She watched for a moment then glanced at her watch. She'd better hurry. Pat and Karl had said dogs could be picked up any time before eleven. Any dogs remaining after that could be claimed in the morning. Millie wouldn't be happy to spend the night in a crate. But she'd better take a quick detour through the grove of oak trees on the far side of the pavilion. It was a favorite place for teenagers to set up their chairs and coolers, out of sight of their parents and other adults. She'd better make sure everyone had gone.

It was dark in the grove. The trees filtered the light that came from the park and muted the voices of the few remaining people. The quiet was almost absolute. No birds chirped, no squirrels ran up tree trunks and there was no soft laughter of teenagers. She sighed with relief. No one was here.

She turned to go back to the still-lit park and the air-conditioned comfort of her car when she caught sight of something lying on

the grass behind the biggest of the oaks. A pile of blankets? No.
A person. Someone asleep? Or passed out. Drat and blast. Just
what she didn't need. How was she going to handle a drunk?
Or worse – a kid passed out on drugs. Should she go for help?
No. She'd find out who it was and what had happened first, then
get help if she needed it.

She walked toward the person slowly, not without
trepidation, but the figure didn't move. Did that mean . . . She
walked closer. A man lay on the ground wearing a chambray
suit jacket – one she'd seen recently, now stained a bright red.
Blood. Blood that came from a hole in the back of the jacket.
Blood that seeped from the back of the man lying there.
Mr Ian Miller. Shot dead. At her otherwise perfect Fourth of
July celebration.

# THREE

Mary sat in her big reading chair, Millie beside her. Pat and Karl Bennington were on the sofa opposite. Her niece, Ellen McKenzie Dunham, fidgeted a little in the wingback chair that sat beside the fireplace, her three-legged hound, Morgan, asleep at her feet. None of them said anything as they watched Ranger sit politely at Karl's side, never taking his eyes off Mary's front door.

Finally Karl sighed. 'I hate this kind of thing. How am I supposed to explain to this dog that his master isn't coming through that door? Not now, not ever?'

Pat laid her hand on his. 'You can't. Don't they forget after a while?'

'Some do. Some never do. I have no idea how long this dog will grieve. Depends a lot on what kind of family he has, if he has one. If it was just him and Miller then it may take a while. German shepherds are pretty smart dogs and very loyal.' He looked over at Mary. 'Do we know anything about this man, other than his name?'

Mary let her hand drop on Millie's head and ran her fingers through the silky hair on her ears. 'I don't. Millie and I met him and Ranger at the dog park only once. He said he was here on vacation, that he lived in Sacramento and he and Ranger were going over to Pismo beach for a few days before they headed home. That's about all. I saw him again today outside Lowell's.'

'Dan will know.' Ellen had been watching the dog with a worried frown. 'I feel so sorry for him. Not Dan, the dog. Although Dan won't be happy. If you're right,' she looked over at her aunt, 'and he was shot in the back, that makes it murder. Not suicide, not an accident. Murder, pure and simple.' She shuddered. 'I wonder who he was and why someone would want to shoot him. And in the back? That's so . . .' She looked at Morgan, who slept on. 'I take Morgan to the dog park a lot but I never met him or his dog.'

'When will Dan be here?' Pat asked. 'It's getting late and we have to do something with him tonight.'

'It's later than late and I have no idea. He said for all of us to wait for him here, that he'd try to get over as soon as he could.' Ellen looked at Mary's old schoolhouse clock and sighed. 'It's already one. If he doesn't show up pretty soon . . .'

The front door opened but it wasn't Dan Dunham, chief of Santa Louisa police, who entered. It was her great-niece, Susannah McKenzie, her long dark curls held back from her face with a bright scarf and her dark blue eyes laughing, followed closely by Neil Bennington, a tall, blond young man with a cowboy hat set on the back of his head, his well-washed jeans and battered cowboy boots proclaiming they were his usual costume.

'What are you all doing here so late? We saw the lights and thought we'd better check. It's been a long day and I thought . . . Hello, Ranger.'

The dog was on his feet, his tail wagging as he walked toward Susannah. She squatted down, allowing him to place a kiss on her cheek while she ran her fingers over his ears and his shoulders. 'Why are you here? Where is Mr Miller? Why . . . Oh, no. Does this have something to do with what-ever is going on at the park?'

Mary sighed. Susannah and Neil had shown up at the park tonight in time to meet Karl and Pat Bennington, Ellen and Dan Dunham and Mary for ribs and salad purchased at the Kiwanis stand. After that they'd gone their separate ways, but here they all were again. All except Dan.

'I'm afraid it does.' That was as far as Mary could go.

Susannah got to her feet and faced Ellen. 'Mom, what's happened?'

'Someone shot Mr Miller during the fireworks display.'

'So that's why the dog's here,' Neil said softly. 'Leave it to you two to think of the dog in a crisis.' He smiled at his parents, then took Susannah by the arm and pushed her down beside her mother. He perched on the arm of the sofa next to her and swung his hat off his head.

Ranger immediately started a low rumbling in his throat.

The hair on the back of his neck stood up and his body got rigid.

'It's OK, boy. I'll get rid of it.' Neil dropped his hat on the floor beside the sofa and held his hand out to Ranger, his fingers down for him to smell.

The dog examined the hand then looked at Neil and listened to the soothing voice. The rumble died away, the hair on his neck lay back down and they all relaxed.

'That dog doesn't like cowboy hats,' Karl observed. 'Lots of dogs don't like hats. They don't seem to recognize even a close friend when they put on a hat. Interesting.'

Susannah looked at him, down at the dog, then back at her mother. 'Never mind hats. What happened?'

But Ellen watched Ranger work his way under the coffee table until he faced Susannah then put his head on her foot. He sighed. So did Mary, with relief. The dog was obviously not going to attack Susannah.

'He seems to know you. So you must have met Mr Miller. How well did you know him?'

'We met him at the dog park.' It was Neil who answered. 'We've taken Morgan with us a lot since we've been home from school this summer. He's even gone on some horse-farm calls with us when we've done a ride along with Doctor Pickering. He seemed to like the horses. But what he really likes is the dog park. He and Ranger became racing buddies. Ranger fell hard for Millie.' Neil grinned. 'Guess he fell even harder for Susannah.' The grin was gone. 'How did Mr Miller get shot? Was it an accident? Is he all right?'

This time Ellen's sigh was more of a groan. 'He was murdered.'

'Mr Miller?' Susannah straightened up from petting Ranger to stare at her mother. 'That nice man? Why would anyone—' She broke off and looked at Neil as if he might have an answer.

He didn't and turned to his father. 'What happened?'

Karl shook his head. 'No idea. I'd never met the man until this afternoon when he came to drop off Ranger. He said the dog didn't do loud noises well and he wanted him to be some-where safe. He'd pick him up right after the fireworks. I guess from what Mary's said he was shot in the oak grove sometime during the display. Probably during the finale. The "1812 Overture" is pretty loud. All those cannons going off.'

'We've been waiting for Dan to give us more information,' Pat told her son. 'We need to know what to do with the dog.'

'That's easy,' Susannah said firmly. 'He's coming home with us. He doesn't understand what's happened and needs comforting. Putting him in a kennel all alone would be cruel. That's OK, isn't it, Mom?'

Mary might have laughed at the stricken look on Ellen's face if the situation hadn't been so sad. But Susannah was right. The dog needed comforting. Her hand strayed once more to Millie's head. Millie had needed a lot of comforting when her previous owner had been murdered and Mary had provided it. Ranger deserved the same.

'I don't know.' Ellen looked and sounded torn. 'Jake's just getting used to Morgan. He was an only cat for years . . . and what will Dan say?'

'Dan will be fine with it. He's a good guy, even if he is a cop and my stepfather.'

'Nice to have approbation,' Dan said, 'even if it is qualified. Which is worse, being a cop or your stepfather?'

Susannah laughed. 'Depends.'

'Oh.' Ellen was on her feet, ready to greet her husband. 'I didn't hear you come in.'

'Evidently none of you did. What is this nice guy supposed to agree to?'

'Taking Ranger home with us tonight so he won't be sad. That's OK with you, isn't it? He and Morgan like each other.' Susannah gave her stepfather her full-watt smile.

He grinned back. 'As long as he doesn't eat Jake, it's fine with me.' He looked at Ranger, who was still under the coffee table. 'Poor guy. Why is he under the table?'

'To get closer to Susannah.' There was a smile in Neil's voice. 'She has a way of doing that to guys.'

Dan grinned at Susannah, who made a face at Neil, then he slid out of his uniform jacket and hung it on the peg beside the front door. His hat went on top of it. He turned back to face the expectant faces watching him and sighed. 'I don't suppose there's any coffee?'

'No, but there's iced tea.' Ellen was on her way to the kitchen before he could respond, but since he didn't stop her Mary assumed iced tea would be acceptable.

They were going through a lot of it this hot night. She'd have to make another container tomorrow.

In the meantime . . . 'What do you know?'

'Not nearly enough,' Dan said a bit mournfully. He pulled a dining-room chair close to the end of the sofa Ellen had vacated, settled down and took a long swallow from the glass she handed him. 'Mary, how are you? That can't have been a pleasant experience.'

'I'm fine.' She wasn't as sure as she sounded. Shock did something to you, something not pleasant, and seeing Mr Miller lying there, so very dead, had indeed been a shock. What happened after she started yelling for help was a bit of a blur but one thing stood out – still did. He'd been shot in the back. 'That poor man. He was lying on his face and all that blood on the ground. That's where he was shot, wasn't it? In the back? There was blood on his jacket and it looked . . . There was a hole in it. Why would someone do that?'

Dan set his empty glass on the side table by the sofa, careful to make sure it was on a coaster, then looked around the room. 'I can only guess but Ian Miller wasn't here on vacation. He was with the California Bureau of Investigation, special crimes division, and had been investigating a series of jewelry store robberies. Evidently he was following some kind of lead. What exactly, I don't know. Makes me wonder if he found what, and who, he was looking for.'

'Oh.' The thought struck Mary hard enough that her exclamation came out as a gasp.

All eyes shifted to her.

'What?' Ellen leaned forward expectantly.

'Do you know something?' Susannah left off stroking Ranger's ears and stared intently at her great-aunt.

'No,' Mary said. 'It's just that Millie and I saw him . . . them . . . Mr Miller and Ranger in front of the jewelry store this morning, right after the dog costume parade. He was staring in the window at the new necklace Jerry Lowell made. He said the necklace was new but the sapphire and diamonds were old. Had old cuts or something. I wondered how he knew. Do you suppose he thought Lowell's was about to be robbed?'

'No idea.' Dan looked around the room, his gaze coming to rest on Susannah, then moved on to Neil. 'You two have toted Morgan around a bunch this summer. You must have met them, since Ranger seems smitten with Susannah. Where?'

'At the dog park.' Susannah looked at Neil, as if for corroboration.

Neil nodded. 'Three or four times.'

Dan glanced at Susannah then at Ranger. 'What did you talk about?'

'Dogs.' Susannah's answer was quick and emphatic. 'I told him Neil only had one more year of vet school and knew all about dogs. He was worried about Ranger's hip but Neil told him he thought he was fine. He'd be sitting crooked if it was hurting him.'

Karl turned to look at the dog, who had worked his way out from under the table and was sitting in the middle of the room, seemingly following the conversation with interest. 'He thought the dog was dysplastic? Why? Look at him. Neil's right. He's sitting perfectly straight. How old is he?'

'Four.' Neil and Susannah spoke together.

Pat laughed but Karl ignored it. His focus was on the dog. 'If he was he'd have shown signs long before this. What made him think that?'

Neil shook his head. 'I asked him. He was pretty vague – just said he'd heard it was common in German shepherds.'

Karl snorted. 'Not like it used to be. There must have been some reason . . .'

Dan barely glanced at Ranger. 'Did any of you see him tonight at the fireworks? In town, today? No? Just Mary? OK. I've got to get back. We have agents flying down from Sacramento and they'll be landing at our airport in . . .' he checked his phone then slid it back in his pocket, '. . . any time now. Ricker is meeting them but I want to be at the park when they get there. Go home, all of you. Go to bed. There's nothing more any of you can do tonight.' He put his chair back by the table, shrugged into his jacket and set his hat back on his head.

Ranger took one look at it and started rumbling in the throat.

Dan looked at the dog. The dog looked back and the rumbling got louder.

'It's your hat.' Neil was on his feet, holding the dog's collar, stroking him, making soothing noises.

Mary felt Millie tense when Ranger started to growl but her head dropped back on Mary's lap when she saw Ranger settle. Was it the hat? Did he always do that when he saw a man in a hat? Police hats were pretty distinctive. He must have seen one before. So why . . . There wasn't time to think about that right now. Dan was leaving and she had one more question for him before he left.

'Dan, you said Mr Miller was investigating a string of burglaries. How do you know that?'

He paused, hand on the doorknob. 'Miller stopped by the office shortly after he arrived in town. Introduced himself, said he was following a lead about a string of jewelry store robberies up and down the state that might be connected but wasn't sure it was going anywhere. I told him to let us know if he needed any help. He said he would. We chatted for a few minutes and he left. I never saw him again.'

'Did he say what the lead was?'

'No, Mary. He didn't. More's the pity.' He closed the door softy behind him.

Mary noticed he hadn't put his hat back on. No one said anything for a few moments, shock and exhaustion having drained them all.

Finally Karl said, 'We need to get going. The clinic still opens at nine in the morning.'

Pat nodded, stretched and got to her feet. 'Neil, you coming home or are you dropping off Susannah?' She paused, smiled and looked at Ranger. 'And the dog, of course.'

Ellen also was on her feet, staring at the dog. 'He has a lot of hair, hasn't he?' She sighed. 'Neil, would you mind dropping them off? I have real estate clients in the morning and I really don't want to have to vacuum the car before I meet with them. I'll take Morgan with me and put the cat in my bedroom before you get there so he doesn't freak out.' She dropped a kiss on Mary's cheek. 'Are you all right? Will you sleep? Susannah can stay with you . . .'

Mary couldn't think of anything she needed, or less, wanted. She made shooing motions with her hands, saying she would be fine, of course she'd sleep, she had Millie didn't she, she'd see them tomorrow, and she didn't stop until they were all on their way. Then she and Millie headed for bed. Millie was asleep before she laid down her head. Not so Mary. She stayed awake a long time, staring at the dark ceiling, wondering.

# FOUR

I t was after eight when Mary finally woke. It wasn't that she wanted to be awake but the sun was streaming in her window and Millie was sitting on her chest, nudging her with her nose and making whining noises.

Groaning a little and holding one hand on the small of her back, she opened the kitchen door, didn't pause to watch the dog shoot down the stairs and onto the grass but checked the coffeemaker to be sure she'd indeed filled it last night, sighed with relief and pushed the button. She watched the coffee drip for a moment before she opened the broom closet and pulled out the brown paper bag of dog food. It felt unusually light. She poured a scoop in Millie's dish, opened the back door to let her in and sighed. 'Not only do I not know how to get to the Grady place, we're almost out of your food.'

Millie paid no attention to Mary. She buried her head in her bowl and started to devour her breakfast.

Undeterred, Mary sipped her coffee. 'I can't believe I didn't even ask the Gradys for directions last night. I must have been more tired than I thought. Never mind. We'll stop by Furry Friends on our way back, but first I'll call Ellen and find out where we're going.'

Two cups of coffee, a hot shower and a couple of Tylenol later, Mary felt almost ready to cope. Directions on the seat beside her, wondering what had possessed her to make an offer to drive the check out to the Gradys, she and Millie headed out of town. It had been at least four years since Ellen had represented the seller on the piece of land the Grady brothers had purchased, but Ellen hadn't forgotten how to get there. She'd also said the house and barn had been falling down when the brothers bought the place and Mary was to see if they'd done anything to fix it up. If not, she didn't see how they could live in it.

Ellen's directions were explicit, down to how to recognize

landmarks instead of signs. A lot of the roads in the sparsely populated area called Paradise Valley weren't marked very well, if at all, and most weren't paved. But Ellen thought they could find it and she had her cell. Who she'd call for help if she got lost, Mary wasn't sure, but having it was comforting. She didn't get out in the real country very often and was always surprised at how undeveloped it still was, and how beautiful. Rolling hills covered with oaks, cattle grazing on what looked like very dry grass, horses eating hay out of large tubs and ground squirrels playing chicken as they tried to cross the road before Mary rolled over them. She muttered a word she rarely used then spotted the large red barn Ellen had described. She turned right and up ahead was a field gate. The sign on it said, 'Grady Pyrotechnics, private property. Trespassers will be shot.'

Hoping that didn't mean her, she got out, pushed the unlocked gate open and drove through then closed the gate. She didn't know if the Gradys kept cattle on their twenty acres but she was in no mood to find out by having to chase one down. Up ahead was a large, two-story barn. That it was old there was no doubt, the wood weathered by years of heat and storms, but it had undergone extensive and recent renovation. The green metal roof was new. So were the sliding doors and the metal-framed windows. The siding that had been replaced had been left unpainted, evidently to weather along with the old boards. It would be a while before they attained that same gray. In the meantime, the barn had a strange patchwork look. It also looked serviceable and somehow stern.

The house was a different story. It had never been much, even when new. It hadn't been new in a long time. It was also gray, but not because it had been painted that color. The original paint was long gone and the bare boards had faded to a dirty, dreary shade. The once-white trim was now mud-colored. The rotted boards on the porch steps looked dangerous and several of them were missing. There wasn't much screen left in the screen door. The contrast between it and the well-kept barn was jarring. But the house had electricity. There was a large electrical pole in the middle of the yard and thick black wires ran to the barn and to the house. On top of the pole were two floodlights – one facing the barn, the other the house. There would be no shadows in the yard when they were turned on.

The useless screen door was pushed open and Gabe Grady stood in the doorway, hand shading his frowning face. Then, recognizing Mary, he broke into a grin. 'Hi. Been expecting you. Any trouble finding the place? We're tucked back in here pretty good.'

Mary snapped Millie's leash on her harness and they climbed out of the car. Millie looked around with interest, especially at the ground squirrels, who could be seen running for cover behind the barn. 'No. My niece, Ellen, gave us good directions. Good thing. My GPS would never have found it.'

'You're right about that. Ellen. Would that be Ellen McKenzie, the real estate lady? She's your niece?'

'It's Ellen McKenzie Dunham now, and yes, she is.' Mary looked around at the fields, the spreading oak in the dirt-packed yard and the lack of any kind of landscaping. A brown pickup truck was parked under a lean-to attached to the side of the barn but there was no sign of any other farm equipment, nor did the field behind the house look as if it had been worked or grazed in a long time. 'She told me about this place when you bought it but I didn't realize just how isolated you are.'

'Yeah. It's perfect. All our fireworks are in that barn. We make some, put together all the displays and store a whole lot of stuff in there that could be dangerous. Last thing we wanted was a bunch of kids getting in there and making their own little celebration. They wouldn't have thought it was so much fun on their way to the hospital. We keep the door padlocked and the yard light on at night, and we're hard to find. Never had a minute's trouble.'

Mary believed that easily. She also believed a group of teenagers bent on creating a little trouble could be very tempted by a barn full of high-powered fireworks. She approved of the Grady brothers' caution.

'Your check is in this envelope.' She handed it to him, along with a clipboard with a form attached. 'This is a receipt, showing the check is for the amount contracted. Take a look at the check, then if you'll sign the form, I'll leave a copy with you. It really was a spectacular show last night, Gabe. Thank you.'

Gabe took the check, examined it, signed the receipt and handed it back to Mary. 'Heard there was some kind of problem last night after it was all over. Heath and I were pulling out when all of a sudden cops were everywhere. Seemed headed for those oaks trees. You know what happened?'

'Someone was shot.'

'Yeah? Who?'

'A Mr Ian Miller.'

Gabe stared at her then shook his head. 'Never heard of him. Who shot him?'

'I have no idea. He was a visitor here. I only met him a couple of times. Tall man, about sixty maybe, had a German shepherd with him.'

Gabe's eyes flickered. 'There was a guy with one of them dogs watching us set up. Just stood there, the dog sitting by his side, staring at us. He was there for a long time. Never said a word. Lots of folks watch us set up but most are full of questions. Not this guy. Made me nervous. You think that was him?'

Mary told Gabe she couldn't say for sure but she didn't know anyone else who had a German shepherd. It probably was Mr Miller. Had he seen Mr Miller talking to anyone, doing anything other than watching him?

'We were pretty busy. Like I said, the only reason I even noticed him was because of the dog. He growled at me when I took off my hat so I kept my eye on him pretty good. He stayed staring quite a while, then he was just gone. Heath noticed him, too. Said the guy was creepy.'

'Where is Heath?' Mary looked around but their white-paneled van with the painted fireworks all over it was nowhere to be seen.

'He had to meet a guy about a job. He'll be back tonight, later.'

A closed look settled on Gabe's face. He was done talking about Heath. She wondered why the abrupt change in attitude but dismissed it. It wasn't any of her business, but that Mr Miller had been so interested in what they had been doing might be Dan's.

'I think you need to tell Chief Dunham about Mr Miller and his dog. Give him a call, all right?'

'Isn't anything to tell. Just some guy we'd never seen before watching us set up, then when he got bored, he left.'

It was obvious that topic wasn't going anywhere either. Mary thanked him again for a job well done, then she and Millie got in the car and left. All the way to town, she wondered. Why would Ian Miller be so interested in how you put together a fireworks show? Maybe Gabe wasn't going to talk to Dan but perhaps she should think about telling him of Miller's interest. If nothing more, it put him on the show-grounds way before the fireworks started and Ranger was with him. She wondered when he'd dropped off Ranger. Karl would know. Did any of it matter? If Dan didn't think so – well, at least she would have done her part. They hit the pavement and she picked up speed as she and Millie headed back to town.

# FIVE

The town seemed almost as full today as it had been yesterday. But then, the Fourth had fallen on a Thursday so lots of folks had made it a long weekend. The merchants would be happy, but she wasn't. There wasn't a parking spot in sight. Maybe if she went down the alley . . .

There were a couple of ways she could enter the alley. One was off Main Street, which would put her right behind Furry Friends, her destination. John and Glen, who owned the shop, wouldn't mind in the least if she went in the back door. Or she could go down the block and cut down Elm Street. That would take her behind Lowell's Jewelry. What she thought she'd see she didn't know, but that was the way she went. Lowell's back door was dirty white and open, but the metal mesh screen door with the heavy lock wasn't. Someone was in the back room, but who she wasn't sure. However, she was sure there was no robbery in progress. Not that she'd thought there would be. She pulled into an empty parking spot in the back of Furry Friends Pet Shop, snapped the leash on a wiggling Millie and entered through the back door.

'Hey,' she called out. 'It's me, Mary, and Millie, too.'

'Come through,' a female voice answered.

Krissie, the dog groomer for Furry Friends, a tall, black woman with a head of elegantly braided hair, stood at the counter with a collar and leash in her hand, staring at the cash register. She looked at Mary with relief. The people trying to buy the dog collar looked at her, and Millie, with confusion.

'Mary,' Krissie almost whispered, 'what do I punch in here?'

Mary took the dog collar and leash, entered the proper inventory code on the register, swiped the credit card and finished the sale. Smiling broadly, she handed the woman the Furry Friends sack. 'I love that collar and leash. Turquoise and sequins look good on almost any color of dog.'

The woman beamed. 'My little Tootsie is buff-colored. She's a cocker like your dog, but smaller. I think. She'll just love it.'

'She'd better, considering how much it just cost me,' the man muttered.

They took their purchase and left, the woman still beaming, the man still muttering.

'Where's John?' Mary looked around the store but there was no sign of John Lagomasino, the owner and Mary's close friend.

'He had to step out. He should be back any minute. I told him I'd mess up if I had to make a sale but he said I'd be fine. Thank God you came in. I have got to learn how to work that thing. Maybe next time you're here, helping out, you can teach me. John goes so fast . . .' She bent down and scratched Millie's ears. 'I see she lost her red, white and blue ribbons.'

Millie wiggled with pleasure then looked around the store. A small dog in a crate in the grooming area started to bark. Millie's ears went forward and so did she, dragging her leash behind her. Mary watched her go then turned back to Krissie.

'I'll be glad to help you. It is confusing. I thought I'd never figure it out. Right now, though, I need Millie's food. You do have some, don't you?'

Krissie nodded. 'John ordered extra. He thought we'd be pretty busy this week.' She started down the aisle toward a pile of brown sacks. 'What size?'

'Might as well make it the large one.'

She slung the bag up on the counter then smiled at Mary. 'You get to ring it up.'

Mary had expected to.

Krissie watched while she put away her debit card. 'I'll take it out to the car for you but I wanted to ask . . . Was a man really shot at the fireworks display last night? John said you found him. Did you?' There was horror in her voice, mixed with hesitation.

Mary was sure Krissie didn't want to sound morbid but curiosity was a powerful thing. Besides, it was bound to be all over town. 'I'm afraid it's all true. Poor Mr Miller.'

'Miller.' The hesitancy was still there but the name meant something to Krissie. Her dark brown eyes opened wide and a soft, 'Oh, no,' escaped as she stared at Mary. 'Was he the man with the German shepherd?'

Mary nodded. 'Did you know him?'

'Not really. He came in the day before yesterday needing dog food. We got talking. He was a nice man.'

'Talking about what?'

'The town, mostly. He said he was retired and thinking about moving. Our town looked like a nice place. I said it was and told him to talk to Ellen. She'd tell him everything.'

Evidently he hadn't. At least, Ellen hadn't mentioned it. 'What else did he say?'

'He asked about downtown. Did we have a lot of new businesses? He thought The Yum Yum was new. I laughed at that one. Ruthie's had that café since Hector was a pup. I told him we had a number of new businesses – the olive oil store, some of the wineries that have opened tasting rooms in town, Miguel's Mexican restaurant. He asked about Lowell's, the jewelry store. I said they'd been here at least five years. Maybe six. Then he asked who owned the We Buy Gold shop. I told him Lowell also owned it.'

Mary blinked. Hector was a pup? That was one of her mother's favorite expressions. She never had known what it meant. 'Why was he interested in the businesses? Was he thinking of starting one?'

Krissie shrugged. 'He asked about a bookstore. I told him our only independent one went out of business because the owner got sick. But I don't think he wanted to be a bookseller. He was mostly interested in the restaurants, the wine shops and the jewelry shop. Why, I don't know.'

The jewelry shop. What, exactly, had he wanted to know about Lowell's Jewelry besides how long they'd been in business? Before she had a chance to ask, the front door opened and John appeared, chatting to two middle-aged women dressed in crop pants, T-shirts and floppy sun hats. Tourists. They thanked John and headed for the dog dishes decorated with oak trees and grape vines that had made California's central coast famous.

'Mary,' John cried, seemingly ready to embrace her. 'Are you all right?'

'Why wouldn't I be?'

'Well, you had such a long day yesterday and then finding Mr Miller . . . You're right. You're fine.' He grinned then leaned over to pet Millie, who had come running at the sound of his voice.

The doorbell tinkled and an elderly couple walked in. She was dressed in wide-legged pants in a wild print topped with an off-white peasant top with embroidery around the neck. Mary felt an almost overpowering urge to ask where she'd purchased them but squashed the thought immediately. She felt honor-bound to purchase her wardrobe at the rummage sales she ran. But she really liked those pants. Not only did they look comfortable, they looked happy. She contented herself with a cheery, 'Good morning.'

The woman smiled back. The man nodded. From the wary look on his face, Mary thought he was afraid they were about to spend some money.

'Such a cute shop.' The woman looked around. 'Oh, you have a grooming area. What a good idea. Our town has one of those pet-store chains that has one, but it's always so crowded and I never know who's going to do our little Pumpkin.'

The man seemed to wince at the name. Did the dog wince as well?

The woman didn't seem to notice. 'This town is simply darling. What a pity we have to leave this afternoon. There are several wineries we haven't visited and I haven't been in The Olive Pit – such a clever name – and I've heard so much about central California olive oil and wanted to try some. Everyone's been so nice.'

'Except the man at the jewelry store.' The man sounded almost relieved. 'He almost threw us out.' A flicker of a smile crossed his face. 'Too bad. My wife had her eye on a rather pretty pendant, too.'

A frown creased the woman's face. 'It was a beautiful piece. I'd never seen one like it before but it was an outrageous price. The man was so . . . nervous. Unpleasant. You'd think we were there to rob him or something. Anyway, we left.' The frown faded. 'But we had a wonderful breakfast this morning at that adorable Yum Yum.'

They all agreed The Yum Yum was indeed wonderful. The couple wandered off but tourist ladies appeared bearing dog dishes decorated with grape vines. John started to ring them up and Mary, Millie and Krissie carried the dog food out the back door to the car. Krissie grinned from ear to ear.

'I wonder what happened that they let Jerry Lowell out on the floor. He's usually either grousing at someone who wants to sell some gold or in the back, working on one of his pieces. He's a genius when it comes to designing jewelry but he's a failure as a human being.'

Mary wouldn't go that far but it was true that Jerry Lowell had become increasingly nervous and irritable over the last couple of years, ever since he'd opened the We Buy Gold shop. He'd never been interested in casual chitchat, nor in any of the jewelry store customers unless they had come in to talk jewelry design or something related to gems. Most wanted wedding rings, Mother's Day presents, Christmas gifts, something like that. He left them to Marlene, his wife, who Mary was told managed the business entirely. But Jerry handled the buying of old gold. She'd wondered if the strain of having to deal with people was more than he could handle. The thing that seemed to make him the happiest was making his special pieces and he had seemingly instilled his love of creating them to his son, young Tommy. But young Tommy wasn't so young any more. He'd been home from London, where he'd gone to school at a college that specialized in degrees or certificates in jewelry design and gemology for a couple of years and had apprenticed at one of London's finest stores. He'd returned, outdistancing his father in knowledge and skill. Maybe Jerry's increasingly bad temper had more to do with that than his difficulty in dealing with the people who wanted to sell him gold. She wondered, briefly, which of them had made the piece in the store window that had held Mr Miller's interest. Not that it mattered.

'Good thing Jerry's got Marlene,' she said to Krissie as she lowered the trunk lid. 'She . . .' Her cell phone rang.

'Susannah. Where are you?' She listened a moment then sucked in a breath. 'You want me to take care of Ranger? Oh, I don't know. He's a big dog and I'm not sure . . . He is too, bigger than Morgan. But I know Morgan. I don't know that dog and he doesn't know me. What if . . . Oh, all right. But where are you going that's so . . . I guess . . . now? No, that's fine.' She clicked off her phone and shook her head. 'It seems Susannah has to go somewhere right now. Ellen isn't home, Morgan's with Dan and she doesn't want to leave Ranger alone. So I'm elected.' She looked at Millie, who sat beside her, looking up expectantly. 'Well, I guess it will be all right. He likes Millie.'

Krissie smiled and patted Mary on the arm. 'He's a nice dog and very well behaved. He'll be fine. German shepherds are really smart.' She glanced at Millie and grinned. 'So are cockers. You'll be fine. But it's a good thing you bought all that food. Shepherds eat a lot.' With that, she turned and went back into the shop.

Mary sighed and opened the back door of the car. Millie jumped in. Mary got in the front and they started down the alley. She hoped Krissie was right. Taking care of a large bereaved dog wasn't something she felt prepared to handle. However, there was a first time for everything and Millie liked him. She picked up speed as she turned the corner, headed for the Dunhams' house and what she hoped wouldn't be too much of a new adventure.

# SIX

Mary placed the covered bowl of potato salad in the box she'd placed on the floor of the passenger seat and closed the door. Next came the dogs. Millie would be no problem. She loved going with Mary and would jump right in. How she was going to convince Ranger to come with her, she wasn't sure. He hadn't been thrilled when she'd picked him up. But he'd followed Millie everywhere all afternoon. Maybe he'd follow her into the car.

She wasn't sure why she was doing this except Susannah had been insistent. They were going to a barbeque at her mother's house tonight and Mary had to be there. She also had to bring the potato salad. Karl and Pat Bennington would be there, of course, and Susannah and Neil. Maybe this would be a good time to see if there was anything new on Mr Miller's murder. Dan had been away all day and she supposed he had been with the special agents from the state. She couldn't imagine what kind of person would shoot another one in the back, or why. Perhaps she'd find out something tonight.

As soon as she snapped the leash on Millie's harness she started to do donuts on the kitchen floor. Ranger watched her in seeming wonder. He politely stood while Mary attached his leash and followed her and an excited Millie to the car. He hesitated a moment then followed her onto the backseat. Mary heaved a sigh of relief.

She pulled up in front of the Dunhams' and Millie jumped into the front. She put her front feet on the side window and looked back at Mary as if to say *hurry up*. She knew exactly where she was. This was Morgan's house. Ranger didn't move. He sat straight up on the back seat, looking around but not with joy. Suspicion, or perhaps unease, seemed to fill him. Mary wasn't sure what to do. Millie she could handle. She might tug on her leash a little in her eagerness to get to Morgan but that was all. What Ranger would do, she wasn't sure. He had spent the night here but that didn't mean it was home. Would he try to run off? Could she stop him if he did? Maybe she needed help.

Help arrived. 'Are you all right, Mrs McGill?'

A young man appeared in the driver's side window, a good-looking young man whose wavy brown hair fell in soft waves almost to the collar of his polo shirt and whose brown eyes had the longest lashes Mary could remember seeing on a man in a long time. It took Mary a moment but she recognized him and immediately forgave him for the start he had given her. She lowered the window a little. 'Tommy Lowell. If you aren't a sight for sore eyes. Do you know anything about dogs?'

Ranger's face appeared in the back window and he greeted the newcomer with a deep bark.

Tommy backed up a step. 'Who's that?'

'His name is Ranger. I don't know him very well and I'm not sure I can get him and Millie into the house by myself. Can you take him? His leash is on his collar.'

Tommy Lowell didn't look as though he thought taking hold of a large German shepherd was a good idea, but after a glance at Mary he carefully opened the back door, all the time keeping it between him and the dog.

'Good doggie,' he said, hope evident. 'I'm not going to hurt you. I'm just going to take your leash so we can go inside. That's a good doggie.'

Ranger looked confused. Having someone on the other end of his leash was nothing new to him, nor was getting in and out of cars, but this tremulous cooing seemed to make him nervous. However, when Tommy gave a small tug he hopped out of the car and stood, waiting for whatever was going to happen next.

Mary got herself and a bouncing Millie out and turned to Tommy. 'I'm going into the Dunhams'. Do you mind bringing the dog in for me? Will I be making you late for anything?'

Tommy seemed to have relaxed now that he was in no immediate danger of being eaten. He grinned. 'I'm going to the Dunhams', too. Neil and Susannah invited me. They're having a barbeque.'

Mary couldn't repress a start of surprise. She had no idea
they knew Tommy. He'd lived in Santa Louisa no more than
a year before he left for England. Neil was older than him so
they couldn't have known each other from school and Susannah
hadn't gone to Santa Louisa High School. However, he had
Ranger and there was plenty of potato salad. 'Well, then, let's
get inside.' She clutched the box securely to her chest and,
with Tommy and Ranger following close behind, climbed the
stairs and opened the front door.

'We're here and I need someone to come get this box before
I drop it,' she called.

Susannah appeared, looking adorable in white shorts and a
striped tee. She took the box, greeted both dogs and smiled at
Tommy. 'Glad you decided to come. Neil owes me five dollars.'

Tommy blinked but immediately smiled when Neil appeared,
a beer in each hand. He handed one to Tommy. 'Come into
the backyard. Dad's getting the barbeque started. He declares
there's an art to it. I just dump in the charcoal and pour on
some lighter fluid and let 'er rip. Not him. He and Dan fiddle
around with it for an hour, getting it just right. We're having
hamburgers.' They disappeared out the back door, followed
by both dogs.

'Is your mother home yet?' Mary opened the refrigerator
and looked around for room for her bowl. The platter of
hamburger patties, another of corn ready for the grill, and a
plate of already sliced cheese, onions, tomatoes and lettuce
answered her question. 'She and Pat in the backyard?'

Susannah nodded and handed her great-aunt a glass of white
wine. Mary smiled and accepted it. After the last few days,
relaxing over a glass of wine while someone else cooked
dinner seemed like a fine idea. 'Where did you and Neil run
into Tommy Lowell? I didn't know you knew him.'

Color ran up Susannah's cheeks. 'We don't . . . That is . . .
we didn't but . . .'

'But what?' Mary took a small sip and leaned back against
the counter, waiting while Susannah collected herself.

She wasn't a girl who flustered easily – actually not at all
– so why would knowing Tommy Lowell, or inviting him for
hamburgers, turn her an interesting shade of pink?

Suddenly Susannah grinned. 'Come on outside. Neil and I have something to tell all of you.' She opened the refrigerator and took out two green bottles. Champagne. Next the cupboard. 'How am I going to carry . . .?'

Neil appeared at the door. 'Give me the bottles. You bring the flutes. Now that we're all here . . .' He grinned at Mary. 'Come on out. Susannah and I have an announcement.'

A cold chill ran through Mary. She knew what they were about to announce. She'd been expecting it for some time. So, why was she feeling so . . . They were right for each other. They loved each other. Their families were best friends. But they were so young. No. They weren't. Susannah would start her last year of college in the fall and Neil his last year in veterinary school. He had already made plans to set up a large animal practice through his father's clinic and help him with the small animals as well. Susannah had been assured a job teaching science at the local high school. They were the same age she and Samuel had been when they married. So, why was she worrying? Well, she wasn't going to. This was a good match and they were exactly the right age. She resolutely pushed herself away from the counter and followed Neil into the backyard, ready to toast the happy couple.

The news was greeted with delight but not surprise. Champagne glasses were passed and toasts were made. 'Tommy is making our rings. That's where we were this afternoon.' Susannah glanced at Mary and smiled. 'And, Aunt Mary, we want to use my great-grandmother's diamond. Is that all right? Grandma gave it to Mother, but she and Dan opted for plain bands. Tommy will make a new setting but I thought . . .'

Mary was thrilled and said so. Her mother would have been as well. Her great-granddaughter would wear her diamond. A testimony to family. Tommy promised to show them all the design soon and invited anyone, who wished, to drop by the shop and see the work in progress. The wedding wasn't to take place until next summer, after both graduations, so they could all relax and enjoy the engagement before the hectic preparation of a wedding started. Only Mary knew they wouldn't. The preparations, or at least talk about the wedding, would begin tonight.

A bowl of guacamole was produced, along with chips, and the conversation gradually drifted off to other things.

Dinner was over, the debris cleared away and, by tacit agreement, they split into separate groups. Ellen, Pat and Susannah began to talk about wedding gowns, venues and invitations. Dan, Karl and Neil's conversation seemed to range from dogs to baseball. Dogs interested Mary but baseball was beyond her. Besides, she was getting sleepy. She'd started to nod when Tommy pulled up a chair next to her.

Her head snapped up and she smiled at him. 'I haven't seen much of you since you returned from London. Did you enjoy your stay there?'

He nodded. 'It was a great experience. The school was wonderful. I learned so much and I am now a certified gemologist.'

Mary had no idea what that was or that there was such a thing, but decided it made sense. You had to know something about gems if you wanted to be a jeweler or design jewelry. Being certified seemed to designate expertise. 'Is your father certified as well?'

Tommy flushed. 'No. My dad, well, he sort of taught himself. He knows a lot about gold and some gems but he's never taken any certified courses. He's really talented at designing jewelry pieces, though, and knows how to work with gold and silver.'

That took Mary by surprise. 'But with all the things you have in the store, surely he must know about value and . . .' She broke off as Tommy shook his head.

'My mom does all the buying for the store. Dad's not interested. He's only interested in making jewelry and now in his We Buy Gold shop.'

'Oh.' Mary wasn't sure what to say and they sat in silence for a moment, both watching the dogs. Millie lay at Mary's feet, her head on Mary's shoe, fast asleep. Ranger and Morgan lay side by side, replete after an evening of rough housing and a large dinner of dog food and left-over hamburger meat.

Soon Tommy asked, 'Ranger. That's his name, isn't it?'

Mary nodded. 'What about him?'

'Didn't he belong to the man who was killed at the fairgrounds?'

Mary nodded again.

'What will happen to him now?'

Good question. 'I'm not sure. He seems to have taken to Susannah and he gets along with Morgan, but she'll go back to school soon and he can't go with her. I don't think Ellen and Dan want another dog. I'm sure the special forces members will take care of him.' She wondered why one of them hadn't claimed him before this, but then Ian Miller had only been killed yesterday and she was sure they were all busy trying to find clues as to who had done it. Someone would claim the dog, and soon.

'I don't know much about dogs but he seemed nice when I brought him in. Do you think he'd let me pet him?'

She looked at Tommy in surprise. 'I don't see why not.' She examined the wistful look on his face. 'You don't have a dog of your own?'

'No.' There were a number of emotions wrapped up in that single word. 'When Mom asked me to come back from England she said she needed me in the store. I didn't really want to but I said I would. I thought I'd get my own place and was going to get a dog. Then she asked me to stay at home for a while. My dad hates dogs. I think he's afraid of them.' He paused as he watched the dogs. 'It's getting late. I'd better get going. Sure has been nice talking with you, Mrs McGill. It's been a nice evening. I wish our family . . . My dad wouldn't be caught dead barbequing a hamburger.' He smiled at her and walked over to say his goodbyes to the rest of them.

Ranger raised his head. Tommy hesitated, took a step toward the dog, leaned over and stretched his hand out. Ranger touched it with his nose. Tommy abruptly turned and took his leave. Ranger watched him go. Morgan snored.

Ellen took the chair Tommy had vacated. 'He's a nice young man but certainly quiet.'

'Yes. Do you know anything about his family?'

Ellen looked at Mary questionably. 'Not much. Jerry's not very friendly but Marlene's nice. I've heard she's the one who runs the store and does it well. That's about all. Why?'

Mary sighed. 'Just wondered. I don't think he's especially happy and wondered why.'

'If I had to live with his father, I wouldn't be especially happy, either. Do you want another glass of wine?'

'I should go. It's getting late.'

'Not that late and I think Dan wants you. He's making "come here" motions.' Her eyes crinkled in amusement. 'You might as well have another half-glass while you find out what he wants.'

Mary accepted a refill and let Ellen move her chair closer to where the rest of the group were gathered. That they had been discussing the murder wasn't surprising. Dan held Mary's glass while she settled herself and Millie, who decided Mary's lap was more inviting than the concrete patio. She took her glass back, holding it a little high so Millie wouldn't knock it out of her hand. 'You wanted me?'

'I did.' He grinned. 'We all did. You haven't given your opinion on where the wedding should be held.'

Mary snorted. 'There's no need for any discussion. Saint Mark's, of course. And Les will officiate. I'm sure he would be glad to perform the service in your backyard, if that's what you want, but you'd never fit half the town in here.'

Susannah groaned. 'I don't want half the town. We thought a small wedding, just the families . . .'

'So did your mother and Dan. It's just not possible.' She leaned over and patted Susannah's hand. 'It will be beautiful and you'll be happy you had all those people later.'

'When it's all over?'

Mary smiled and turned to Dan. 'That's not why you cornered me. Is it something about Mr Miller? What we're going to do about his dog?'

'Yes. And I don't know. Let's take Mr Miller first. Yesterday morning, when you saw him in front of Lowell's window, did he say anything else other than what you already told me? Did he do anything?'

Mary let her smile die away and thought back. 'No. Just what I told you. Why?'

Dan made a grumbling noise, leaned back and took a long drink from his beer can. 'No one knows what he was doing here. I hoped he might have said something that would throw some light on that.'

'What do you mean? You said he was a special agent for the state. The people he worked with must know. He was investigating jewelry store robberies.'

'Yeah. Only there has never been a jewelry store robbery in our town.'

Neil, who had been holding Susannah's hand, let go and picked up his beer. 'Maybe he had a line on the gang or whoever is breaking into these places and thought they'd be here this weekend to rob Lowell's.'

Dan nodded slowly and set his empty can on the table. 'Certainly a possibility but, if so, he didn't let his brother officers in on it.'

'Isn't that a little odd?' Ellen, who had been listening to this exchange closely, frowned. 'If one of your people had a lead on a case you were working they'd never dream of not telling you.'

'True,' Dan said. 'But evidently Miller was a bit of a loner. At least, according to Eric Wilson.'

Pat finished the last sip of her wine and twisted a little to look at Dan. 'I thought that was some sort of unbreakable rule. You always have a buddy, always tell someone what you are working on. What about his partner? What about his friends? Didn't he tell one of them where he was going and why?'

'Eric Wilson was his partner and he says Miller didn't have any friends. Guys he worked with but not friends. Says he was a cold fish. Aloof. Secretive. Didn't open up to anyone.'

'Not even his dog.' Karl had been silent through most of this but that wasn't surprising. Karl had been observing the dog. 'That dog isn't grieving, he's confused.'

'That's not fair.' Susannah almost bristled. 'We saw him at the dog park several times. He was as nice as could be to Ranger. Made sure he had water and let him run wild with Morgan. I'm sure he loved him.'

Karl looked at her then at Neil.

Neil sighed. 'He was nice to the dog when we were at the dog park, no doubt about that. He took good care of him but I'm not so sure about the love part. Ranger obeyed him, Miller expected that. He certainly didn't abuse him but there was a sort of businesslike aura about their relationship. I think Ranger was probably loyal to Miller but I don't think he loved him, and I don't think Miller loved Ranger. Just a sense I got.'

Karl nodded. 'Miller was undoubtedly good to the dog but Ranger isn't going to die grieving for him. He'll make the transition to another family just fine.'

'What other family?' Mary pushed Millie down and prepared to stand. It was time to go. 'Did any of those people who came down here offer to take him home?'

Dan shook his head. 'No. So, I guess Ranger stays here for a few days, at least. Besides . . .'

Ellen spoke up. 'Dan thinks Ranger might be able to tell us something. What, I don't know, but Jake hasn't completely freaked out so I guess he can stay a while.'

The cat might not have, but Mary thought Dan had. That dog wasn't going to tell anyone anything, but at least he'd be safe and, if how Susannah treated him was any indication, loved. She sighed. It was time she and Millie went home. They also had nothing more to tell Dan but Mary had a lot to think about. Tommy Lowell and Ranger were at the top of her list.

# SEVEN

Mary woke early, or rather Millie did. It was Saturday. Mary had nothing scheduled except a haircut and that wasn't until eleven. It had been a trying week. She had planned to spend some much-needed time waking up leisurely. But Millie needed to go out and as long as she was up . . .

She pushed the button on the coffeemaker and listened to the familiar gurgle, smelled the familiar smell and stretched. It was a beautiful morning but the day would be hot. Maybe they'd go for a walk before breakfast. Her breakfast. She knew Millie had no intention of waiting for hers. She could eat while Mary got dressed and had a cup of that wonderful-smelling coffee.

She wasn't the only one up early. There was a line outside The Yum Yum waiting for their justifiably famous breakfasts. Ruthie had supplied chairs and coffee and the people in line were happily sipping and chatting while they waited. The line wasn't quite as long in front of Miguel's. However, he had put tables out on the sidewalk and in the small patio on the far side of his tiny restaurant. Mary's mouth watered at the thought of his *huevos rancheros*, but even though Miguel waved at her and indicated a small table, she and Millie kept going. She needed some alone time and she wasn't going to waste it. She wasn't going to answer the phone or the door. She was going to make a poached egg, fix some toast, slice a peach and read her library book. Then she would get her hair done, make a much-needed trip to the grocery store and go home and put her feet up. She wasn't going to think about Susannah's wedding, or what would happen to Ranger, or who killed Mr Miller. Especially not that. But it was odd.

That thought stayed in her mind while she got out the yogurt, sliced peaches on it, put a piece of bread in the toaster and heated up the coffee. She sat at the kitchen table and opened her latest library book, but the words refused to have meaning. Instead, Dan's voice, talking about Mr Miller, how he was a loner who went his own way and told no one where he was going or why kept reverberating in her ear. Why would he do that? If he thought he was on the trail of the robbers, wouldn't he want backup? If he thought, for some reason, Lowell's Jewelry store was the next to be hit, did he think he could stop it alone? He must have had some pretty solid evidence, and he must have known who the thieves were because he ended up dead. But how did they find out he was on their trail? None of this made sense.

She finished the last bit of toast, gave Millie the yogurt carton and started cleaning up the kitchen. She had an hour before she had to be at the beauty shop. Just enough time to put in a load of laundry and make out a grocery list. She'd think about Mr Miller and Ranger later. She stopped, the dishwasher door open. Why would she think about them at all? Solving who murdered him wasn't her job and there were competent people working on getting Ranger a good home. She needed to think about the things she was in charge of, like her after-the-event report to the Fourth of July committee. Writing it would take some doing, and she had a lot of people whose information she had to get before she could finish it. She would think about that, and her haircut. With a decided nod to herself, she finished cleaning the kitchen.

# EIGHT

The beauty shop was almost empty, which suited Mary just fine. She'd geared herself up for a barrage of questions about the murder and the fewer people there were to ask them the easier it would be to avoid answering. Speculation had run wild throughout town – a stranger in their midst, gunned down like on a TV show, the kind no respectable person would acknowledge they watched but about which they seemed to know a lot. Just Lucille, her long-time hairdresser, and Leigh under the dryer. Luckily, she was held captive there, at least for a few minutes. Lucille would have questions but they'd be to the point and soon over. Leigh would have a hundred theories, not one that made sense, and she'd repeat more rumors than even Agnes, Dan's front office person, could come up with. Mary wanted to sit back, get her hair washed and cut, and relax.

'Where's Millie?' Lucille ran her fingers through Mary's hair, assessing what, Mary didn't know or care.

'Visiting John at the pet shop. She loves John and Glen and, of course, she feels right at home there.'

Evan, Millie's previous owner, had owned Furry Friends until he was rudely murdered. That was when Millie had come to live with Mary, an arrangement that seemed to suit both of them. Glen Manning, president of the local bank, and his partner, John Lagomasino, took over the shop when Evan died. John had been a surgical nurse at the local hospital but had gotten burned out by what he termed 'all that blood.' However, the hospital had other ideas. They called him in on a fairly regular basis when they had a particularly difficult surgery. However, John seemed to prefer the pet shop. He and Glen had been close friends of Evan's and were breeders of cockapoos, so running a pet shop and grooming parlor seemed to come naturally to them. Millie enjoyed staying at the pet shop, the guys liked having her and she didn't have to be left alone

at Mary's house. The arrangement had saved more than one
sofa pillow from destruction.

Lucille nodded and pulled the lever that tilted Mary backward over the shampoo bowl. 'OK. Tell me.'

'Tell you what?' Mary knew exactly what Lucille wanted
to know but it was hard to talk upside down. Besides, she
wasn't sure how much she should tell.

Water ran, shampoo was applied, strong fingers expertly
rubbed Mary's scalp, and the next thing she knew she was sitting
right side up again, a towel wrapped around her shoulders while
another surrounded her head.

Lucille stood in front of her. 'You can talk now. What on
earth happened out there?'

Mary sighed. There was no way out. Scissors wouldn't touch
her head until she'd told some of the story. 'I don't know very
much.'

'But you found him, didn't you? You must know something.
Who was he?'

'A tourist. His name was Miller and he had a German
shepherd called Ranger. I met him once at the dog park. He
said he was here on vacation, that he lived in Sacramento.
He told Krissie at the pet shop he was interested in moving
and asked questions about the town. She told him to call Ellen
but he never did. Who shot him, or why, I have no idea.'

The towel came off and a comb started separating strands
of hair. 'Good thing you came in here. It's gotten long.' She
pulled a strand out straight, examined it then let it fall. 'I think
I saw him. That dog isn't one you'd forget. Where was it that
night?'

'He'd left him at the Benningtons' free Fourth of July kennel.
Said the dog got nervous about loud noises.'

Lucille began to snip. 'I had a German shepherd once. That
dog hated loud noises, too. One Fourth we found her in the
bathtub. Guess she thought that was the safest place. I had to
laugh, until I tried to clean all that dog hair out of the tub.
Doesn't Dan have any ideas? I heard there were some kind
of special agents who flew in. What's that all about?'

Drat and blast, but she might have known. Someone at the
airport was bound to have noticed a special plane of men

coming in late on the Fourth. Especially as they were met by one of Santa Louisa's finest. 'They're from some kind of special statewide police force, based in Sacramento. They came in to help Dan and his people.'

'Why does Dan need help? He's one of the best chiefs of police any small town could wish for.'

'Dan says because they have a lot more forensic equipment than he does.'

'Uh-huh. Now why are they really here?'

'I guess Mr Miller was a special policeman as well. He was getting ready to retire but that wouldn't matter. The police don't take it lightly when one of their own gets killed.'

The scissors snipped faster and there was a gleam in Lucille's eyes. 'Was he here on assignment? Is that why he was killed?'

Mary swallowed another sigh and hoped she hadn't told too much. 'I really don't know, but since he was getting ready to retire it could be he really was just looking around.'

'And got himself killed because he was thinking of moving? Hardly.' Luckily the blow dryer started and Mary didn't have to respond. When it stopped, Lucille was ready to move on. She stood back, inspected Mary, used the tail end of a comb to tuck an errant strand back where she thought it belonged and smiled. 'Looks good, if I do say so.'

Mary nodded and smiled as well. It did look good, but what she really liked was how easy it would be to care for.

She was writing out her check when Lucille commented, 'The fireworks show was the best we've ever had. All the events were fun. Even the stupid dog parade. It was a good day. You did your usual wonderful job, Mary.'

Before Mary could answer, she was interrupted by Leigh, holding out a curler she'd removed, oblivious to anything other than her hair. 'I think I'm done.'

'Yeah. I think you are. Just hold on a minute, Leigh. I'm finishing up with Mary.'

'What are you two talking about? The fireworks show or the murder?'

Mary groaned, but silently. Leigh wouldn't really listen but she'd repeat whatever she thought she heard as gospel truth. She needed to make this as noncommittal as possible. 'I don't know anything about the murder but Lucille was saying how good the fireworks show was.'

Leigh looked at her as if she didn't believe her, which she probably didn't, but she didn't comment. At least not about the murder. She had plenty to say about the fireworks. 'I guess they went off all right. At least they were loud enough. Half the kids in the audience were crying.'

'Oh, I don't think so,' Lucille said. 'I had two of my grand-kids there and they loved it. Especially the end when the cannons went off and the sky lit up with the flag. That was pretty darn good. Those Gradys did a bang-up job.'

Leigh gave a snort and took out another curler. 'Those Grady brothers are a couple of no-goods as far as I'm concerned. Why, I practically had to drag Gabe Grady off my grand-daughter one day last week, and all Heath did was stand and watch.'

A jolt zinged through Mary. Gabe Grady had tried to assault a fifteen-year-old girl? 'What happened?'

'He was standing right there in the drugstore, laughing and talking to her, brazen as could be. Told her the lipstick she wanted to buy would look good on her. I told him to keep his opinions to himself. She was underage and he had no business saying anything to her.' She paused, her lips pursed. 'That child wouldn't speak to me for a whole hour. Said I'd embar-rassed the life out of her. I told her I'd probably kept her from a fate worse than death.'

Mary should have known. Gabe hadn't been doing anything except maybe a little mild flirting. Leigh had blown the whole thing out of proportion. Gabe was a good-looking guy and Mary was sure he was an expert at flirting. No wonder April had been furious with her grandmother. 'That doesn't sound too serious, if all they were doing was talking.'

'First talking, then heaven alone knows what comes next. Gabe's a grown man. He doesn't need to be talking to fifteen-year-olds. You mark my words, Mary McGill. There's something fishy about those two brothers. Living way out there all alone, roaming around the country setting off fireworks . . . I've never heard that they've joined any church in town, either. They're worth keeping an eye on, that's what I think.'

The edges of Lucille's mouth twitched, whether from laughter or irritation Mary wasn't sure, but she didn't really want to listen to any more of Leigh's silliness. Lucille had to but Mary was going to pick up Millie and go home. 'If you say so,' she said to Leigh, grinned at Lucille and left.

# NINE

The farmers' market was in full swing. The park was packed with locals and out-of-towners, reveling in the local produce and handcrafts. The local merchants were reveling, too. The wine shops were full; so was the olive oil store.

There were several people looking in the real estate office window and more than one admiring what Mary thought was the necklace in the jewelry store window. Only the necklace was gone. Instead, the window held several pewter pieces Mary had never seen before, surrounded by cute little American flags. She paused as she walked by on her way to the pet shop to admire them. Pewter was a weakness of hers. These looked old but it was hard to tell. Had they borrowed them from Central Coast Fine Antiques? Very possibly. She didn't bother to look at the price tags but kept walking, wondering why the necklace had been removed, but was soon distracted. Should she go to the farmers' market first or get Millie? Farmers' market. It was so crowded Millie might get stepped on and Mary needed some vegetables.

She was weighing the merits of several large tomatoes when she heard her name called. 'Mary. I thought you might be here. Crowded today, isn't it?'

Dan made his way through the crowd, many of whom looked at him curiously in his uniform lightweight jacket open due to the heat, his chief's hat pushed back on his head. A man whom Mary had never seen before followed close behind. He was almost as tall as Dan but a good ten years older. He wore a navy blue suit with a white shirt and striped tie. A poor choice for this hot day. He didn't walk with the long, purposeful stride Dan had but somehow seemed . . . loose. His hands, suspended from thick wrists, seemed to flap as he walked. His shoulders sagged. He turned his head from side to side as he ambled toward her, seemingly looking at everything, in no hurry, but he still kept up with Dan. His face, when he was close enough for her to see him clearly, had formed jowls and his nose had thickened. Tiny broken red veins crisscrossed it. His eyes were covered with dark sunglasses but Mary immediately got the impression that, in spite of his unimpressive appearance, he was a man to be reckoned with. She didn't have time to pursue that thought.

Dan was already introducing him. 'This is Special Agent Eric Wilson. He's from the California Bureau of Investigation, Major Crimes unit. He was Ian Miller's partner and wondered if he could ask you a couple of questions.'

The expression on the man's face didn't change but Mary could almost feel his eyes studying her. An uncomfortable feeling.

'I don't think I have many answers but I'll be glad to try. However, I need to pick up Millie.'

The man seemed momentarily startled but his face settled into impassivity almost immediately.

'Let me pay for these. My car is parked behind Furry Friends. It was the only place in town with an open parking place. I'll meet you at my house. Fifteen minutes?'

Dan laughed. 'Do you think Millie's ready to come home or is John ready to have her go home?'

'I think she's ready for her dinner, and if I'm not around to harass then she'll start on John. I'll see you there.'

She turned to pay for her tomatoes, quickly adding a green pepper, and hurried over to the pet shop. What Mr Wilson thought she could add to what she'd already told Dan she had no idea but it would be interesting to find out.

# TEN

She had barely finished scooping Millie's midday snack into her dish when the door opened.

'We're here.' Dan walked in, followed by Mr Wilson.

Mary straightened and smiled at them. 'Perfect. I've just finished giving Millie a little something. Now she won't drive us crazy telling us she's starving to death. Iced tea?'

Eric Wilson looked at Millie, her head buried in her bowl and long ears brushing the floor, with obvious distaste. 'Thank you, no. If you don't mind, Mrs McGill, we don't want to take up too much of your time. Is there someplace we can . . .' He looked around the small kitchen. There was no place to sit except at the white table under the kitchen window, and there were only two chairs.

'I'll have some, Mary, and thank you.' Dan's sideways glance at Wilson made Mary wonder how Dan felt about the man.

She didn't think it was especially friendly. 'I'll get it. Why don't you two go into the living room? I'll be right in.'

Dan led the way, followed by Agent Wilson. Mary quickly poured two glasses, added sugar to Dan's and carried them into the room. She handed Dan his then seated herself in her large reading chair, made sure there was room for Millie when she'd finished her snack, and waited. She didn't have to wait long.

Agent Wilson took a notebook and pen out of his jacket pocket, flipped it open and looked at her, his face expressionless. 'You stated that you saw Ian Miller on the morning of July Fourth, standing in front of . . .' he glanced at the notebook, '. . . Lowell's Jewelry. The dog, Ranger, was beside him and he was looking at a necklace in the window. Is that correct?'

Mary thought the statement sounded unnecessarily pompous but nodded.

'Would you state why you were in town that morning?'

Mary looked at Dan, whose face was a blank mask. He barely inclined his head at her but it was enough. 'I was one of the judges for our annual dog costume parade. It was the first event of the day.'

'A dog costume parade?' Agent Wilson sounded incredulous, almost horrified.

Dan covered a smile by taking a sip of tea.

'I can describe some of the costumes if you think it would be helpful.' Mary knew her remark was a bit tart but didn't care. Dog costume parades were neither unheard of nor horrible. A little silly, perhaps, but they certainly didn't warrant Agent Wilson's reaction. She didn't care much for this man.

'That won't be necessary.' Agent Wilson's ears turned pink, from embarrassment or irritation, Mary wasn't sure. She almost missed his next question as Millie chose that moment to jump up and sit beside her.

'Why did you stop to talk to Special Agent Miller?'

'I didn't. At least, I wasn't going to, but Millie wanted to say hello to Ranger.'

Millie picked her head up off Mary's lap at the sound of her name but evidently decided nothing interesting was happening and dropped it back down.

'Do you remember your conversation?' The pen was poised above the notebook, ready to make notes, but Mary had nothing important to say.

'We commented on the necklace, then I told him about the Benningtons opening their veterinary clinic that evening to dogs whose owners didn't want to leave them alone. Some dogs are really bothered by fireworks. Mr Miller took the phone number, we said goodbye and I left. I never saw him alive again.'

Special Agent Wilson laid the pen on top of the notebook, having not made a single notation, and leaned forward a bit. 'Did he make any comments about the necklace?'

'Just that it was beautiful workmanship and looked new but the stones were old. He said the diamonds were rose-cut but I have no idea what that means. That was all.'

There was a pause, as if Agent Wilson was waiting for Mary to go on, but there wasn't anything more to say, so she sat back and let her hand drop down on Millie's head. Millie sighed.

Finally, he said, 'Then what happened?'

'Nothing. Millie and I went home. We had lunch, then later I dropped her off at the vet clinic and went to the park. The next time I saw him, he was dead.'

Again, a pause as Agent Wilson consulted his notebook. 'There is no necklace in the jewelry store window now.'

Mary's eyes narrowed. There was no reason she could see for the man's accusatory tone. 'I am aware of that, but if you're asking me where it is or why they changed the window, I don't know. However, if you go into the store I'm sure they'll be glad to show it to you and explain why they took it out.'

Wilson flushed a deeper pink. 'I'm sure they would, but I'm asking you . . .'

'I think Mrs McGill has told you everything she knows.' Dan stood, stretched his back and set his hat back on his head. 'My stepdaughter and her fiancé met Miller at the dog park, but I spoke to them last night and all they talked about was dogs. I don't think this is getting us anywhere. You can talk to the Lowells if you want, but if I was them and had an expensive piece of jewelry in my window with so many strange people in town, I think I would change it out as well.' He walked over, dropped a hand on Millie's head then patted Mary's shoulder. 'We won't take up any more of your time. I imagine Ellen will drop by later.' He turned to the other man and there was no mistaking his meaning. They were through here. 'Shall we?'

After they left, Mary sat for a few minutes, trying to make sense of the whole scene. That Wilson was rubbing Dan the wrong way was evident, but what did Wilson think she could tell him that she hadn't already? Or was he simply used to harassing people? She took a sip of her tea and grimaced. He had left a bad taste in her mouth and sugaring her tea wouldn't erase it. What was going on in the park? They couldn't have come up with much concrete evidence if they were reduced to badgering old ladies. Maybe Dan had told Ellen something. She'd give her a call.

Ellen walked in before she could pick up the phone.

'What's going on around here, anyway? Dan just texted me to say one of those state cops was here questioning you and got a little pushy. He was worried you might be upset. Are you?'

'Of course not.'

'I didn't think so. Did you make iced tea? I'm dying of thirst.'

They settled at the kitchen table and Mary related her opinion of Special Agent Eric Wilson. 'He was almost rude. It was as if he thought I was keeping something back, but what that might be, I have no idea. I only met the dead man twice.'

'Was the woman agent with them? I forget her name . . . Baxter. Emma Baxter. Now, how could I forget that? The Baxter place was one of my first really good sales.'

'There was no woman with them. Baxter? I don't suppose she could be any relation to the Baxter family . . . Ellen, was it the Baxters' property the Grady brothers bought?' It hadn't occurred to her, when Ellen gave her directions to the Gradys' ranch and told her the house and barn were such a wreck, that it might have been the Baxter place she was talking about.

Ellen nodded. 'It wasn't an easy sale. Evidently, old Clem hadn't believed in paperwork. No will, no one could find the deed, behind on taxes, and Mrs Baxter . . . I forget her name . . . was no help. She was no better than a quivering mass of jelly, poor thing. She knew nothing about their finances, or lack of them. Didn't even seem to know what a deed was. I don't think she'd made a decision harder than which pot to wash first in years. Maybe he made that one for her too. According to everyone, including his son, he wasn't a nice man.'

'No, he wasn't.' Mary thought back, remembering Clem cursing everyone he came across. 'They had three sons. He drove them all off when they were hardly out of their teens. Drove everyone off. A sad, angry man.'

Ellen smiled. 'According to his son, Cody, he was a crook.'

'What? I never heard that. Lazy, mean-spirited. Lots of things, but I never heard . . . What did he do?'

'I have no idea. All I really cared about was getting a clear title and making sure the well still drew water. The buyers, the Gradys, paid cash, so I was spared that nightmare. The place was such a wreck, I'm not sure we could have gotten financing.' She drained the last of her tea, got up and put her glass in the sink then turned and looked at her aunt. 'The Baxters were lucky someone like the Grady brothers came along. Most people would have been scared off by all the work and all the money making that place livable would entail. But the Gradys wanted someplace private because of the fireworks.' She walked to the table and picked up her purse, fumbled for her keys then addressed Mary. 'Why all the interest in the Baxter place, which is now the Grady place?'

'I'm not sure,' Mary said slowly. She also got up but didn't move away from the table. 'It just seems so . . . odd. All of it.'

'All of what? That someone named Baxter is back in town?'

'Yes.' Mary looked at Millie, who stood by her empty dinner dish and whined. Mary walked almost without conscious thought toward the broom closet and Millie's food sack. 'That and Special Agent Miller coming to town telling Dan he's on the trail of jewelry store robbers but not telling his partner or any of the other agents he might have a lead. Then he gets shot in the back. Who shoots a man in the back like that but gangsters and terrorists? There's something about all this that doesn't feel right.'

'Murder never feels right. But I don't see how Miller's admittedly strange behavior has anything to do with the Gradys buying the old Baxter ranch. Mr Miller was a state cop, those jewelry store robberies he told Dan about were in different regions in the state, and evidently he was an expert in tracing stolen jewelry. The only thing you'd find on the Grady ranch would be fireworks and ground squirrels. Are you seeing something I'm not?'

'No. I don't see any connection.'

She stood and stayed staring at Millie's food sack after Ellen left, wondering what was making her uneasy. Millie gave a sharp bark.

'Oh, I'm so sorry. I guess I was wool-gathering.' She dipped the cup into the bag then stopped. 'Wait. You already ate breakfast and lunch. For heaven's sake, what's the matter with me?' Ignoring Millie's hopeful gaze at her empty dish, she poured herself another glass of iced tea, returned to the living room and sat in her big chair, a disappointed Millie beside her. 'I really don't see a connection. But still, Mr Miller was murdered and there has to be a reason. Those Baxter boys were always wild things. You don't suppose they could somehow be connected to the robberies, do you? What am I thinking? Baxter's a common enough name and those boys are grown and middle-aged. This woman, whoever she is, has no connection with that old family.'

Millie groaned and put her head down on Mary's knee.

# ELEVEN

I t was a beautiful morning. The radio said so. Mary rolled over, opened one eye, shuddered and shut it off. She'd forgotten to turn off the alarm last night. It was seven on a Sunday morning. She had a whole hour before she had to be up. Church didn't start until nine-thirty. Millie, however, was wide awake, and since Mary had moved she expected her to get up. She also expected breakfast.

After three licks on the forehead and a little pawing, Mary gave up. She hadn't forgotten to fix the coffee. Thank goodness for small favors. If she couldn't sleep in she could at least read the morning paper while she slowly savored her coffee. Another thing to be thankful for. Many of her friends' doctors had strongly advised them to stop drinking coffee – some had turned to decaf, while others avoided it altogether. She sighed in relief as she set her mug on the table and opened the paper.

The front page was devoted to the murder. Somehow their new young reporter had found out that Ian Miller was a special agent for the California Bureau of Investigation and was having a wonderful time speculating why he had been in Santa Louisa, who could have killed him and whether a criminal gang was hiding out in their quiet little town. Or was the killer hidden among the many tourists that filled the town this weekend? The facts were few but that hadn't stopped him. The only thing he hadn't speculated on was the fate of Miller's dog.

Mary put down the paper and wondered how Ranger was doing. Such a nice dog. She'd always been a little leery of German shepherds. So big and, according to the ones you saw on TV, good at sniffing out drugs, taking criminals down, snarling and growling. Ranger wasn't a bit like that. He was a gentleman. She hoped he'd end up in a good home.

She turned to the local section and smiled. The review of how the Fourth had gone was glowing. She didn't have another event scheduled until early fall. Unless you counted the concerts in the park, but the bands were all scheduled, the parks and rec people ran the wine and food booths and, although she was on the board, she really had almost nothing to do except show up. Two months without a committee meeting except for her wrap-up meeting for the Fourth of July committee. She was going to the library first thing Monday morning to stock up then get that old chaise out of the garage and spend a whole lot of time sipping iced tea and reading.

The phone rang. 'Susannah, how nice to hear from you.'

'Aunt Mary. What are you doing this morning?'

'Sipping coffee before I get into the shower and get dressed for church. Why?'

'Because Mom and Dan and I thought we'd pick you up. We're going to breakfast – well, brunch, afterward.'

'Oh.' What a pleasant idea. 'Where? Miguel's?'

Susannah laughed. 'Miguel's would be great. Oh. One thing.'

*Here it comes.* 'What one thing?'

'Well, I know how much Millie hates to be alone.'

There was hesitancy in Susannah's voice but laughter as well. Mary had a good idea what was coming next and braced herself.

'We thought we'd bring over Morgan and Ranger so they could stay with her. Keep her from chewing up your sofa pillows.'

More laughter. 'Oh, I don't know. I think that's . . .' She looked at Millie, who was on the sofa, tongue hanging out of one side of her mouth and her eyes expectant, ready to go wherever Mary was going. Only Millie wasn't welcome in church and she certainly wasn't welcome at Miguel's, even on the patio. Mary groaned and gave in. 'Fine. The service starts at nine-thirty. Better be here no later than a quarter after.'

She'd get out the old quilt she had stored in the cedar chest, put it over the sofa, lock all the pillows in her bedroom and hope for the best. She glanced at the clock, then at Millie, shook her head and started toward the shower.

# TWELVE

The service went well. Reverend Lester McIntyre did an admirable job talking about the brutality of murder and led the congregation in a beautiful prayer for Mr Miller and his family. He made a plea for anyone with the slightest idea they might have any information to talk to Dan Dunham immediately then turned the sermon into the wisdom of the Ten Commandments.

Dan, Ellen, Susannah, and Mary stopped for what they thought would be a brief moment in the church hall. It didn't work out that way. People wanted information, along with their coffee and donuts, and it wasn't long before Dan was in the middle of a circle of people bombarding him with questions. Most wanted reassurance that Dan thought the murderer was from out of town and had moved on. Mary was the center of another circle, questions coming at her from all directions, wanting more information on what Mr Miller was doing in town. Neither of them was doing very well coming up with answers. Finally, Ellen came to Dan's rescue, Susannah to Mary's, and they pulled into Miguel's parking lot. The aroma of Mexican food wafted from the kitchen door and Mary's stomach growled.

'Let's sit on the patio, if there's a table.' Ellen led the way through the doorway and stopped at the empty hostess stand. 'I think there's one empty in that corner.'

'Hey, Susannah.' A pretty girl, her dark hair done up in heavy braids with red, white and green ribbons woven through them, came up, her arms full of menus. 'Four? These your folks?'

'Hey, Connie. Yeah. This is my mom, Ellen Dunham, my stepdad, Dan, and my great-aunt, Mary McGill. Everyone, this is Connie Garcia. Her dad is Miguel. She's going to graduate from Cal Poly next year also, only she's going to teach Spanish.'

Connie grinned. 'Seemed like a natural major and who knows? Maybe some of the kids will actually learn something. Patio? Follow me.'

They did, but Mary stopped and grabbed Ellen's arm. 'Look. There's the Grady brothers. I guess Heath got back in town safe and sound.' She motioned toward the far corner of the room where three people sat at a table, deep in conversation.

Ellen squinted as she peered into the dimly lit corner. 'I didn't know he'd gone. Isn't that Jerry Lowell with them?'

'I think so. Hard to tell in this light but . . .'

The man turned to say something to Heath.

'That's him. I didn't know they were friends. I wonder where Marlene is.'

Ellen shrugged. 'Probably at home doing dishes. They must know each other, but if body language is any indication I wouldn't say they're too friendly.'

Ellen was right. Jerry sat rigid in his chair with what looked like a full plate in front of him. The Gradys looked relaxed. Gabe lounged in his chair, his hat pushed back on his head and what looked like a Bloody Mary in his hand. There was no mistaking the celery sticking up out of the glass, even at this distance. Heath sat on Jerry's other side, talking. The expression on his face seemed bland but Mary didn't think his words were, at least not judging by Jerry's reaction. Ellen took her by the arm and tugged. 'They're all waiting for us. Come on.'

With one last glance, Mary allowed herself to be guided out onto the patio, where the others were already seated, menus in hand.

'What was so interesting in there?' Dan looked up from his menu as she sat down but didn't give her time to answer. 'I'll have a Bloody Mary. Ellen, what do you want? Susannah wants a Screwdriver. Mary?'

It wasn't until the drinks arrived and they had ordered that he asked his question again. 'Who did you see in there that had you so intrigued?'

'Not intrigued, exactly. Just a little surprised.'

'Jerry Lowell was having breakfast with the Grady brothers.' Ellen took a sip of her Margarita and smiled. 'Lovely. He didn't seem to be enjoying it very much. Too bad. The food here is really good.'

'What do you mean?' Dan leaned back, looking around at the crowded tables and took a sip of his Bloody Mary. His interest seemed idle, at best. 'What were they doing?'

Ellen and Mary looked at each other.

Ellen shrugged. 'Jerry seemed upset but the Gradys didn't. Gabe was slouched in his chair, evidently enjoying a Bloody Mary, and Heath was talking. I have no idea what he was saying but it didn't look as if Jerry liked it.'

Dan set his glass on the table, sat up a little straighter and turned his full attention to Ellen. 'Didn't they buy the old Baxter place? You had the listing, didn't you?'

Ellen nodded. 'It was one of those joyful experiences when both the buyers and sellers were difficult. I was more than glad when we got that one done.'

He was quiet for a moment while he stared at her, then he nodded and picked up his glass. 'I'd forgotten that. What are the Grady brothers like?'

Ellen licked a little salt off the side of her Margarita glass and stared into it. 'It's hard to describe. Heath was always polite, whereas Gabe . . . Well, as far as I can tell, the only things Gabe takes seriously are his fireworks, his electronic devices and his pursuit of "pretty women." But Heath is one of those people who always seems to be suspicious of something, or someone, and there's just this aura of if you try to take me, you'll be sorry. A faint chip on his shoulder that he's daring you to knock off, and if you do, all hell will break loose.' She took a sip of her drink, puckered her mouth then hurried on. 'I'm not explaining this well, and it was only a feeling I had, but he isn't an easy person to be around.'

Dan nodded slowly, but before he could say anything he was interrupted. Pat, Karl and Neil arrived.

'I told Susannah we weren't going to be able to get away, but all dogs going home this morning got picked up and everything got done early, so we decided to see if you were still here.' Pat grinned, looked around for a chair and spotted a recently vacated table. 'Quick, Neil. Pull that table over here.'

He and Dan obliged, Karl brought chairs and Susannah waved to Connie. 'It this all right?'

Connie nodded and hurried to get a fresh tablecloth and menus. Neil pulled his chair a little closer to Susannah's and started telling her about his early morning call to a neighboring horse farm, Karl and Dan began rehashing last night's baseball game and Mary, Ellen and Pat began a discussion on which flowers would be suitable for a summer wedding. The Gradys and the Lowells were forgotten.

It wasn't until later that afternoon that Mary thought about them again. Their table was vacant when they'd left. Why hadn't Tommy and Marlene been with them? None of it was her business and there were plenty of things waiting for her to do that were.

The phone rang. Wondering which committee thought they needed an emergency meeting, she answered.

It was Susannah. 'Aunt Mary, I forgot to ask you this when we picked up the dogs. I need to go into the jewelry store tomorrow to get my ring sized. I thought you might like to come with me. I want you to see what we picked out.'

Mary quickly agreed. Susannah and Neil would pick her up around ten-thirty, if that wasn't too early, and Neil would take the dogs to the dog park while they looked at the ring. Mary almost snorted. Ten-thirty too early? She assured Susannah that would be perfect and that both she and Millie would love it. Humming slightly under her breath, she went into the kitchen to get Millie's dinner.

# THIRTEEN

There was only one couple in the jewelry store and they didn't seem like immediate prospects for a sale. Mary smiled a little as she watched the giggly girl hanging on the young man's arm. They stared at engagements rings, her with rapture. He looked torn between pride and terror. Mary doubted if they would make a purchase today and maybe not anytime soon. Evidently Marlene agreed with her. She told them politely to take all the time they needed then turned to Mary.

'Susannah brought you in to see if you approve of the setting they've chosen for your mother's diamond?' Her smile was practiced but warm, especially as she turned it on Susannah. 'Where's Neil?'

'We left him in the park playing with the dogs. Is Tommy around? He said I could show Aunt Mary what we picked out.'

Slightly embarrassed, Mary gave a little laugh. 'They certainly don't need my approval but I'm anxious to see it.'

'I'm sure they don't but it's nice they want you to see it. Many young couples today don't want to share anything with their families.' There was a hint of bitterness in Marlene's voice. She smiled, however, as she turned to Susannah. 'Tommy's not here but I'll go get the book. You don't want to see the mold, do you?'

Her smile was broader when Susannah shook her head. She went toward the back of the store and Mary and Susannah started to peer into the cases.

'They have some beautiful things.' Susannah sounded a little wistful as she looked at an onyx pendant with a small diamond in the middle, filigreed gold around the outside. 'The best ones, though, are those Tommy and his father make. Tommy told us a little about the process but he left me behind when he started to talk about lost wax.'

Mary quit admiring a complex gold bracelet to stare at her. 'Lost what?'

'Lost wax. Evidently they carve the new designs in wax then press small rubber pads or something around it to make the mold. Somehow the metal gets involved, also heat, and the wax melts . . .' Her voice trailed off and she started to laugh. 'I didn't understand a word he said but it sounded complicated. Anyway, you can use the molds over and over and we picked out one Jerry made. He's used it several times and Tommy says it comes out beautiful. It's simple and the diamond isn't set too high so it won't get caught on things.'

'Well, well. Look what we have here.'

A male voice sounded behind Mary but was clearly not addressing her.

'I do like summer. The views are a lot nicer than in winter and this view is just fine. What's your name, pretty lady?'

Susannah whirled around, eyes blazing, hair flying. 'Are you addressing me?'

'Oh, yeah. You're a feast for the eyes in those shorts and that nice T-shirt. Don't think I've seen you around here before.'

Gabe Grady seemed about to let his hand drop down on Susannah's shoulder but he broke off as Mary also turned to face him.

'This is my niece, Gabe. Her name is Susannah. Her mother is Ellen McKenzie Dunham, your real estate agent. Her step-father is Police Chief Dunham. We were looking at Susannah's engagement ring.' She made sure there was frost on every word as a deep red flush crept up Gabe's face.

'Ah,' he stammered, sneaking a sideways glance at a fuming Susannah. 'I didn't know that was your . . . I mean, I didn't know . . . I didn't mean anything, just . . .'

Marlene walked back into the store, a picture album in her hand. 'Hey, Gabe. If you're looking for Jerry, he's around the corner in the We Buy Gold shop.' She stopped, looked closer at the red-faced Gabe and watched while he pushed his cowboy hat onto the back of his head, showing off a heavy gold watchband.

'Yeah. I guess I'd better . . . Thanks, Marlene. Sorry, Ms McGill. No offense, I hope.' This last he addressed to

Susannah, who said nothing. She didn't have to. Her glare was enough. With a slight nod, he turned and quickly left the shop.

The three women watched him go. Marlene sighed and turned to Susannah. 'He come onto you?'

Susannah nodded.

'Gabe . . . he thinks he's quite the ladies' man. Somehow he's never figured out all that sexist stuff just makes a girl want to either run or hit him with something. Thinks for some reason he's the most desirable man alive. He's an idiot.' She proceeded to lay the book on the counter, opened it and flipped a few pages. 'Here it is.'

It took Mary a minute to readjust. It had been a long time since she'd seen a pick-up attempt. She didn't remember them as being so overtly sexist but supposed they were. This one hadn't worked out very well for Gabe. She glanced at Susannah, who still looked flushed but was more composed than Mary felt.

She looked at the page and forced herself to concentrate. 'Why, it's perfect,' she exclaimed as the picture of the ring came into focus.

Susannah beamed. 'Then you think Great-Gramma would approve?'

'I think she'd be delighted. What do the wedding rings look like?'

'Plain, with a repeat of this leaf pattern etched on the top. We didn't want anything that could get caught on something, like a horse's halter. Neil says he knew a vet who got his ring caught, I forget on what, and lost his finger.'

There was a nice thought. Mary took another look and decided they were a good, safe choice. 'When will Tommy have the engagement ring finished?'

Marlene picked up an invoice and studied it. 'In about two weeks. You came in to be sized, didn't you? We'll need to size Neil as well but that can wait a bit. I did have a couple of other questions about how you want the diamond set . . .'

Mary tuned them out. She was beginning to get nervous about leaving Millie so long. Not that Neil would let anything happen to her but it was time to get back. She started moving down the counter, looking at the jewelry while Marlene and

Susannah talked about details that held no interest for her. The door tinkled and she looked up. A middle-aged couple came in. The woman wore beige silk pants with a loosely matching V-necked top. A gold pendant with a large green stone in the middle hung from a heavy gold chain around her neck. Thin gold bracelets decorated both wrists.

She talked excitedly and steered the man to the display case directly opposite Mary. 'There it is. Isn't it lovely? The price seems reasonable. Fifteen thousand. Don't you think so?'

The man didn't seem astonished at this statement but Mary was. What was the woman looking at that seemed a bargain for that huge sum? She edged farther down the case so she could get a look. The necklace that had been in the window. The woman was staring at it then looking at the man with her. 'What do you think?'

'If the stones are as good as you think, then yes. The design is quite good.' He glanced around at Marlene, who had left Susannah and was bearing down on the couple.

'Would you like to see it out of the case?'

The man nodded. 'Do you have a jeweler's glass I could use?'

Marlene also nodded, produced a ring of keys and unlocked the case.

Susannah appeared at Mary's side. 'I think I'm finished here. Let's go.'

They were out the door and halfway across the park when Mary grabbed her arm. 'Susannah, did you hear what that woman said? Fifteen thousand dollars for that necklace was a good buy. How can that be?'

'Tommy told us about it. Evidently there's a lot of gold in the necklace, the diamonds are old but exceptional quality and large, and the sapphire is a really good one. But with jewelry it's not always just about how much gold or the size of the stones. According to Tommy, it's the artistry involved. You don't expect to pay for a painting based on how much the paint cost. That's not the way I've ever thought about it, but then, I've never been one for jewelry. Aunt Mary, who was that man in there? The idiot who thought he was God's gift to women?'

'Gabe Grady, one of the Grady brothers. They put on the fireworks show the day before yesterday. Your mother had the listing on the ranch they bought.'

'Are they the ones you were talking about at breakfast? The ones who were with Jerry Lowell?'

Mary nodded. 'Yes. I had no idea they were friends. They don't seem to have much in common.'

'Judging by the bracelet and chain that idiot was wearing, maybe they're customers. I wonder if he does that a lot. Comes on to women in that way, I mean.'

Mary thought back to Leigh's outrage over Gabe's comments to her granddaughter. 'I rather imagine he does.'

Neil was in the middle of the dog park, sitting on top of the picnic table, Millie beside him and Morgan and Ranger stretched out under it. Tommy Lowell sat on Neil's other side, the two of them deep in conversation.

Neil looked up and smiled at Mary. 'What do you think?'

'I think it's perfect. Hello, Tommy.'

Tommy greeted her back, or Mary thought he did. It was hard to tell over Millie's howls of welcome.

'For heaven's sake, dog, I've only been gone half an hour. You'd think—'

Millie howled again and threw herself at Mary. Neil laughed and caught her.

'You'd better sit down and let this thing finish telling you how much she missed you before she knocks you down. You really are going to have to break her of this before you get hurt.'

Mary knew that. She'd been told by Dan, John and Glen, and Karl Bennington, but it was easier said than done. Secretly, Mary liked that Millie didn't want to be parted from her. She sat, let the little dog jump onto her lap and greet her. Then she settled down with Mary's hand on her head. She heaved a huge sigh and closed her eyes. Neil shook his head.

Tommy watched with interest. 'Does she always do that?'

'I'm afraid so. I felt so bad for her when she first came to live with me, I let her get away with a lot. But we're not very often apart so . . . she gets a little excited.'

'To say the least.' Susannah pushed Neil over and perched

herself on top of the table beside him. 'Aunt Mary loves the rings.'

Tommy didn't exactly beam but he looked pleased. 'They're one of my dad's designs but I've got an idea how I can update it a little. I want to set the diamond down into the ring more, bring the leaf motive in a little . . . I'll probably have to recast the mold but that shouldn't be too hard.'

Mary found she was staring at him. Not too hard? It sounded impossible to her. She'd never really thought about jewelry design before but, of course, someone had to create it. 'Did you do the necklace that was in the window July Fourth?'

'Yes. Do you like it?'

Mary nodded. 'It's beautiful. There were some people looking at it when we left. Seriously looking. Do you often make pieces that valuable?'

Susannah was staring across the park at the jewelry store. 'Does your mother ever get nervous being by herself with pieces like that in the store? I mean, with no one else there. If she ever got robbed . . .'

The color seemed to drain from Tommy's tanned face. 'My mom's alone? Where's my dad? Where's Crystal?'

'She told Gabe Grady your dad was in the We Buy Gold shop. Who's Crystal?'

'Gabe. What was he doing there? He's . . . You said someone's looking to buy the necklace? My mom's alone? Why he does that . . . damn and blast.'

Ranger had crept out from under the table while Millie was greeting Mary to sit beside Tommy, who stroked his head. The dog looked up in surprise as Tommy jumped to his feet. 'I'd better get over there.' Then he looked at the dog. 'I'll be back.' He let the dog gate slam behind him as he left then almost broke into a run as he crossed the park.

Mary, Neil and Susannah watched his rapid progress until he disappeared into the store.

'Well,' Susannah said finally, 'I guess that answered my question.'

Neil took off his sunglasses, wiped them off with the end of his T-shirt and replaced them. 'I don't know if it was his dad not being there that upset him or Gabe looking for his dad.

He seemed pretty relaxed until then. We were talking about dogs. He doesn't know much but seemed pleased Ranger took to him. Something sure set him off.'

'It's an expensive piece.' Mary couldn't help thinking of the other jewelry store robberies Dan had talked about, the ones Ian Miller was investigating when he was killed. Could somehow . . . No. Those people walked in looking like what they were. Wealthy tourists. 'I expect when you have that many valuable things in a store you're always a little on edge. Although, it does seem reckless somehow for Marlene to be alone, especially with this many people in town. Who's Crystal?'

'No idea,' stated Neil.

'Isn't she the girl we met when we went in the first time? She was showing someone bracelets or something.'

Neil looked a little blank. 'Maybe. Anyway, we'd better get going. I told Doctor Pickering I'd go on calls with him this afternoon to Hilltop Morgan Horse Farm.' He slid off the table and reached for the dogs' leashes. 'We're going to float teeth. You coming with me?' he asked Susannah.

'Ugh. No. I have no interest in helping hold a horse while you file calcium deposits off its teeth. Besides, I told Mom I'd help her. You ready?' This she addressed to Mary, who still stared across the street at the closed door of the jewelry shop.

'I think Millie and I will do a few errands. We can walk home. You two go on.' She snapped Millie's leash on her harness and set her on the ground. 'Where's Dan? Is he out at the fairgrounds?'

'No.' Susannah looked at her with one eyebrow slightly raised. 'He's at the station.'

Mary could almost feel her wanting to ask why but she didn't and Mary didn't volunteer. She just smiled. 'Thanks for letting me see the rings. I'll see you later.'

Susannah and Neil headed toward the parking lot. Mary and Millie started down the sidewalk in the other direction toward the library and the police department that was the next block over.

# FOURTEEN

I t was quiet in the lobby of the police station. Agnes, Dan's receptionist, was seated at her desk, the buttons on her intercom silent, a paperback open in front of her. As usual, she was dressed in a light blue shirt and darker blue pants held up with a wide black belt. There was no insignia on the shirt. Agnes wasn't any part of law enforcement but that wasn't how she saw her position. Mary had asked Dan once if he'd ever considered letting Agnes carry a gun. He'd asked her if she thought he'd gone insane. Mary smiled and wiggled her fingers as she and Millie started down the hall to Dan's office.

'Mary, I think . . .'

Mary ignored her. She was in no mood to gossip with Agnes. She had some questions she wanted to ask Dan and, if she was lucky, she might get him to take her home. She knocked once on his closed door and heard a faint, 'Come in.' She did. Dan was in but he wasn't alone.

'Mrs McGill. How nice to see you again.' Special Agent Wilson pushed back his chair and came toward Mary, hand outstretched and face creased in a smile. 'I'd hoped we'd meet. I owe you an apology.'

Mary's hand was encased in his and her arm shaken. Her instinct was to pull it back, but good manners and a firm hold by Wilson kept her from it. Millie, however, wasn't restrained by either. She growled softly, but with meaning.

Wilson let go immediately. 'Your little dog is a bit possessive. Probably a good thing.' He took her arm, gingerly, one eye on Millie, and guided her to the chair he had vacated. 'Sit here. We were just finishing up. But before I leave, I wanted to say I'm sorry about yesterday. I didn't mean to be so . . .'

'Aggressive?' Mary suggested.

The smile this time wasn't so broad. 'That's one way of putting it. I'm afraid the shock of Ian's death had me a bit on edge. I hope you'll forgive me.'

'Of course.' Mary glanced at Dan, who watched Eric Wilson with what she recognized as distaste.

A sound came from the person sitting in the chair on the other side of Dan's desk, one Mary hadn't noticed until now. A young woman sat in it. The sound could have been a cough, a suppressed laugh or a snort. Whatever it was, it wasn't respectful. Mary glanced at her then looked back at her again. Hurriedly, Mary assured Wilson she had nothing to forgive, that she understood completely, but her attention was on the woman. Short-cropped blonde hair, slender, long, tapering fingers that ended in well-kept but closely clipped nails, large blue eyes and a thin, straight nose that turned up slightly at the tip. 'Miss Baxter?'

The woman started and the smile evaporated. 'How did you know . . .?'

'That you're a Baxter? You're every inch a Baxter. Which one of the boys is your father?'

She grinned, a little ruefully. 'Cody. When he heard I was coming here he said I didn't have to worry about being recognized as one of the notorious Baxter tribe. No one in this town would dream a Baxter would end up a cop, let alone a state cop. Guess he was wrong.'

Mary nodded. 'When your father and his brothers were in high school, most folks thought they'd end up in the penitentiary. Evidently, they didn't. At least, he didn't.'

'None of them did. And you are . . .?'

'Mary McGill. This is Millie.' Mary gestured toward Millie, who sat by her ankle, inspecting the woman with what appeared to be interest.

'So you're Mary McGill. My father's told me about you. You actually taught him to cook?'

A picture of Cody Baxter, spatula in hand, remains of fried egg on the middle-school kitchen ceiling, appeared in Mary's memory. She didn't get too many boys in her home economic classes but Cody Baxter had smilingly stated he needed to learn how to cook. She wasn't sure he'd learned much about cooking but he'd enjoyed flipping fried eggs. She sighed. 'I guess you could call it that. What is he doing now? And the other boys, how are they?'

The woman smiled. 'My dad's a dentist. Cam is a Lutheran minister and Casey is a captain with the California Bureau of Investigation. They're all married with kids and I'm the only girl.'

The fleeting idea the Baxter brothers could somehow be mixed up in robbing jewelry stores evaporated. 'How wonderful. You must tell your father – all of them – I said hello. How is your grandmother?'

'In a care facility. She's pretty far gone, doesn't recognize any of us. It's really sad.'

Agent Wilson had been listening to this with increasing displeasure. 'I didn't know you knew this town, Baxter. You should have told me.'

'I've never set foot in it until we came last night. My father grew up here but we never came, not even to visit our grandparents.'

How sad. But, given that all three boys had left home as soon as possible, not surprising.

'Your uncle is Captain Casey Baxter?' There was an odd mixture of expressions on Agent Wilson's face as he stared at Emma Baxter. A wary look overlaid with exasperation and something else. 'Somehow, I never connected . . . You didn't think to mention that, either?'

'Sir, it never occurred to me. My uncle – none of my family – has anything to do with this case.' There was exasperation in Emma's voice as well.

A confrontation seemed to be building but was defused by a knock on Dan's door. Without waiting for permission, the door opened and Sergeant Ricker appeared. He nodded at Mary, ignored the two special agents and addressed Dan. 'The coroner's office just called. Seems Sacramento doesn't want them to do the autopsy on Miller. They want to, and they want the body sent up right away. Our guys need you to tell them what to do.'

'Tell them to release the body right away, of course.' The aggressive tone Wilson seemed to favor was back.

Dan sighed. 'They still on the phone?'

'Nope. Said you should call them back asap.'

'OK. Wilson, I think we need to talk to whoever made that "request." Mary, do you have your car?'

She shook her head.

'That's what I thought. It's too hot for you and Millie to walk home. Agent Baxter, do you have a car?'

She shook her head but didn't look at Dan. She watched Wilson's face get redder. Why? Mary wondered. Because Dan seemed to be questioning the release of Mr Miller's body to somebody else? She didn't know how those things worked but it seemed as if there was going to be a dispute and Dan wanted her out of the way. Never mind. She'd find out all about it later.

'Maybe she can drive me home in your car. She'd have it back here long before you're going to need it.'

The corners of Dan's mouth twitched. 'Good idea. Emma . . . you don't mind if I call you Emma?'

She shook her head again.

'Good.' He opened his desk drawer and pulled out a more than full key ring, removed a car key and handed it over. 'Mary knows which car is mine. Thanks.'

The door had barely closed behind them before the sound of raised voices followed them down the hall.

# FIFTEEN

They pulled into Mary's driveway before she had decided which of the many questions she had for Emma Baxter she'd ask first.

'My, that was so much more pleasant than walking on this hot afternoon.' She smiled at Emma and tightened up on Millie's leash.

The dog knew she was home and she wanted out of the car, now.

'Why don't you come inside for a few minutes? I have iced tea in the refrigerator. I made it this morning, and it'll give you a chance to stay away until they finish arguing about whatever it is they're arguing about.'

Emma hesitated and pulled out her cell. She grinned. 'Fifteen minutes. They should have it resolved by then. We all know how it's going to come out but I don't blame Chief Dunham for trying to keep the body here. After all, it's his murder.'

Dan's murder? It probably was but that wasn't quite the way she would have put it. Mary unlocked the front door and, with Millie leading the way, passed through the house to the kitchen. It was blessedly cool. She had hesitated to put out the money last year for the air-conditioning system but Dan and Ellen had persuaded her. Right now, she was glad they had.

'Sit down there.' She gestured toward the old white table, unsnapped Millie's leash, ignored her as she sat down beside her empty dinner dish and pulled two glasses from the cupboard. 'Sugar?'

Emma shook her head and looked around. 'I love rooms like this. It looks like real people live here.'

As opposed to what? But Mary knew what she meant. Her kitchen would never appear in *Better Homes and Gardens* but a lot of good meals had come out of it over the years. Still did.

She set a glass in front of Emma and lowered herself into the other chair. 'How long have you been with the bureau?'

Emma took a sip before answering. Her expression changed from determinedly cheerful to glum. 'A couple of years. I signed on as a rookie right after I graduated from college and was assigned to Miller and Wilson a couple of months ago.'

'Then you didn't know Mr Miller very well?'

'He wasn't an easy person to get to know.' Emma picked up her glass and held it in both hands, staring into it. 'He and Wilson had been partners for – oh, ten years or more. Only, something happened. I don't know what but they barely spoke. I've spent the last couple of months walking a tightrope between them.'

'That can't have been very pleasant,' Mary said with what she hoped was a sympathetic voice. 'Did they quarrel?'

'No. At least, not in front of me. I think it was more than that. Ian – Agent Miller – figured out the connection between all those jewelry store robberies and I think Eric Wilson felt . . . I don't think Ian told him he was even working on them. When Eric found out . . . it wasn't good.'

'What do you mean, connection? Dan said . . Chief Dunham . . . there had been several robberies. Was there some doubt they were all done by the same person? Or persons?'

Emma buried her face in her glass as if buying time while she decided how to answer. 'Robberies happen all the time. Jewelry store robberies are often smash-and-grabs, mainly because most stores are so well alarmed. But these were different. There have been twelve of them in the past twenty-six months over four states. It took a while to realize . . . Anyway, after three reports came into our office with the same method of entry, all in very different jurisdictions in the state but all seemingly committed by the same person, or persons, Ian got to wondering if there were other robberies that fit the pattern and started looking harder at out-of-state jewelry stores. He contacted other state law-enforcement agencies, telling them what he was looking for, and came up with nine more. He was an expert on tracing stolen jewelry, so this was his kind of case.'

Mary wasn't sure what she'd just heard. 'What do you mean, method of entry? What was so distinctive about that?'

Emma's smile was broad. 'It's so bizarre it's almost funny, but not quite. These people, whoever they are, have a metal saw. They cut the bottom off the back door of the jewelry store, then someone evidently crawls in below the motion detectors, which are almost always installed either up high or at the height of the door handle, disarm the alarm system then set the cut section of the door back in place. No one knows they're inside and they can spend all the time they want choosing what to take. They must do a lot of research because they can really clean a store out of a lot of their best pieces. Mostly gold, but lots of good gemstones – almost all diamonds – have gone missing as well.'

Mary set her glass down and stared at Emma. 'They do what? Saw the door?'

Emma nodded and her laugh was rueful. 'Sorry. It's not funny but the sheer audacity of this just bowls me over. A grown man, squeezing through the bottom of that door then replacing the panel he sawed off. But he – or they – must have some pretty awesome computer skills. They have been able to hack into every one of those alarm systems and turn them off. Then, when they leave, they turn them back on. The stores seem to be chosen carefully. They all carry high-end jewelry and they're all stand-alone stores. No strip malls, no alleys that trucks might go through when they're cutting their way in. More than half the robberies have been on long weekends or holidays. The thieves have been gone hours before anyone finds out they've been robbed.'

Tea abandoned, Mary stared at her. 'Let me get this straight. These robberies – the ones where the robbers sawed off part of the doors – happened over four states? All in the last two years?'

'With this entry method, yes. I'd be surprised if these were their first robberies, though. The guys appear to be pros.'

Mary shook her head as if maybe she could shake away the conflicting thoughts swirling through it. 'If there were that many robberies, all done the same way, why was it so hard to realize the same people were committing them?'

Emma sighed and took another sip of her tea. 'This is good.' She took another, larger sip. 'Four states, that's why. Four different agencies investigating them, not one state talking to another. They struck three in California, each time stores that specialized in high-end estate jewelry. One shop in Beverly Hills, one in Palos Verde and another in the San Francisco Bay area. I guess that got Ian thinking and he started checking with other states. He found what he was looking for all right but he didn't find any of the jewelry. No one else has, either. Wilson thinks Miller had a lead of some sort and that's why he was killed, but what that was none of us know. Yet.' She drained her glass, pushed back her chair and set the glass on the drain board. 'Thanks for the tea. I was just about dying of thirst.' She paused, stared at Mary, started to say something, stopped then blurted out: 'I'll be here another couple of days. If you have time and don't mind, could we meet again?' A bright red flush ran up her neck into her hairline. 'I'd like to ask you . . . I never really knew my grandma when she was . . . normal. My dad won't talk about his childhood much – my uncles won't either – and they refuse to discuss my grandfather. I wondered if . . .'

'If I knew them and could tell you something about them?' Emma nodded.

Mary drew in a deep breath and let it out slowly. 'I never really knew your grandfather but I've heard lots about him. Your grandmother was the older sister of one of my high-school friends. I knew her slightly but I knew your aunt well. I don't know how much help I can be but yes, I'll tell you what I know about your family. Why don't you call me when you have some time? We can meet at The Yum Yum for lunch or coffee or something.'

'The Yum Yum.' Emma laughed out loud. 'My dad still talks about it. Said he's never had a hamburger half as good since he left here. I thought he was making up the name but I guess not. I'd love to have one of those hamburgers. If you'll give me your number . . .'

Mary got a pen and notepaper and started to write.

Emma laughed. 'Just tell me – I'll put it in my phone.'

'Oh. Of course. I forgot you can do that.' She looked at

Emma's phone, wondering not for the first time if you could really rely on it. 'Or you can always ask Dan, Chief Dunham. He's my nephew and knows how to get in touch with me.'

The smile disappeared from Emma's face and a faint look of alarm took its place. 'I didn't know that. Mrs McGill, if you don't mind, please don't mention what I've told you about the robberies. I don't think any of it is classified but I'm always talking too much and—'

'You have nothing to worry about.' Mary smiled. 'I won't mention it but I don't think there's one thing you've said that won't be on the local news tonight or in the paper. In the meantime . . .' She put her finger to her lips.

'Thanks.' Emma leaned down and gave Millie a pat on the head. 'I think someone wants her dinner.' With that, she left.

Mary glanced at the clock then shook her head. 'It's not even close to your dinnertime.'

Millie looked crestfallen but Mary ignored her. She sipped her tea, staring out of the window, thinking. All those robberies. She had no idea how much money all that jewelry would be worth and, more to the point, where it was. She didn't think for one moment thieves who could plan so many robberies so professionally wouldn't be equally as efficient in turning it into cash. But how? Why had none of what they'd taken shown up? Or had it? The necklace in the window; the one Ian Miller found so fascinating. Could the stones in it be stolen? If they were stolen, did that mean the Lowells knew? No. She didn't know Marlene well but her reputation for being a fair and honest businesswoman was well-established. Tommy had been gone most of the years they'd been open in Santa Louisa, away at school in London and then working there. He'd been back less than a year. She thought back. When had they come to town? Five years ago? Six? They'd bought the store from the Hudsons when Bart Hudson died. None of his children had wanted to run it. None had even stayed in town. The Lowells had changed the store a lot over the years but she was sure not with stolen jewelry. She finished off her tea, put her glass and Emma's in the dishwasher and headed for the phone. Maybe she'd leave a message asking Dan to stop by on his way home. They had things to talk about.

# SIXTEEN

Dan waved away Mary's offer of iced tea and opened the refrigerator door. He emerged with one of the beers she always kept for him.

'Thank goodness this day is over.' He pulled out the chair opposite her and pulled the tab. Foam lined the edge of the can and quickly the edges of his mustache. 'That tastes wonderful.'

'Bad day?' Mary had replaced the pitcher of tea in the refrigerator and poured herself a glass of her favorite Chardonnay. She tasted it and smiled. 'Did you get your dispute with Mr Wilson settled?'

'It wasn't exactly a dispute, more of a tactical disagreement which I was bound to lose. But I managed to delay everything long enough so my ballistics people got a good look at the bullet that killed Miller. The bullet, with Miller, will, of course, go to Sacramento for their people to do with it what they will. But at least I know what kind of gun I'm looking for.'

'What kind?'

'Some kind of high-powered rifle. Hit a deer or a man with that thing and they're done for.'

Mary shuddered. She didn't disapprove of hunting, if whatever was hunted was going to be used in some way, but the thought still made her squeamish. The idea of something being killed just because someone had a gun and could made her furious. The thought that someone with that kind of gun used it to shoot Mr Miller in the back made her a little faint. 'They certainly identified the bullet fast.'

'They only identified which *kind* of gun. It doesn't tell us which gun. Big difference. But if we can find a suspect and he, or she, has such a gun, we can send it up to Sacramento and see if they can get a match. In truth, their lab is a lot more capable than ours. And, since Miller was one of their own, they might even put a rush on it.' He took another long drink. 'If we can find the gun.'

Mary took a small sip and let her eyes stay on the remains in her glass. 'Tell me more about these robberies Miller was looking into.'

Dan laughed. 'You mean you didn't pry enough out of poor little Emma?'

Startled, she set her glass down quickly. 'I don't know what you're talking about.'

'Yes, you do, but it's fine. Did she tell you Wilson's theory about the Lowell necklace? That the sapphire and diamonds might be from one of the robberies? There were at least two stores robbed that specialized in antique pieces.'

'She never mentioned the necklace.'

'Did she tell you that none of the stolen pieces have shown up? Not at any of the pawn shops known to accept stolen goods, nor on any of the black markets we know about. Not one piece?'

'She might have mentioned something about that.'

Mary hoped Emma wouldn't get in trouble for talking to her but, at least, she truly hadn't broken her word.

'Out of twelve robberies we are sure were committed by the same person or people, not one piece. So, when Wilson heard Miller had been looking at the necklace with such interest, he immediately decided those stones belonged to one of the robbed stores. If you think he was aggressive with you, you should have heard him with Marlene. Didn't work out so well, though.'

'What do you mean? What happened?'

Even Millie seemed interested. She left her bowl, which she had been sniffing hopefully, to sit beside Mary's chair and stare at Dan. He laughed – at the remembrance of what had happened or at Millie's expression, Mary wasn't sure.

'Wilson barged into the jewelry store and confronted Marlene, demanding to know where they got the sapphire and diamonds. At first, Marlene was speechless, but then she got mad. She said she didn't know, that Jerry handled all of the custom jewelry buying and selling and she ran the store. He was next door at the gold shop but she'd call him and ask him to come over and talk to Mr Wilson. I could hear Jerry yelling over the phone. It wasn't long before he stormed in, waving receipts in front of Wilson's face, going on about who did he think he was, calling his wife a thief. Made quite a scene.' Dan smiled a little broader then bent down and scratched Millie's left ear.

Mary thought about it for a minute. That Jerry Lowell made a scene didn't surprise her but it seemed a little excessive if he had receipts. Of course, Jerry would take it personally and he wasn't the easiest person to be around. Poor Marlene. 'Where did Jerry get the jewels?'

'According to the receipts, the sapphire was in a gold brooch he bought a few months ago. He says he doesn't usually keep those kinds of stones but the owner didn't want it and he thought he might use it in a piece someday. I guess Tommy beat him to that. The diamonds were in another piece he bought. He says he pays for diamonds if the owner wants to sell them at the right price. Usually he has to recut them, but Tommy said the old cut was perfect for what he was doing so he let him use them. Says he buys gold pieces with gems in them all the time, that's his business and where did Wilson get off . . . He went on for a while. Wilson asked if he could have copies of the receipts for his purchase of the pieces of jewelry he bought and Jerry threw him out. Said if he was under suspicion of something he could damn well come back with a warrant.'

'Could he? Come back with a warrant?'

'Oh, yes. Actually, he wouldn't need one. The law states that resale shops have to produce receipts for the pieces they buy for three years. Also sworn statements from the sellers that they own the jewelry and have the right to sell it.'

'That makes sense. So, what happened?'

'Jerry finally let Wilson look at the receipts. Wilson grumbled but there wasn't much he could do, so we left. I'll go back and apologize to Marlene tomorrow, when Wilson isn't around, but the Lowells are off the hook.' All trace of amusement was gone. He swallowed the last of his beer, got up and put the can in Mary's recycle trash can, turned and leaned back against the sink. 'That whole scene could have been avoided. If he'd let me do it my way, we'd have still gotten the information we wanted and probably more, and no hard feelings. Now, if we need to ask either of the Lowells anything else, ever, we'll have a hard time getting an answer.'

'What more can you ask them?'

'Beats me. Marlene says she never saw Miller or his dog. Jerry says he noticed a man and a dog looking at the necklace in the window, but he didn't speak to him and had no idea who he was. I'm not sure what they could tell us.'

Maybe some general information about jewelry stores, how their security worked, how and where they bought their inventory – that kind of thing – but then, Mary decided the police probably already had that information. 'What do you do now?'

'Good question. We have no physical evidence at the murder scene. There are tons of footprints all over that grove of oaks, a trillion cigarette butts and even more candy wrappers, papers that held hotdogs, empty cups, all kinds of trash, but nothing that could reasonably be tied to the shooter. There was one bullet and that went right through him and ended up in the oak tree he was under. The blood you saw came from the exit wound, not the entrance. We don't have any leads on who committed the store robberies, either, and although we think it's the same person or persons, at this stage it's nothing but conjecture. Wilson's tearing his hair out and I don't blame him. After all, Miller was his partner.'

Mary nodded and took another sip. Should she tell Dan what Emma had said? Might as well. Dan was aware they'd already talked about all this. 'Emma didn't seem to think they were all that close – Miller and Wilson.'

Dan straightened a little and there was definite interest in his eyes. 'Elaborate.'

'She didn't say much. Only, they're supposed to be mentoring her, I guess that's what you'd call it, and she said Miller had been the one who made the connection between all those robberies, did all the work contacting people from different states, putting it all together. He didn't tell anyone what he was doing until he had all the information, not even Mr Wilson, who was evidently miffed.'

'From what I've seen of Wilson, miffed would be mild. I wonder what else Miller didn't tell him.'

'I wonder why he didn't. Partners don't usually act that way, do they?'

'No, they don't.' There was a thoughtful look on Dan's face. He gave Mary a hug.

'Dan, wait. How is Ranger?'

His smile was the first genuine one she'd seen all day. 'He's doing fine. Susannah and Neil take both dogs everywhere. Ranger seems to love it. Don't forget to lock your door.' And he was gone.

Mary ignored the door. Instead, she sat and thought. Millie lay beside her chair, her head on Mary's foot.

She'd forgotten to ask Dan if the necklace was still at Lowell's. He hadn't mentioned that it was gone. Did that mean the tourists hadn't bought it? That wouldn't surprise her. She didn't think she and Samuel had paid as much for this house as the Lowell's were asking for the necklace. Of course, they'd bought the house many years ago. Still . . . had Tommy somehow squelched the sale? Why? That would have been a nice one. Why did Eric Wilson think the stones were stolen? The only thing he had to go on was Ian Miller looking at the necklace in the window. He was knowledgeable about jewelry. Maybe he was only admiring it.

Mary sighed, removed her foot from under Millie's chin and stood. It was time she thought about dinner. Millie's first. Millie agreed. Mary filled her dish and watched while she devoured it. Maybe she'd make a salad. It was hot and she didn't want to cook. She walked over to the refrigerator and looked in but she didn't actually see anything. The thoughts that kept rolling around in her head wouldn't let her. Where was all the stolen jewelry? Dan said none of it had shown up at the usual places. She wasn't sure where the usual places were but obviously the police did. Why hadn't it? She didn't believe the thieves would wait a year and a half to turn all the jewelry into cash. How did you do something like that? She shut the refrigerator door and stood in front of it, empty-handed.

She assumed they'd take the expensive jewels out of the setting, probably the not-so-valuable ones as well. Could you identify loose diamonds and other jewels? She had no idea. Emma had said they mainly took gold pieces. There must be a reason for that. What did they do with them? How did you go about finding out? The Internet? Ellen claimed you could find out anything on the Internet but she didn't have a computer. Could she get that kind of information on her phone? Maybe someone could but she couldn't. She'd learned how to do a lot of things, but after she'd figured out how to access her bank account and to use the GPS she'd gone no further. So, how . . . The library. They had computers and a head librarian who knew how to use them. Luke would get a visit from her first thing in the morning. Humming a little under her breath, she opened the refrigerator door once more but removed nothing. Had one of the thieves really killed Ian Miller? Had he gotten a clue as to their identity? If that was true, were the thieves people who lived in this town? People she knew? Was that why Miller was here? She was certain he hadn't come to see the dog costume parade or the fireworks. He had suspected someone of something, either the robberies or something connected to them, and that someone had killed him. It was the only thing that made sense. She looked at the bag of spinach she held and put it back. Somehow, she'd lost her appetite.

# SEVENTEEN

Mary walked out of the pet shop feeling a little guilty for leaving Millie with John while she visited the library. Luke would be delighted to have her but rules were rules and dogs weren't allowed. John, however, was always glad to see her, and Millie loved having the run of the pet shop.

Mary glanced both ways and stepped off the curb, planning on taking a shortcut through the park. She caught sight of the roaring van just in time to throw herself back on the sidewalk.

Staggering a little to find her balance, she looked up in time to see a white van, its side emblazoned with images of bright-colored fireworks, speed up the street. The Grady brothers' van. What on earth . . . Where had it come from? The alley. It must have. The turnout of it was obstructed by the two buildings that faced the street, but there was a stop sign to which the Grady who'd been driving had plainly paid no attention. Trying to catch her breath, Mary watched the white van, decorated with the exploding fireworks on the back doors, as well as the side, drive through another stop sign, ignore the driver of the pickup that came to a screeching stop to avoid him and head for the bridge that would take him out of town. She thanked her lucky stars Millie wasn't with her. She always liked to be in the lead and what might have happened sent a shiver down Mary. Did that idiot always drive like that? What could possibly have possessed him? She turned to look down the alley. Where had he come from? Lowell's? It was the store on the end, and the alley was certainly one way to get to their back door. So was the back door of the We Buy Gold shop, although the front of that store faced the side street. Jerry and the Gradys had seemed at odds at breakfast. But that explosive driving looked like rage, not mild disagreement. Taking a deep breath and looking more carefully up and down the almost deserted street, Mary crossed and walked down the brick path through the park toward the library.

It was almost empty. Mary wasn't sure if it was because it was Tuesday and, for some reason, people stayed home, or if the town felt empty because all the visitors had left. However, an almost-empty library suited her purpose perfectly. Luke was behind the checkout counter, leaning on his elbow, thinking about what she had no idea, but she didn't think it had anything to do with the library.

'Hey.'

Luke started then smiled. 'Hey, yourself. Where's your faithful companion?'

'At the pet shop. John loves having her and she loves being there. My sofa pillows love not being chewed to a pulp.'

Luke laughed. 'Fred used to do that but when his big boy teeth came in he quit. I'm surprised Millie hasn't.'

'I think it's more irritation she got left behind than the need to chew. How is Fred?'

'About to be a father again. Pam's little poodle is ready to burst. Poor little thing. She'll be glad to get this over. Should be any day now.'

'Let me know when we can come visit. I'm sure they're going to be beautiful. But that's not why I'm here.'

'We've had the book sale and we're not doing another can tree until Christmas, so it's either a donation for something or you want information.'

Mary smiled. 'Information. Ellen says you can look up anything on the Internet, but since I don't have a computer I thought I'd ask you to help me.'

'Does this have anything to do with the murder?'

*Drat.* The gossip network in this town was every bit as fast as anything the Internet could come up with and probably about as accurate.

'More curiosity than anything. I'm not sure exactly what I want to know, but maybe you can narrow it down.'

Luke's mind wasn't wandering now. 'I'll try. Let's start with a general category. Like fireworks, or picnics, or murder.' He grinned at her.

'I don't want to know one more thing about murder. After

finding that poor man . . .' She didn't try to repress the shudder that ran through her. 'No. I want to know about gold.'

Luke took his weight off his elbow, stood up straight and stared at her. 'Gold? That's a pretty broad topic. What about gold?'

Mary had been wrestling with how to say what she wanted to know without mentioning robbery but hadn't come up with anything. She hoped she wasn't letting out information she wasn't supposed to have. 'How you could change a bracelet or ring or necklace you had into something else entirely. Like another necklace. How would I go about—'

'First, you'd get yourself a microwave.'

Mary's jaw dropped open. 'I don't think you understand. We're not talking about cooking.'

Luke grinned. 'But we are talking about melting. I'm not talking about your kitchen microwave, but jewelers and people who work with gold and other metals use microwaves to melt the metal. Then they can pour it into the jewelry molds they've already made or make gold bars or gold coins and let it harden. That's the first step. I've read that a lot of old jewelry is recycled that way, so if what you really want to know is how whoever is robbing those stores is moving the gold out the door, I'd think recasting it, either into other jewelry pieces or into ingots or coins, would be the way to go. It's hard to trace something that's melted.'

Stunned was the only way to describe how Mary felt. She'd never thought about liquid gold but it made sense. It would be pretty hard to make a slender gold chain with a chisel and hammer. 'How do you know all that?'

Luke's grin got wider. 'Lowell's is making Pam and my wedding rings. I got to talking to Tommy . . . you can't really talk to Jerry . . . and got interested in the process. So I got on the Internet and looked it up. I still don't understand it very well but it's fascinating.'

'Do the Lowell's have that kind of microwave?'

'Don't know, but probably. Jerry does a lot of the custom work in a workshop he has set up behind the jewelry store. I hear he has more alarm systems on both of those stores than there are on Fort Knox. But they have some pretty expensive pieces in the store and he buys lots of gold. Not sure what he does with it. It would be interesting to find out. But it's in that workshop that he makes most of his pieces then brings them into the store to sell. Tommy started out working there when he came home but I hear he's looking into getting his own workshop. Seems he and Jerry have different ideas on how to do things.'

Mary didn't find that much of a surprise. Jerry was a solitary man without many social skills. His only interest seemed to be in designing and making jewelry and, of course, his gold-buying shop. Mary doubted he'd have to be too polite to those customers. People who had something they wanted to sell could either take what he offered or go down the road. Tommy had just spent four – or was it five – years in London, going to school and working with a lot of expert jewelers in what she was told was one of England's most exclusive shops. Of course he had some ideas of his own. He was probably a great deal more skilled than his father, which wouldn't help their relationship. Why had Marlene asked him to return and why had he agreed? He hadn't seemed too happy about it.

Luke's attention shifted from Mary to the checkout desk, where a man with an armload of books was beginning to drum his fingers on the desk.

'I've got to go. My only Tuesday help hasn't shown up yet. Volunteers aren't always reliable.' He called out to the man, 'I'll be right there,' then turned back to Mary. 'I'm sorry I can't help you, but if you know how to work the computer . . . you don't. You really need to learn. You need to get one. You have no idea how much easier it would make your life – all those committees, all the things you do.' He broke off and grinned. 'You wouldn't have had to get dressed and come down here. You could have looked up everything you wanted on it.'

Luke started for the desk, Mary at his side.

'I've thought about getting a computer but I have no idea how one works or where to go to learn. Or what to buy . . . It seems overwhelming. I guess I'll just keep coming in here and hope you have time to help me.' She grinned at Luke.

The man shoved his books at Luke then turned toward Mary. 'Everyone should have a computer. Do you have a cell phone?'

Startled, she nodded.

'Can you work it?'

'Some things – the GPS, my bank account, and I'm learning how to email pictures.'

'Then you can learn how to work a computer. Go see Mo Black, Black's computer services. He'll help you choose the right one and give you a fair price, and every computer he sells comes with four free lessons. If you need more, you can go to one of his classes or take a class at the community college.' He gathered up his books, grunted at Luke's apology for making him wait and left.

'Who was that?' Mary watched the man go through the glass doors into the vestibule between the library and the city offices then out onto the street. 'And who is Mo Black?'

'That's Mr Benson. He comes in here every two weeks, checks out a whole range of books from fiction to biographies to "how to" books. He's a retired teacher from somewhere – I forget where – but he's right about Mo Black. Mo and his nephew, Dave, have the computer store next to the Chamber of Commerce. I bought Pam's laptop there. Talk to them. You won't pay any more than you would at the chain stores and they'll help you learn what you need to know. Once you get going, you'll love it.'

She would? She wasn't one bit sure about that, but she had been thinking about it. Maybe she should go in and talk to Mr Black. It couldn't hurt. A woman cleared her throat behind her. Mary turned, smiled and moved over. 'Thanks, Luke. Tell Pam I got the invitation to your wedding. I wouldn't miss it for the world.' Feeling more than a little dazed, she left the building, intending to go straight to the pet shop, collect Millie and go home.

# EIGHTEEN

'So, I bought it.'

Mary sat opposite Ellen in her kitchen, each sipping a glass of iced tea. The way Mary felt, a glass of her beloved Chardonnay would have been more bracing, but it was only four in the afternoon. Too early. Besides, she was hot and thirsty.

Ellen stared at her aunt and sipped. 'You bought a computer?' She set her glass down and stared some more, a perplexed look on her face. 'I told you to get one months ago. What brought this on so suddenly?'

'It's all Luke's fault.' The gloom in her voice caused Millie to raise her head off Mary's foot and stare at her. Evidently deciding it wasn't an emergency, she dropped it back down.

'Why is it Luke's fault?' The perplexed look was gone. Confusion took its place.

'Maybe not all his fault. Part of it was that man in the library, Mr Benson. He told me to go to Black's. Said if I could operate my phone I could a computer and they'd teach me. So did John. He said if I mastered their cash register, which was all computerized, I could learn to operate my own computer. So I stopped in, just to see what they were all about. I walked out the proud owner of a laptop, a keyboard and a mouse. A mouse!' She shook her head and sighed.

The corners of Ellen's mouth were starting to twitch. 'I know the Blacks but I never thought of Mo Black as that good a salesman. Or did you talk to Dave? He's a nice young man.'

Mary sighed again. 'It wasn't salesmanship, it was the websites.'

Ellen raised an eyebrow. 'Come again?'

'He showed me the websites . . . that is what you call them, isn't it? He's done them for several of the businesses in town and then he showed me the one for the city. Did you know they have a button you can click to see all the activities in town? The library has its own but the Kiwanis, the Purebred Dog Club and all the activities the parks and rec committee put on are all on the city website. I didn't know we were up there. It's a marvelous way to let everyone know when something is going on. He said I could make a list of my volunteers by committee and just email them when I need to get hold of them. You put them in folders, just like you would in a filing cabinet, only I never did figure out where the folders come from. You can also do something called cut and paste instead of copying the same message over and over . . .' Her voice trailed off. 'It looked so easy when he was doing it, showing me. He just whizzed through all of it and said he'd teach me. I hope to heaven I learn. This wasn't cheap.'

The corners of Ellen's mouth twitched. Mary was sure she was going to laugh but she nodded, finished her tea and pushed back her chair. 'No, it's not, but it's worth it. You'll learn. And when you do, you'll love it. What other websites did he show you? Our real estate office? He did our site.'

'Yours and Lowell's and a couple others. I had no idea they were so pretty and had so much information.'

Ellen carried her glass to the sink, rinsed it out and put it in the dishwasher. 'I've got to go; I still have to go to the store. Neil will be there for dinner and that young man can really eat. Did you bring it home? Are you going to play with it tonight, because you might want to wait . . .'

Mary shook her head emphatically. 'Mr Black is bringing it out tomorrow around two. He's going to charge it tonight. I'll get my first lesson. I must admit, I'm a bit nervous.'

'Don't be. Once you get the hang of it you'll be on it all the time. Just think of the things you can look up.'

'What do I have to look up?'

'You must have wanted to look up something today. You were in the library and you haven't finished the library books you took out last week.' Ellen waved toward the small pile of books sitting untouched on the sideboard.

'Oh. Well, yes, I thought I'd ask Luke if they had any books, or if you could find out . . .'

'Find out what?'

Mary hesitated. 'I got to thinking about my mother's ring.

Not the diamond but the ring part. What would happen to it? What do you do with old jewelry like that? Luke told me they melt it down. In a microwave, of all things, then it gets poured into molds to make other jewelry or ingots. Do you suppose that's why no one has found the jewelry that's been stolen? The thieves melted it all down? Can you tell Dan?'

'He already knows. He asked Tommy that very question the other night when we had the barbeque.' She paused and the expression on her face changed. 'What do you want to do with grandmother's ring? The setting, I mean. It won't be of much use to anyone without the diamond. I guess you could keep it for sentimental reasons but somehow . . .' She watched her aunt.

Mary didn't know what to say. The idea of the ring being melted down was for some reason unsettling. It was a part of her memories of her mother, of her childhood. On the other hand, what would she do with it? Send it to one of her sisters? What would they do with it? Put it in a cedar chest, hoping someday one of their children or grandchildren would buy another diamond and reset the ring? Highly unlikely.

'Maybe I should ask my sisters,' she finally said but with no certainty.

Ellen laughed. 'You know what they'll say. You decide. Tell you what, why don't you take the ring in to Jerry Lowell? See what he'll give you for it then take the money and do something Grandma would have liked. She was a huge supporter of our library. Use it to buy books in her name.'

Mary immediately brightened. 'What a wonderful idea. That's exactly what I'll do. Mother would have loved that, just as she'd have loved Susannah having her diamond. I'll go see Jerry Lowell tomorrow. Oh. Where is the ring?'

Ellen walked over and gave her aunt a kiss on the forehead. 'At the jewelry shop. No one picked it up after they took the diamond out of it. Go in and ask Marlene for it then take it around to Jerry. I have no idea how much it's worth but not much, I'd guess. Probably enough for at least one book, though. My mom and the other aunts will all love the idea.'

Then she was gone.

# NINETEEN

They had loved the idea. All but Anne, the youngest of Mary's sisters.

'I don't know why it bothers me, it just does,' she'd kept saying. 'I keep remembering her with that ring on. Melting it down seems so . . . harsh.'

But eventually Mary and the other two prevailed. What was Anne going to do with it? She had all boys and they were all married. Her grandkids didn't want an empty setting – neither did she – and she would still remember their mother with the ring on her hand no matter where it was. Besides, think how proud she would be to have donated a book or two to the library. Mary sighed with relief when it was finally decided.

She was at the jewelry store when it opened. Marlene was openly surprised to see her and even more surprised when she noticed Millie by her side. Mary thought she was going to say something but instead she smiled.

'You're here bright and early. Is it about Susannah's ring or can I do something else for you?'

'In a way.' Mary smiled back, relieved Marlene hadn't said anything about Millie. 'It's about my mother's ring. The one the diamond used to be in, or is coming out of.'

Marlene raised her eyebrows slightly as if the ring was not of much importance. 'Oh? Do you want it back?'

Heat ran up the sides of Mary's neck. 'No. It's not that. I talked to my sisters . . . Ellen suggested we sell it. To Jerry. It's supposed to be a high grade of gold but I don't know what that means. None of us want it, and Ellen suggested we take whatever money we could get and donate it to the library in my mother's name. Only, I don't know how to go about this.'

Marlene's smile was suddenly a lot broader. 'Come through to Jerry's shop. He'll acid test the ring for you then weigh it. That will give him an almost exact idea of what it's worth in today's gold prices. It's not a heavy ring so it won't be worth much, but it should certainly buy a few books. What a lovely idea.'

Mary started around the corner but Marlene stopped her.

'Oh. I'm so sorry, but the dog can't come. Jerry . . . I'm sorry, Mary. He'd have a fit. He doesn't allow dogs in his store or his workshop. I don't care if they come in the jewelry store but he won't tolerate them. Can she stay in the car? This won't take long.'

Stay in the car? At ten-thirty on a July morning in Central California? No. She couldn't. But Mary didn't say anything. Millie could once more visit the pet shop. She'd like that a lot better than a gold store anyway, but she couldn't help but feel insulted. For the dog? Yes. Just a little. It was Jerry's right, but what harm could Millie do, sitting by Mary's side while she found out how many library books they could afford to donate?

'I'll take her down to the pet shop.' She knew her voice sounded stiff but that was how she felt.

Marlene didn't seem to notice. Relief was the only emotion she registered. 'Good. I'll get the ring and meet you in the We Buy Gold shop. It's right around the corner.'

Mary knew that but she said nothing. She picked up Millie's leash and headed for the pet shop.

A few minutes later, Mary walked through the door of the We Buy Gold shop and stopped abruptly. She wasn't sure what she'd expected – maybe a dingy little store with rows of . . . what? Gold chains hanging around? Old gold watches on display? Dust on the shelves? There was none of that. Instead there was a small counter atop a glass case and a weight scale on top of that. A chalkboard hung on the back wall, showing the date and what seemed to be the current price of gold in ounces. There was a cash register and a receipt book on the counter, and a smiling Jerry behind it. Everything was clean, neat and professional-looking. She took in a deep breath and approached the counter, where her mother's ring lay on a black piece of cloth. Somehow this professional business approach was more intimidating than the haphazard shop she'd expected.

'Marlene says you want to sell your mother's ring. That right?'

Mary nodded. 'We thought we would. My sisters and I . . . What are you going to do with it? Would you ever try to reset it or something?'

Something flickered in Jerry's eyes that made Mary sorry she'd asked. She knew what would happen, or thought she did, and they'd agreed among themselves that they were all right with that, but suddenly nostalgia took hold of her. Not Jerry.

'I sell all these things to a smelter in LA. They melt it down, refine the other metals out and sell the gold to . . . never mind. I have no use for it, Mary. I buy diamonds sometimes and keep some of the stones folks don't want if I can use them in a piece I want to create, but everything I buy here gets melted down, either in my workshop or in the smelter. No exceptions.'

His eyes had gotten hard, like granites. This was business and there was no room for sentiment.

She inwardly sighed. 'How much is it worth?'

Jerry almost smiled. 'I've weighed it and done an acid test, so we know how much is gold and how much is other metals. I wrote it all out for you. Here.'

He pushed a page of the receipt book toward her. She picked it up and gave a small start of surprise. It wasn't a huge sum but it was more than she'd thought. They would be able to buy several books. She looked at Jerry and nodded.

He nodded back. 'Now we have to comply with the law. I need your fingerprints and you have to sign this.'

'What is it?'

'Your sworn statement you have the authority to sell the ring.'

He rolled her thumb in ink, pushed it down on four forms, had her sign two of them and handed her cash. Before she knew it, she was on the sidewalk, the money in an envelope in her purse, along with a copy of the receipt.

# TWENTY

Mo Black arrived exactly at two. By three, Mary had a colossal headache and a belly full of determination. She was going to conquer this black box if it was the last thing she ever did. Given the way she felt right now, it might be.

Mo had arrived with a small printer as well as the laptop, keyboard and mouse. He looked around.

'Where you goin' to set up?'

Set up? 'I thought we'd set it on the kitchen table for now. Then, when I get dinner ready . . .'

Her voice faded away under his incredulous gaze.

'You need a desk.'

That was emphatic enough. 'Why?'

'You need someplace to put the printer. Then you need to plug the keyboard into the laptop, connect the mouse and get a pad to run it on. All that takes room. After you learn how to operate it you can take the laptop with you but you probably won't. At least, not very often. So, we need to set it up.'

Mary looked around the kitchen. So did Mo. There was nowhere except the table.

'The dining room?' There didn't seem much hope in Mo's voice but he followed Mary through the door. There was only one possible location. The credenza.

Mo stared at it without saying a word. He didn't have to. The rigid set to his jaw said enough. His eyes narrowed slightly as he walked into the living room and looked around. 'Your bedroom?'

Mary shook her head. This was a small house. The kitchen was small, the dining and living rooms adequate, but her bedroom had just enough room for her bed, a chest of drawers and her rocking chair. She couldn't even get Millie's bed in without falling over it. As Millie preferred hers, it didn't matter, but the computer wasn't going in. It would have to go in the spare room. That was where she kept her sewing machine, the day bed that pulled out into a double bed for company and a chest of drawers that contained all her sewing things, a lot more things she'd forgotten she had and two overflowing bookcases. She hadn't had overnight company in ages and hadn't sewn anything in even longer. Maybe it was time to put it all away. She led him down the small hallway and opened the door.

Mo walked in and smiled. 'Yeah,' was all he said.

'We can put the sewing machine . . .'

Mo was way ahead of her. 'My mom had one of these.' He had the top on the old Singer secured before she knew what was happening. 'The closet?'

She nodded and it was out of sight – the laptop, the printer and everything else spread out on Samuel's old desk.

'I don't suppose you have Wi-Fi?'

Mary had to think. 'Does that mean no wires?'

He nodded.

'I think the man who connected my TV said something about it. I told him I might get a computer. Would this tell us?' She opened the bottom drawer of the desk and removed the folder of information and paperwork the TV and phone man had given her. Mo took it, nodded and went to work. Before Mary knew it she was seated at the desk, staring at the open computer, her hand on the mouse. Her first lesson was ready to begin.

After Mo left, Mary headed for the kitchen and the Tylenol bottle. Dazed was a good word for how she felt, but also exhilarated. She'd had no idea this would be fun but it was. It was also going to be useful once she learned more. A whole lot more. For now, she'd better practice. Her second lesson was scheduled for tomorrow afternoon. Tomorrow morning would be taken up by the wrap-up meeting of the Fourth of July celebration committee and, as chairwoman, she had to be there. Her final reports were ready. She should probably go through them one more time. But first she'd see if she could remember anything Mo had taught her.

# TWENTY-ONE

The meeting went well. Milt Chadwick, treasurer for the parks and recreation steering committee, reported that they had stayed within their budget, which Mary considered a minor miracle. The vendors were pleased, had all made donations to the park and rec committee and all of the events were considered a success, especially the fireworks. It went exactly as planned. Except for the murder of Ian Miller.

It was almost nine and people were leaving. Only Mary, Milt Chadwick and Joy Chambers were left. Mary drained the last of her coffee and pushed her chair back, careful to miss Millie who was asleep under it, and took her mug to the sink in the city hall meeting room. Another meeting was scheduled for first thing the next morning and she wanted to make sure they left the room clean.

'We'll help with that in a minute.' Joy tipped her mug back and forth, as if looking for one last drop, sighed and looked at Mary. 'I hear you bought a computer. How are you doing with it?'

Mary leaned back against the counter. She fleetingly thought it was a good thing she didn't have any secrets to hide. In this town they wouldn't remain secret for more than a day. She frowned. Someone was keeping a secret. One serious enough that it resulted in murder.

'Yes. I bought it from Mo Black and he's already given me one lesson. It's complicated, but when I figure it all out I think I'm going to like it.'

Milt laughed. 'Almost no one figures it all out. If you can answer your emails, do your banking and sort of work Windows, you'll be doing fine. Has he taught you how to get on the Internet yet?'

'That was first. I have a username and a password. I'd already set up an account with the bank on my phone so getting into my account online wasn't hard. Then we got into websites. I had no idea the library had so many . . . what do you call them? Those buttons. You can find anything.'

'Are you going to put up your own website?'

Mary couldn't tell if Joy thought that was a good idea or the silliest one she'd ever heard. 'I hadn't thought about it. Do you think I should? What would I put on it?'

'Of course you should.' Milt, at least, was positive. 'You could put on your calendar – you know, what committees you're chairing, notices of meetings, results of committee decisions, that kind of thing. I'm sure there's lots of things.'

Her calendar? 'Why would anyone be interested in a list of my committee meetings?'

'If they were supposed to attend one and couldn't remember the date, they would be. It could be sort of like a community calendar.' So Joy did think it was a good idea.

It was something Mary would have to think about when she got better at all this. One lesson hadn't even scratched the surface of what she needed to know. But Joy was warming to her subject.

'Half the people in town who have websites have some kind of calendar. Even Ruthie does.'

Mary blinked. 'Ruthie has one? Why?'

'Specials. She has a list of holidays and days of the week when she has specials.'

'If you want The Yum Yum's special, all you have to do is read the chalkboard.'

Joy shook her head. 'If you want her cheese and broccoli quiche you don't want to drop in every day to read the chalkboard. You can look it up online. Same with lots of things. Why, even those Gradys have a calendar. That way, if some town or event wants fireworks, they know right off if the date they want is already booked. Saves everybody time and fuss.'

Mary didn't remember anyone looking at the Gradys' calendar when they booked them, but admittedly she hadn't known they had one when she'd called. Maybe she'd gotten lucky.

'It's something to think about. However, I need to learn a lot more before I attempt something like that.'

She turned, filled the sink with soapy water and began to gather up all the mugs.

Joy brought over a tray of empties and started dumping used napkins in the trash. 'Does Dan have any idea who shot that poor man?' She picked up a dishtowel and proceeded to wipe as fast as Mary could wash.

'If he does, he hasn't shared that information.'

Milt handed Mary his empty mug. 'I'll take out the trash. Is there anything else that needs doing?'

'I don't think so. You go on home. We're almost finished here, then we're going to leave as well.'

He hesitated, the look on his face one of doubt. 'Mary . . .'

She handed Joy the last mug, faced him and waited.

'That man who's been with Dan since the Fourth – who is he?'

'He's Eric Wilson, a member of the California Bureau of Investigation major incident crimes unit.'

'Oh.' There was a lot in that little word.

'Why? Is something wrong?'

'No. No, I'm sure not. It's just that . . .' The look on Milt's face was indecisive.

'Milt, what are you not sure about?'

'It's just that . . . I think I've seen him before. Here. In town. I've been thinking about it and I'm sure he's the same person.'

Mary heard her sharp intake of breath. 'Where did you see him?'

Milt looked uncomfortable. 'In the alley behind the computer shop. I remember because I'd parked back there and saw the guy when I went in. I wondered about him then. He didn't seem to be going anywhere, just sort of hanging around. We don't have too much crime in this town but there are several shops that open onto that alley and I immediately wondered what the guy was up to. I mentioned it to Mo Black, just so he'd watch the back door. The guy was still there when I left with my computer. Mo helped me out to the car with it, and he went over and talked to him. I sort of waited a minute, you know, to make sure everything was all right, but it seemed to be and I drove off. I'm sure it was this man who's been around town with Dan.'

'Have you mentioned this to Dan?'

'No. I didn't think it was important, just . . . interesting. Do you think I should?'

'Never mind. I'll mention it but I'm sure you're right. It's probably not important.'

'Hey, how's that dog – the one Miller had? He seemed a nice kind of dog.'

Mary told him about Ranger. Milt nodded, took out the trash and left. Mary and Joy finished the kitchen and left as well, Millie leading Mary eagerly toward their car. She opened the back door and Millie jumped in, then she placed her tote bag with all her files in it on the passenger seat. She remembered little about the drive home. She was too busy wondering why Mr Wilson had come to town but never mentioned it. She had little doubt Milt had recognized him but what was Wilson doing in the alley? What had he wanted with Mo Black? When was all this? But, most importantly, did Dan know?

# TWENTY-TWO

This was the way she'd planned to spend her summer. She hadn't crawled out of bed until almost eight. Mercifully, Millie had slept in as well. She made herself a light breakfast of fruit and yogurt and was sitting peacefully at her kitchen table, eating a piece of toast, sipping a second cup of coffee, about to open the library book she'd been trying to get to for a week. She had no place to go and nothing scheduled.

The phone rang.

She thought about not answering it but some habits were hard to break. 'Hello?'

It was Emma Baxter. Would today be a good day to meet for lunch? Wilson had gone back to Sacramento for the day, she was at a loose end and she'd love to meet Mary at The Yum Yum – her treat. Mary looked at her library book, shut it and said she'd be delighted. Twelve-thirty? Perfect. She'd meet Emma there. She hung up and sighed. Oh, well. She didn't have anything she had to do other than get through the library book before it was due, and if she could help Emma find out a little something about her roots, so much the better, although Emma might not be too pleased with what Mary had to say. Her grandfather hadn't been a model citizen and her poor grandmother had not had an easy time. If her father and uncles didn't want to talk about their childhood, she certainly didn't want to talk out of turn, but some things . . . Like what the boys had been like in school, how smart they were, how the fried egg thing was an accident . . . But maybe she'd skip how they were always on welfare and their father drank up all the money and never could hold a job. She was going to have to walk a fine line, indeed.

'You're in luck.'

Millie looked at her with what seemed to be anticipation.

Mary laughed. 'Yes, you're going, but only as far as the pet shop. You can harass the kittens while I have lunch with Emma.'

Millie seemed to smile as she watched Mary head for the shower.

Emma dropped the remains of her half-eaten hamburger on her plate and picked up her iced tea. 'My grandmother didn't have an easy time of it, did she?'

Mary finished the last of her BLT and pushed the plate to one side. 'No, she didn't. She lived like a pioneer woman most of her married life and I think it broke her heart when the boys left, but I also think she knew they had to or they'd end up like their father.'

Brow furrowed, eyes gleaming suspiciously, Emma looked at Mary. 'Why didn't she leave him? I know my father tried to get her to several times but she wouldn't. Why?'

Mary shook her head. 'I don't know. I really never knew either of them. Her sister, your aunt Bea, was a friend of mine and she told me things. She tried to get her to leave, also. She couldn't understand it and it almost drove her to distraction. Finally, she gave up. I think the boys did also.'

Emma shook her head. 'The poor thing.'

'She made her choice.' Mary tried to make her voice kind but firm. Eva Baxter had chosen to stay and there was nothing her sons or granddaughter could do about it – not then and certainly not now. 'Tell me about your father and your uncles. I haven't seen them in years. I didn't see your father when he came to sell the ranch and take your mother away. I guess he didn't want to come back because Ellen said they did all the rest of the sale by fax or electronically. Does he like being a dentist?'

Emma grinned, a white, straight teeth grin. Testimony to her father's talent? 'I guess he does. It certainly wasn't what I wanted to do, although one of my brothers is in dental school. I wanted to do what my uncle Casey did, and here I am.'

'I'm sure it's a lot more exciting.'

'Sometimes. Often it's a lot of paperwork and tracking things – and people – down. But sometimes . . .'

There was a lull while Emma seemed to retreat into her own thoughts.

Mary tried to think of something to break the silence. 'Why did Mr Wilson go back to Sacramento?'

'Oh.' She came back with a start. 'He took Miller's laptop and his cell phone to the lab. There may be something on one of them that can give us a clue as to why he was here.'

Mary nodded. 'I assume you went through his room. Where was he staying?'

'Place called The Harmony Ranch. Not very glamorous, but clean and they take dogs. And, no, we didn't find anything else. No notes, no pictures, not one blasted thing. I hope he left something on his computer.'

'Yes, The Harmony Ranch. A good place. I know Heidi, the owner. How about the dog? Who's going to take him? Does Miller have any family who'd want him?'

'Not that I know about. He was divorced years ago but I don't know who she is or where she is. As far as anyone in the department goes, I'm not sure. I know Wilson won't. He's never liked that dog and Ranger isn't too fond of him.'

Mary leaned forward a little, studying Emma's face, wondering if she should bring up what Mitch had told her and decided she should. 'Did Mr Wilson say anything about his visit to Santa Louisa a few weeks ago?'

Emma had been watching her tea sway in her glass as she tipped it from side to side, but now it hit the table with a small bang as her head jerked up to stare at Mary. 'Say what? Wilson was here? In this town? When? How do you know that?'

'A friend told me. He wanted to know who he was. Said he'd seen him in town a while ago and wondered why he was with Dan.'

'He's sure it's the same man?' Mary didn't know how to read the expression on Emma's face but it was a lot more than mild interest.

'He's positive and I believe him.'

'Mary . . . Is it all right if I call you Mary?'

Mary nodded and waited.

'Did your friend tell you where he . . .' She waited but Mary didn't respond. 'Where was Wilson and what was he doing?'

'My friend saw him in the alley, the one behind the jewelry

store, the pet store and the computer shop. Wilson seemed to be loitering and it made my friend nervous.'

Emma was very still. She seemed to be thinking hard and whatever she was thinking didn't seem, from the expression on her face, to please her much. 'That's all you're going to tell me, isn't it?'

'Well, it's not like I was told in confidence, but . . .'

'Are you going to tell Dan?'

'Should I?'

'I think it might be a good idea.'

Unease crept up Mary's neck and settled in the back of her head. There was something going on here that she didn't like. That Emma hadn't known Wilson visited Santa Louisa only a few weeks ago was obvious, but he had berated her for not telling him her family originally came from this area. Why? She could hardly quiz Emma. She'd absolutely tell Dan about Wilson and who saw him and what he was doing. Then she'd quiz him about what it all meant. He might or might not tell her whatever he knew. In the meantime: 'I'll mention it to Dan.'

Emma nodded, the expression on her face grim, and picked up the check. 'I've got to get back. I've already taken longer for lunch than I should have. Thank you, Mary, for everything. I'll be talking to you?'

There was a large question mark on the end of that sentence that couldn't be ignored. Mary nodded and pushed back her chair.

It took only minutes and they were on the street, Emma ready to head toward the police department and Mary to her car, but they were both stopped by a voice calling Mary's name.

A tall, dark-haired young man wearing sunglasses, a large smile and leading – or rather, being led – by a German shepherd, was baring down on them at a slow trot.

'Look who I have.' Tommy Lowell proudly came to a stop in front of Mary. He grinned at her then smiled at Emma, who smiled back. 'Hello. I'm Tommy Lowell. This is Ranger.'

'Ranger, I know.' Emma bent down and rubbed Ranger between his ears.

He wagged his tail in greeting.

'I'm Emma Baxter.' She straightened up and looked Tommy Lowell over slowly. 'Nice to meet you, Tommy Lowell.' She turned slightly toward Mary. 'Thanks for everything. I've got to run.' Then she addressed Tommy once more. 'Do you have Ranger often?'

'This is the first time. He's a nice dog.'

'Yes. He is.' She looked at Ranger thoughtfully then back at Tommy. 'Maybe we'll meet again.'

Mary, Ranger and Tommy watched her hurry down the sidewalk and disappear around the corner.

'Who was that?' Tommy hadn't yet taken his eyes of the now-empty corner.

'She's one of the special agents looking into Mr Miller's death.'

Tommy whirled around to stare at her, Ranger seemingly forgotten. 'She's a cop? Is she looking into the jewelry robberies as well?' His face had gone white and he looked a little sick.

'How do you know about the jewelry robberies?'

'Everybody in town knows about them. That Miller guy was here investigating them and Dan thinks there's a connection.' He turned to look at the empty corner once more. 'Wouldn't you just know it,' he mumbled, then he and Ranger walked slowly down the street the other way.

# TWENTY-THREE

'Isn't that Tommy Lowell?'

Mary startled and turned quickly.

Heath Grady was standing beside her. She had been so intent on wondering why Tommy would be upset that Emma Baxter was with the police that she hadn't noticed him walk up. She nodded.

'Since when did he get a dog?' Heath sounded as if the idea of a dog was somehow offensive.

'It's not Tommy's. It belonged to Ian Miller, the man who was killed at the fairgrounds.'

Heath pushed his cowboy hat back on his head and cocked one hip. He watched Tommy until he and Ranger disappeared around the corner. 'Yeah. Gabe told me about that. The guy with the dog who watched us put the show together. So the dog doesn't live with them? It's not little Tommy's dog?'

Mary nodded, wondering why Heath sounded so speculative and why the sneer? Tommy wasn't little, in any way, but the way Heath said his name . . .

'What'd that guy do that someone wanted to kill him?'

Mary gritted her teeth. Heath was certainly in a mood today.

'I don't know. I'm not sure the police know, either, but they're working on it.'

'Sure.' Heath sounded as if he held Tommy in disdain and the police as well.

Where had that come from? It hadn't sounded as if he even knew Tommy, so why the sneer? As for the police, unfortunately there were a lot of people who didn't hold them in high esteem. Some had reason not to, but others just seemed to distrust the police for no particular reason. She wondered which camp Heath belonged to. Or did he hold most other people in disdain? That was a possibility. He and Gabe looked alike: both tall, lean, with large blue eyes and dark brown thick hair, but there the resemblance ended. Gabe wore heavy jewelry and his jeans were a little too tight. His smile for the girls, even much older 'girls,' was a little too familiar, his handshake for the guys or clasp on their shoulder a little too quick. Heath was just the opposite. No jewelry, jeans bleached almost white with washing, his smile rarely given to anyone and his hand never extended. That faint look of disdain wasn't only for the police department or Tommy.

'What brings you to town?'

His eyes narrowed and, for a moment, she thought he was going to tell her it was none of her business, but he didn't. 'Had some banking to do.'

'Oh. Is Gabe with you?' She looked around for the white-paneled van that looked like a rolling fireworks show, the one that had almost run her over the other day, but it wasn't in sight. She didn't think Gabe would miss a chance to get to town and what little action Santa Louisa could supply.

'He's at home, packing the van. We've got a job this weekend.'

'You two certainly keep busy. Don't you ever worry about leaving the ranch all alone while you're gone so much? I mean, all those fireworks and everything and you're so far out.' Much to her fury, her voice faded away under Heath's soft, mirthless laugh.

'Anyone fool enough to try to get on our land or in that barn or the house would get a pretty unpleasant surprise. Gabe isn't good for a lot of things but he's a whizz with electronic stuff. The White House isn't protected nearly as well as our place.'

The look on Heath's face almost dared her to ask how, but she decided she didn't care. 'Well, it's nice to see you again but I've got to pick up Millie and get home. Good luck with your show.'

Heath grunted. She smiled at him. Feeling a lot safer knowing the van wasn't in town, she crossed the street into the park on her way to Furry Friends and Millie.

# TWENTY-FOUR

'One of the Gradys almost ran you over? Thank God you didn't have Millie with you.'

'He didn't mean . . .' Glen Manning's face was fire red as he glared at John. 'Of course we're glad you didn't get run over.'

John stared at Glen, then at Mary. 'Oh, I didn't mean . . . it's just that she sometimes tries to run ahead and . . .'

Mary laughed. 'I know what you mean. I thought the same thing. Something else we've got to work on.'

Mary was perched on the stool in front of the cash register. Millie lay quietly on the floor beside her as the humans talked. She'd finished her extravagant greeting and seemed content to rest before she and Mary left for home.

'I hope you don't mind Millie visiting so often. I feel we're imposing but she loves to come and I know she's safe here.'

'We don't mind in the least. We love having her, and since you're always helping us out when we need someone to watch the shop when we're called away, it's the least we can do.' John wiggled his fingers in Millie's direction. Since ear scratching wasn't involved, she closed her eyes.

Glen didn't seem to be paying attention to Millie or John. 'I've seen that van come roaring out of the alley exit before. I think it's Gabe driving but it's hard to tell at a distance. They look alike and they both wear those huge cowboy hats, but Gabe seems to be the reckless one. Heath is all business, at least when he's in the bank. He knows to the penny how much they have and watches it like a hawk. The way he looks over his accounts you'd think we made a habit of shorting him every month.'

'Most folks are careful like that these days. Money doesn't go as far as it used to.' Mary didn't add she was one of those who watched her money carefully. It would be easier as she learned to use the computer more efficiently.

Glen snorted. 'He doesn't need to be all that careful. That business of theirs is a lot more lucrative than I'd have ever imagined.'

'How much is he worth?' John's eyes gleamed. He loved gossip and sensed he was about to hear something really interesting. He wasn't.

'I can't tell you that. It's privileged information, and besides, it's none of your business. However . . .'

John practically licked his lips in anticipation of the next piece of news.

'Heath is a good businessman and knows how to diversify his holdings. Financially, they're as solid as anyone in this town.' He gave John an almost wicked grin. 'Yes, I'd say G and H Enterprises is doing just fine.'

Mary almost laughed. Glen got his point across and hadn't really told them a thing. But all this didn't solve the problem of Gabe – if it was Gabe – driving like a madman.

'I suppose I could tell Dan but I don't think he can do a thing about it unless he, or someone, sees him. I'll tell him to keep an eye out.'

She slid off the stool, leaned down, snapped Millie's leash on her harness and picked up her purse in preparation to leave.

Glen seemed to have other ideas. 'Speaking of Dan, has he any leads as to who killed that man? The word is out he was a special agent for California's major crime unit. Is that true?'

'Uh, yes.'

'Was he really here looking for jewel thieves?'

'Put like that, it sounds sort of romantic, doesn't it?' John grinned at Mary as if they'd shared a joke.

Mary didn't think it was romantic to get shot in the back and that Miller had been poking around her town made her more than worried, but she smiled back at John anyway. 'Gossip didn't fly around this town this fast when we had a party line. Where did you hear that?'

'My dear Mary, it's all over town.' John's smile got broader.

Glen's frown got deeper. 'Heidi, over at Harmony Ranch, was in the bank and she told me. Said they turned the murdered man's – Miller, was that him? – room upside down. She had no idea what they were looking for but all they found was his laptop and some dirty underwear. And a dog bed and dishes.'

'Oh, good. Does Dan know that? Ranger – that's the dog – is staying with them.'

'Dan was there so I guess so.' Glen paused. 'You know that man with Dan? The other state policeman? He's been in town before. Do you know why?'

'Why he was here? I have no idea. How do you know he was?'

'He wanted to cash a check and the only branches we have are in San Louis Obispo county, so getting a check cashed was a bit of an ordeal. I finally got it done for him.'

'Why didn't he use his ATM? There's a fee but they work anywhere.' John looked a little confused, as if such a simple thing shouldn't be a drama.

'You can only get so much cash at any one time with your card. He wanted more. Why he couldn't use it for whatever he wanted to buy, I don't know. But we got it done. He got his cash and was on his way. When I saw him with Dan yesterday, I remembered him and wondered. I had no idea he was a policeman.'

Mary was a little breathless. First Milt said Miller was skulking around in the alley behind Lowell's and now Glen said he'd wanted to get a large amount of cash but didn't want to use his ATM card. What was all that about? What was he doing here, anyway? The whole thing was confusing. She glanced at the clock on the register and gasped. Mr Black would be pulling into her driveway any minute for her second lesson. She felt like the white rabbit as she called out 'I'm late' to John and Glen and, with Millie trotting rapidly beside her, made a dash for her car and home.

# TWENTY-FIVE

Mary walked in her back door as her doorbell rang. Millie careened through the house, barking. She only quit when Mary picked her up and opened the door to let in Mo Black.

'Noisy, isn't she?' He held his hand out for Millie to smell.

She evidently decided she knew him because she quit barking and wagged her stub of a tail. Mary set her down and she immediately headed for the guest bedroom, now the computer room, and lay down on the old quilt Mary had left folded by the desk.

'I guess she remembers me.' Mo Black and Mary followed Millie into the room.

'Sometimes it takes her a minute to decide it's all right for someone to come in. I think you're now on her acceptable list.'

Mo grinned. 'Good thing.' He laid a folder on the desk, stood back and indicated Mary should take the chair. 'Let's see you log on.'

Mary worked her way through logging into several websites and accessed her bank account. Mo pronounced her ready to email. 'Do you remember how to do that?'

She didn't. At least, not at first. Finally, she remembered and there it was. An empty email list. No. There was one email, welcoming her to the wonderful world of instant mail.

'Today we're going to practice sending and receiving emails and setting up separate folders of email addresses for different purposes. You'll need that for all your committees.'

An hour later Mary had successfully emailed Ellen twice, had an email back from her, which she opened, and started two lists. Now all she needed were the addresses of people to put on them. She felt euphoric, as if she'd accomplished something monumental, and was completely exhausted.

Mo got up, stretched and handed Mary the notebook. 'These

are printouts of everything we've gone over today. When you
try to do this stuff by yourself and realize you have no idea
what to do next, just look in here. There are lessons on Word
and some other things, but don't try them until I come back.
Which will be . . . Do you remember how to find the calendar?'

She didn't, but there it was, on page five. She entered it.
Day after tomorrow, at four p.m. She smiled and stood. 'Before
you leave I'd like to ask you a non-computer question, if you
don't mind?'

Mo Black's face changed from friendly to wary and all
traces of a smile vanished. 'Depends on what it is.'

Feeling somewhat embarrassed, but why she didn't know,
Mary plowed on. 'There's a Mr Eric Wilson in town and I
was told you were talking to him in the alley behind Lowell's
a few weeks ago. Can you tell me if that's true?'

'Can you tell me why you want to know?' There was no
mistaking the bitterness in his voice. It might have been a
nosy question but she hadn't expected this degree of antago-
nism. She had to think for a second how to phrase her answer.

'Mr Wilson is with the California Bureau of Investigation.
It was his partner who was murdered at the Fourth of July
celebration. He's here investigating his death. We . . . that is,
Dan Dunham . . . understood he'd never been in town before
but I was told he had been seen talking to David. I wanted to
know if Mr Wilson was . . . not telling our own police something important.'

Mo didn't say anything for what seemed a long time. A
hardness had developed around his mouth and seemed to cloud
his eyes. 'My nephew, Dave and I, we've known – if that's
the correct term – Eric Wilson for about ten years. He was
one of the arresting officers of my brother and his wife. David's
parents. Dave was seven then. He keeps showing up from time
to time like a bad penny. That was him in the alley, talking
to me.'

Mary was too stunned to say anything for a moment. 'But
why? Is he worried about David?'

If that was it, why had he not mentioned it?

Mo's snort wasn't laughter. 'He's been certain for years I
had some part in what my brother and his wife were doing.

He tried to tie me to them then and he's still trying. He thought Dave was also somehow involved. Tried to have him put in juvenile hall but there wasn't one shred of evidence against either one of us. Still isn't, but no one's been able to make Wilson believe it.' He turned to go but paused when Mary held up her hand.

'Mr Black . . . Mo . . . what did your brother and sister-in-law do to . . .' Heat crawled up her cheeks. It was an impertinent question but it had escaped before she could stop it.

Mo Black didn't seem to think so. Instead, a small grim smile appeared. 'They were convicted of robbing a series of jewelry stores.'

# TWENTY-SIX

'I don't see the connection.'

Ellen pushed her empty pie plate to one side and picked up her glass of iced tea. It was too hot for coffee.

She, Dan, Mary and Emma Baxter all sat around Mary's dining-room table, eating lemon blueberry pie and drinking iced tea. It was also too hot to bake but that's what Mary did when she was upset. Somehow it helped settle her nerves, and her conversation with Mo Black had left her upset.

'More pie, anyone?' She pushed her chair back, ready to refill plates.

Millie looked up hopefully from her spot under the table by Mary's chair. Ranger and Morgan lay on each side of the kitchen door. Hoping some crumbs would drop their way as she passed in and out?

Everyone groaned. The pie was delicious but rich.

Ellen pushed her aunt gently back down in the chair. 'I'll get the iced tea pitcher.'

Emma got up, started to collect plates and followed Ellen into the kitchen.

Dan stared at Mary. 'I don't see how you do it. You found two people who are willing to swear Eric Wilson was in Santa Louisa not more than a couple of weeks ago while Wilson gave us to believe he'd never heard of this town until he got the call that Miller was dead. It's not exactly a lie but as close as it gets to one. Only, why?'

'Why was he here or why didn't he tell you?'

'Both.' He sighed and leaned back. 'It's interesting and I guess I'll have to ask Wilson about it when he returns, but I'm with Ellen. I don't see the connection.'

Emma stepped over the dogs and sat back down. 'Why do dogs always lie in doorways?'

No one had an answer to that question either.

'I can think of one possible reason he was here.' The

behavior of dogs abandoned, she returned to the behavior of people. 'Wilson was furious when he found out Miller had made a connection between that string of robberies. He could have been trying to find out if the Blacks were implicated.'

Ellen stepped over the dogs and slid into her chair. 'What would that have to do with Miller's murder?'

Emma shrugged.

'Were Miller and Wilson partners when Mo Black's brother was arrested?'

That the wheels were turning in Dan's head as he tried to fit the puzzle pieces together, Mary had no doubt, but these pieces didn't seem to belong to the same puzzle.

Emma looked blank. 'Don't know. That was way before my time.'

'But you know how long they'd been partners?'

She nodded slowly. 'Over ten years. My uncle said they'd been close friends at one time but had a falling out a long time ago. I don't know over what. Anyway, they remained partners but the personal friendship was dead. Miller has gone his own way ever since.'

'A falling out but not such a big one they weren't still partners. That doesn't sound like a big enough motive for murder.' Mary had absentmindedly scratched Millie's ears as the dog tried to climb into her lap. She pushed her down. 'There's not room enough in this chair for both of us and the crumbs are gone.'

Millie sighed and crept back under the table.

Ellen set her empty iced tea glass back down and looked at Dan. 'Do you think the Blacks could be implicated? That Black shot Miller because he was on his trail?'

Dan shook his head. 'First, we don't know Miller was. Second, if anyone was on Black's trail it was Wilson, and if Emma's right he was on Miller's trail as well. But what good killing Miller would do either of them, I can't see.'

'Suppose that . . .' Ellen didn't get any further.

'Suppose we don't go any further ourselves until we get some evidence. Wilson should be back tomorrow or the next day and, with any luck, they'll have found something on Miller's computer or phone. There wasn't one thing in his hotel room that was helpful. Except possibly that laptop and phone. And, of course, the dog bed.'

Ellen laughed. 'Which you brought home and Ranger has ignored. Morgan likes it, though.'

Dan grinned. 'Ranger likes having his own dinner dish.' His grin faded as he stared at the dog. 'Another mystery is why no one on Miller's team has offered to take Ranger or offered any information on who might.' He turned to Emma. 'Did Miller have a family?'

'I heard he was divorced but have no idea when or where his ex might be. I don't know who would have a claim on Ranger or who might want to adopt him. I can't. I live in an apartment complex that frowns on goldfish. How about the guy who we met walking him?'

'Tommy Lowell?' Mary looked at Dan, then Ellen. 'He seems to like the dog. Would he take him?'

'I don't think his father would let him.' There was more than a hint of disapproval in Ellen's voice.

It was annoyance more than disapproval that Mary felt. 'Tommy Lowell is a grown man. He lived in London for years before he came home. He's a certified . . . something and can rival his father in jewelry design in every way. I doubt he'd need permission to take a dog.'

Dan burst out laughing. 'Tommy would be happy to hear you stick up for him, I'm sure, but I agree. I doubt he needs sticking up for. Ellen's also right, though. Jerry Lowell has pretty fixed ideas of what he wants and what he doesn't. If Tommy wants the dog and his father doesn't, I'll bet Ellen could find him a little house someplace to rent. He might be a lot happier that way.'

Mary remembered what Tommy had said. His mother had asked him to move back in with them. Why, she didn't know. Would Tommy really move into his own place over a dog? Time alone would tell.

That was as far as the conversation went that night. Ellen yawned. Dan smiled, pushed back his chair and suggested they call it a night.

Mary locked the door after them and went into the kitchen to clean up, but the girls were way ahead of her. Glasses and plates in the dishwasher, remains of the pie in the refrigerator, drain boards wiped down – there was nothing left to do. Relieved, Mary let the tiredness that had been creeping up on her for the last hour or so take over. She and Millie would also call it a night. She vowed tonight she wasn't going to lie awake, worrying about who killed Mr Miller. If it was someone from town, what would that mean for the town? She was going to slip into her lightest nightgown, leave the ceiling fan on and go right to sleep.

Only she didn't.

# TWENTY-SEVEN

**M**ary sat in front of the computer, muttering. The notebook Mr Black had given her was open on the desk and she was trying to follow directions on how to set up and save a list of committee members. She could make the list, and she thought she'd saved it but found, to her dismay, she couldn't find it again. What had she done wrong? She didn't know but her frustration level was growing. This computer business had sounded wonderful when she'd decided to do it but the learning curve everyone talked about felt more like climbing Mount Everest.

The back door opened. She could barely hear who it was over Millie's frantic barks but it was someone they knew. That was Millie's welcome bark, not her warning one. Mary pushed her chair back, glad of the interruption, and headed toward the kitchen to greet their guest.

It was Ellen. 'Hi. I'm on my way home for lunch but thought I'd stop by. Got a second?'

'You came just in time. I'm trying to learn how to work that wretched machine and was about to throw it out of the window. Let's have a glass of iced tea. Maybe I'll be calmer after having one and talking with you for a minute. What brings you here, anyway?'

Ellen took two glasses out of the cupboard while Mary got the tea out of the refrigerator then filled them. They sat at the kitchen table, Millie under Mary's chair, and smiled at each other.

'All right.' Mary took a sip of her tea. 'What's up?'

Ellen smiled. 'Nothing, really, but after our conversation last night I thought you might be interested. I got a voicemail from Tommy Lowell this morning.'

From the mixture of amusement and disbelief on Mary's face, Ellen thought she was probably very interested.

'What? What did he say?'

'First, that he couldn't pick up Ranger today until after work. That was no surprise. It was what else he said . . .'

'I'm waiting.'

'He wants to buy a house.'

Mary set her glass down on the table, hard, and stared at her niece. 'He what?'

'He wants to buy a house. One in town, with a yard. One where he can walk to work. Two bedrooms is fine. Can I help him?'

Mary wasn't sure what to say. Buy a house? With what? Did he have enough money to do that? He was young. Maybe he didn't realize . . . what was she thinking? He was well over twenty-one, had lived on his own in another country and had worked in a business light years more sophisticated than Lowell's small-town jewelry store. He most likely knew exactly what he wanted and how to get it. 'What did you tell him?'

'I sent him to Glen Manning. Glen will tell him about loans, then he'll tell me what Tommy can afford. Prices have gone through the roof in the last few years and a small house in town is no longer a bargain. We'll see, but I thought it was interesting. Do you suppose it's the dog or he's just sick and tired of listening to his father complain?'

What a curious thing to say. Mary wouldn't doubt Jerry Lowell complained and was probably jealous of his more accomplished son, but how did Ellen know?'

'How do you know he complained? What about?'

Ellen looked into her glass of tea and her cheeks got pink. 'Dan and I bought our rings at Lowell's. There's nothing fancy about them, just two plain gold bands, but Marlene was really nice to deal with. Jerry ignored us. She and I got sort of friendly and one day, when she must have had it with him, she made a few comments.'

'Well? You can't stop now. What did she say?'

'That Jerry had nothing to do with the business. He ran his custom jewelry design business out of the workshop behind the store and sold his jewelry through the store but he was more interested in the gold-buying store than the jewelry store. I guess it's making good money, but Marlene said she was responsible for everything else and was getting tired. She wanted Tommy to come back and help run it. Jerry didn't. When Tommy returned, he made it as hard for him to work as he possibly could and she was getting sick of it. I doubt it's gotten better, hence Tommy wants something of his own.'

Mary thought about that for a moment but it didn't make much sense. 'I don't understand. How does he make it hard?'

Ellen shrugged. 'I got the impression she meant he didn't want Tommy using the jewels and the gold for his designs. Although, why he'd care when all of it must belong to the Lowell's store, I have no idea. But you saw that necklace. I think it has a lot to do with what Tommy does with the jewels. He really is an artist.'

Mary nodded. Maybe that was it. Maybe Tommy was sick of dealing with a morose father and wanted his own place. That was understandable. But all this gave her an uneasy feeling, one she couldn't identify.

Ellen looked up as the old schoolhouse clock chimed out noon. 'I've got to go. I have a showing at one and still have some preparations to make. Pat wants us all to come to her house for dinner tomorrow. She wants to talk wedding plans and look at the ideas Susannah is coming up with. She's already bought about two pounds of bride magazines and is marking them up. Neil is beginning to get that glazed "I'm out of my depth" look grooms get. It's a good thing they're off to school in a few weeks. They can concentrate on something other than the bride's dress, how many bridesmaids to have and caterers. This is going to be a long year.'

Ellen gave her aunt a kiss on the forehead and Millie a pat on the head and was gone. But Mary didn't move. She sat for a long time, sipping her tea and thinking about Tommy Lowell and his relationship with his father. Whatever it was, it evidently wasn't warm and fuzzy. Suddenly, she straightened up so quickly the chair creaked under her. When had Tommy come home? Not quite two years ago? She thought that was right. And when had the burglaries started? About that time. Could it be possible . . . no. Absolutely not. She didn't think Tommy liked his father much and certainly wouldn't commit robberies with him. But the stones in the necklace . . . Had they really come from pieces Jerry bought for his We Buy

Gold shop? What was it Jerry had said? He only bought diamonds. All the other stones were either kept by the owner of whatever it was they wanted to sell or he disposed of them some other way, but to him they were worthless. That sapphire didn't look worthless. It was large, a deep blue and beautiful. Had whoever owned it really just given it up? Or had it been in another piece of jewelry entirely? Millie whined. She crawled out from under the table, put her front feet on Mary's chair and her head in Mary's lap.

'Worried about me?' Mary's hand dropped to stroke Millie's silky head; her fingers scratched the back of one ear. 'Don't. I'm fine. It's just that . . . Oh, dear. I think we've managed to land ourselves in the middle of a particularly nasty muddle.'

# TWENTY-EIGHT

'So you think because Tommy Lowell wants to buy a house he may be implicated in a series of jewelry store robberies, not one of which was committed within one hundred miles of here?'

'Put like that, it sounds ridiculous.' Mary glared at her nephew-in-law, Dan, who sat in her air-conditioned living room, tie loosened and shirt unbuttoned, sipping a beer. He grinned at her.

'She didn't mean it like that and you know it. And what makes you think he isn't? He has enough money for a down payment and he didn't get it working for his mother in the jewelry store.' Ellen glared at her husband as well, picked back up her wine glass and sipped.

Mary had called Dan, asking him to drop by on his way home, and he had evidently phoned Ellen, who had shown up at around the same time, Morgan and Ranger with her. The three dogs lay in the middle of the room, seemingly listening to the conversation. All three heads were on their paws but all three sets of eyes were alert and all six ears were cocked.

She sighed and took a sip from her own glass. This wasn't going the way she'd hoped. 'Look, Dan. I'm not accusing Tommy, or Jerry for that matter. I'm exploring possibilities and trying to fit in some facts.'

'What facts?'

'The fact Mr Wilson was in town a couple of weeks ago and didn't bother to tell anyone about it. We have two very reputable people who'll swear to that. Three, actually.'

Dan leaned forward in his chair and set his beer on the table. 'Mitch saw him in the alley; Glen helped him cash a check. Who's the third one?'

'Mo Black. That was the next thing I was going to tell you. It seems Mr Eric Wilson arrested Mo's brother and sister-in-law about ten years ago – for robbing jewelry stores. According to Mo, he was sure then, and still is, that Mo and possibly David, his nephew, were somehow involved. David would have been around ten or twelve so I don't see how he could have been, but maybe Mo . . . Although, that doesn't seem likely. But we have jewelry stores again. I don't like all these coincidences.'

Dan got very still as he stared at Mary. 'Well, well. They do seem to be piling up, don't they? Have you told Emma about this?'

'Emma? No. Why should I?'

'Just wondered.'

'Why would Wilson suspect a young boy?' Ellen looked not only horrified but almost angry. 'How could he be involved?'

Dan looked unhappy. The sigh he heaved was deep and long. 'It's been known to happen. Kids get dragged into their parents' criminal activity for lots of reasons. One is they're small enough to fit into places the grown-ups can't go. Small hands, small bodies, small spaces.'

'Like the Artful Dodger.'

Ellen and Dan both looked at Mary. Then, suddenly, Ellen nodded. '*Oliver.*'

'Oh.' Dan smiled. 'The musical.'

'The book. And it was called *Oliver Twist*.' There was the faintest trace of disgust in Mary's voice but she immediately went on. 'I suppose David could have somehow helped his parents but he was young. He would just have done what he was told. You could hardly blame him for that.'

'Some people could, and would. Besides, if a child really is involved, CPS wants to know a lot more about the kid. They'd do a battery of psychological tests. Examine whoever was going to take the child thoroughly, do follow-up . . . all kinds of things.'

'I don't think Agent Wilson was doing the kind of follow-up you're talking about.' Mary added a little sniff for emphasis. 'The way Mo described it, it sounded a lot more like harassment.'

'What does that have to do with Tommy Lowell?' Ellen got up and headed for the kitchen. She picked up Mary's almost empty glass on the way. 'Refill?'

Mary started to say no but nodded instead. That would be all for her tonight, but right now a little more sounded good. 'I don't think anything. I'm only trying to sort out who might have had a motive to murder Mr Miller.'

'If we're looking at motive, neither Tommy Lowell nor Mo and Dave Black have one. From what you say, the Blacks would be more likely to murder Wilson and if Tommy Lowell and his father are committing the robberies, why would they go after Miller?'

'Because somehow Miller got on their trail?' Ellen handed her aunt a full glass, Dan a fresh beer and set her own glass on the coffee table before stepping over the two large dogs who had moved over between the sofa and Mary's chair, where Millie had joined Mary.

The beer can lid popped and Dan took a drink. 'I don't think so. I don't think Miller was that close to anyone. From what I've learned so far, there aren't any clues as to who these guys are. No fingerprints, no sightings of a suspicious car . . . well . . . maybe one.'

Ellen brightened up. 'Oh, good. Finally. Something. What kind of car?'

'Two reports of a white-paneled van seen in the vicinity of the jewelry stores about the right time. We wouldn't have paid much attention to the first one but the same kind of van seen two times makes us at least take notice. Only . . .'

'Only what? It's something, isn't it?' There was an eager look on Ellen's face that Mary didn't think was justified but she waited to hear what Dan had to say.

'There are hundreds, maybe thousands, of white-paneled vans on the road. Neither of the ones seen had anything to identify them, except they were white and paneled vans. The stores were in two different states and the robberies months apart. There is nothing to make us think they're connected to the other robberies other than we don't have anything else. The chances they were driven by the same driver and that driver was connected with the robberies is up there with winning the lottery.'

'But, for now, it's all you've got?'

'It's all the Bureau's got. I'm not involved in solving the

robberies, just in finding out who killed Miller. And I'm only on the fringe of that investigation.' Dan didn't sound too happy about that.

His cell phone rang.

'Damn and blast.' He leaned over on one hip and took it out of his pocket, looked at the dial and answered.

Ellen was muttering about another dinner ruined but Mary watched Dan's face. His expression changed from mildly irritated to startled to rock hard.

'You're sure? OK. I'll be right there. Any of the state boys still here besides Emma? Don't let 'em touch a thing. Get our team over there, secure the scene and call the forensic guys in San Luis Obispo. Keep the family out of there. I'm on my way.'

Ellen had quit muttering. 'What's happened? Something bad – I can tell by the look on your face.'

'It's not good. Marlene just found Jerry in his workshop. Shot.'

Mary managed to set her glass down without dropping it. She didn't think she could speak for a moment but finally managed. 'Is he . . .?'

'Dead? Yes.'

'Can we help?' Mary glanced at the dogs but they'd be fine where they were. She'd worry about their dinners later. 'Is Marlene . . .'

'I don't know, but yes, you can help. Take Ellen's car. Park behind the pet shop and walk over. I think having someone with her will help Marlene a lot. She doesn't have any family here, except Tommy, and I don't want anyone throwing a lot of questions at her. I want to talk to her first.' He was on his feet, buttoning his shirt and pulling his tie back in place. 'Tommy. I wonder where he is.' The speculative look that thought brought passed and a hard, no-nonsense look took its place. 'Don't go past the yellow tape. Just wait for me. I'll find out where she is and call Ellen. You two can stop her falling apart until I can get to her. Ellen, keep your cell handy.'

They watched him go out the front door, then Mary sighed. 'I can't believe this. Why would anyone want to shoot Jerry Lowell?'

'Off the top of my head, I'd say it has something to do with Miller's murder, but what I have no idea. Thank God that's Dan's job. Let's go see if we can help Marlene. That poor woman.' She looked around, gathered up her purse and turned to Mary. 'Let's go.'

'Should we take the dogs?' All three dogs were sitting in the middle of the room, looking anxious. The mood of the humans had changed quickly and they weren't too sure what to make of it.

Ellen seemed to hesitate, then said resolutely, 'No. I have no idea what we're going to have to do or where we'll be. I don't want them staying in a hot car or us having to worry about them. If for some reason we can't get back soon, I'll call Pat.'

Mary nodded. 'I'll just lock the back door.' She ran into the kitchen, threw the lock on the door, grabbed her keys off the key holder and stuck them in her purse. She called out to Millie as she passed by, 'The sofa pillows are off limits,' and followed Ellen out the front door.

# TWENTY-NINE

I t looked like half the town was gathered in the street in front of Lowell's Jewelry and the other half was crowded into the park, all of them staring at the store and muttering quietly among themselves. There were police cars in front of the store but not neatly parked. They were blocking the middle of the street in a haphazard pattern, two firetrucks and an ambulance among them. The entire block was taped off with yellow crime-scene tape. Uniformed officers milled up and down the street behind it, reminding everyone by their presence that no one was allowed behind it. As far as Mary could tell, no one was even close to it.

Ellen pulled into the alley off Main Street. The alley behind Furry Friends Pet Shop hadn't been blocked off but it was full of people. It seemed as if every owner or patron of every shop that backed into it was in the alley, staring at what was happening behind the yellow tape at the other end. There was one open parking spot. John, Glen and Krissie, who held a half-groomed schnauzer in her arms, stood in it. John started to wave when he saw them and pointed to it. Ellen quickly pulled into it.

'I think I'd better call Dan, tell him we're here and see what he wants us to do next.' Ellen turned off the engine, unlocked her seat belt and opened the door. She sat sideways on the seat, watching the happenings at the other end of the alley while she punched in numbers.

Mary climbed out of the car and joined the other three. 'Do you know what happened?'

'Just that Jerry Lowell was shot.'

Mary had never seen Glen Manning look so solemn. Maybe shocked was a better word. His face was white and drawn, his mouth pinched.

'We heard he was dead but someone else said he was still alive, just badly hurt. I think he's still in there but we're not sure.'

Mary was pretty sure, from what Dan had said, that Jerry was dead, but she didn't think it was up to her to confirm it. 'Do you know who shot him? And why?'

'No, to both.' John didn't look much better than Glen. 'I started down there to see if I could help the EMTs but they know their job. I'd just be in the way. Besides, he's dead.'

'How do you know that?' There were tear tracks down Krissie's face and she clutched the dog a little too tight but her voice was steady. Also a little indignant. 'You can't be sure.'

John looked at her, then at Mary. 'If he was still alive he'd probably be headed for surgery. The ambulance hasn't moved and I haven't had a phone call telling me to get my butt over to the hospital and get ready. He's dead.'

'What happened?' That he was dead Mary had accepted. But she wanted more facts than that before they had to face Marlene. 'Who found him?'

'Marlene.' Glen seemed almost overwhelmed with sadness.

Mary fleetingly hoped there was someone left in the bank or that they'd locked it. It didn't look as if there was anyone left in any of the shops. They were all in the street or in the park. Even the sidewalk across from the park was full of people. Word had spread fast.

'How do you know Marlene found him?'

'Because she came out of the back of the gold shop screaming at the top of her lungs. You could hear her all the way down here. John went out to see what was going on and about then the first cop car pulled up.'

Mary turned to John. 'Did you see anyone else? Anyone leaving or in the alley?'

John shook his head. 'Just Mo Black. He was holding Marlene, who was sobbing into his shoulder. I could hear her screaming all the way down the alley that he was dead. I assumed it was Jerry but had no idea he'd been shot. I thought a stroke or heart attack and was on my way down to them when the first car pulled in. It was Gary and that new guy. They ran to them, then Gary went into the gold store and the other guy started to talk to Mo. I went up to them and offered to help, but about then the EMT guys arrived and I returned to the shop.'

'When did you find out Jerry was shot?'

Glen and John looked at each other, then at Krissie. 'I guess . . . someone ran into the bank shouting there'd been a shooting at the gold shop. I called John right away. He knew something had happened but not that Jerry had been shot. The police were starting to fan out, telling everyone to keep inside, but whoever did it is long gone. I'm sure we're all going to get questioned and all the shops around here will be searched and whatever else they do. I just can't believe it. How did you hear?' Glen seemed to be returning to his own unflappable self.

He stared down the alley, watching the police as they came out of the flower shop and waited. Another two policemen came out of the wine shop and shook their heads. They crossed the driveway that led to the street, the one the Grady van had sped out of and almost run over Mary. She watched them approach as she answered Glen.

'Dan was at my house when he got the call. He wants Ellen and me to take Marlene someplace away from all this and try to keep her calm until they can question her. Have you seen Tommy?'

He gave her a funny look but shook his head. The policemen headed down the alley toward them just as Krissie stated she had to go back inside. The dog was tired of being held and she needed to put him somewhere. 'I don't dare try the clippers on him right now. My hands are shaking. If they want to talk to me . . .' she nodded at the approaching officers, '. . . tell them I'll be back as soon as I put this guy in a crate.'

Ellen came up, cell phone in hand. 'Dan says they've given Marlene some kind of shot to calm her down and for us to go around in front to the EMT truck. They have her lying down and want to keep an eye on her for a few more minutes, then, when they think she's OK, we're to take her to your house.'

Mary nodded. 'What else did Dan say?'

'That Jerry had been dead for some time when Marlene found him and they have no idea who shot him. They're looking but they're sure the shooter is long gone. Dan's got teams out talking to people now but I could hear him gritting his teeth.'

'Did Dan say if Emma is with him?'

Ellen shook her head. 'He did say he'd like to know where Wilson is, though. I edited that statement a little. He seemed to think Wilson should have come back to town last night.'

'He's back.' Glen's statement couldn't have been more matter-of-fact. 'He was having breakfast at The Yum Yum around eight this morning. John and I saw him as we were leaving.'

'Then where's he been all day? Why isn't he with Dan now? That man is something else. I wonder . . .' Ellen never finished her statement.

A white van covered from front to back with pictures of exploding fireworks pulled off the street down the short exit that led to the alley where they all stood. The Gradys had arrived.

'Hey,' John hollered. 'Slow down before you kill someone.'

The van came to an abrupt halt. The driver could be seen looking up and down the alley, presumably for someplace to park. There wasn't one. The driver's door opened and so did the passenger side. A Grady brother exited from each side, cowboy hats pulled down on foreheads, tight jeans covering long legs, boot heels crunching on the loose asphalt.

'They're going to leave the van right in the middle of the alley,' Ellen exclaimed. 'They can't do that.' She started toward them but Glen grabbed her arm.

'Wait.' He pointed down the alley.

Both groups of policemen were descending on the van, arm gestures clear they wanted it gone and gone now. The Gradys seemed to be digging in their heels. Loud exclamations could be heard, the Gradys demanding to know what was going on. They'd just heard about Jerry on the news, the police insisting they move the van and the Gradys refusing until they got information. One sentence came through loud and clear.

It was Heath, his voice angry and forceful. 'We heard on the radio that Jerry Lowell is dead; he's been shot in our store. I want to know if that's true and I want to know if it's been robbed.'

Their store? Mary stared at the arguing group, stunned. Their store? The Gradys? She turned toward Ellen, who looked as surprised as Mary was, then at Glen.

He nodded. 'Heath's right. G and H Enterprises owns the We Buy Gold shop. I don't know if Jerry Lowell was the manager or had some kind of small interest but the Grady brothers hold the business license and run all the money through their bank account. I can't say I blame Heath for pitching a fit. I'd want to know if I'd been robbed, too.'

The police won. The Gradys got back in the van, turned around and roared out of the alley onto the street. Where they were going to park, Mary had no idea, but she was sure they weren't leaving. She didn't know how long Dan and his people would keep the store and the street around it closed off, but probably for a while. From the set of Heath's chin, she'd bet money he planned on sticking around until he could get back in that store.

Feeling more than a little queasy, she turned to Ellen. 'I think it's time we found Marlene and took her to my house. She needs some quiet time to gather herself so she can face what's coming.'

Marlene wasn't the only one.

# THIRTY

**M**arlene sat on Mary's sofa, breathing in and out of her mouth, an occasional sob interrupting her breath. Her eyes were open and stared straight ahead but Mary didn't think she saw anything or anyone in the room. She saw an entirely different scene.

Mary tried to remember how she felt when Samuel had died. It hadn't been expected, either, and although it had been a massive heart attack which no one, even his doctor, had seen coming, she wasn't sure it made much difference, at least not to how Marlene felt right now. Jerry was dead. She'd found him. Mary had found Samuel dead on the bathroom floor, his razor still in his hand. She hadn't believed it – at least, not at first – but after she rolled him over and pumped on his chest she'd realized he wasn't coming back. Then what had she done? She couldn't remember. The next hour, day, week was a blur. She'd had to do things, answer questions, make decisions, but she wasn't sure what she'd done, who she'd answered or what she'd decided. The next clear thing was Samuel's funeral and that day she'd rather forget. That was the day she knew, really knew he was never going to return.

Was that how Marlene was feeling right now? Numb? Unable to function, to feel, to grieve? As if her body, her mind had shut down? That was the way she looked. She hadn't even responded when Tommy arrived.

'What happened?' He'd sat beside his mother on the sofa, had taken her hand and tried to put his arm around her but she hadn't responded, just turned her head slightly to look at him.

'What happened? I don't know. He didn't come back to the store after closing time.' She fell silent. She turned her head away from Tommy and resumed staring at nothing.

'Mom?'

She seemed to startle at the sound of his voice and turned her head toward him once more.

'You locked up the store? Is that right?'

She nodded.

'So it was five?'

Another slight nod.

'What did you do?'

Marlene gave a deep shudder and a tear appeared in the corner of one eye. She put up her hand to brush it off. 'I went into the workshop. He wasn't there, so I went out into the alley and into the back door of the gold store. It wasn't locked, which I thought was odd. He always kept it locked. I called out but there was no answer so I went in. He was there, by the cash register, on the floor, blood all around him.' She heaved another sigh then resumed staring across the room. She let her hand stay in Tommy's but it wasn't as if she knew it was there. She didn't seem to be aware of anything but what she was seeing in her mind's eye. What that was, Mary was certain she knew.

'Mom.' Tommy tried again but Marlene didn't respond. He turned to Mary. 'What should I do?'

'Nothing. She's in shock and the techs gave her some kind of shot. She'll come around but then she's going to be in so much pain it will take a while. Just let her work it through.'

'But we need to know what happened.' There was pain on Tommy's face as well but his was mixed with anger. He placed his mother's hand gently in her lap and leaned forward. He clenched his hands into fists and his eyes blazed. 'Someone killed my father – shot him – and we need to know who and why.'

Mary wondered if Tommy had an idea of why but maybe not who. Marlene hadn't brought him back from London because she wanted company. Something had been wrong and she wanted help. But what kind of help? Her thought was distracted by Ranger. The dog had been watching Tommy and Marlene, lying beside Morgan, his head between his paws. Now he started to whine. He got to his feet, walked over to Tommy and put his head in his lap, then sat and put one paw on Tommy's knee and looked into his face. Tommy gasped then took the dog's paw, stroked it then leaned forward and buried his face in the dog's fur. Ranger moved in closer and stood, almost as if he wanted to climb into his lap. The fur on Ranger's shoulder, where Tommy's head was buried, looked damp. She sighed and looked over at Ellen, whose eyes looked as if they were going to overflow any minute. They all needed the tissue box. She pushed herself to her feet, but before she could start for the kitchen the doorbell rang. Dan? To talk to Marlene? She brushed the back of her hand over her own eyes as she opened the door.

It was Emma Baxter. 'Dan . . . Chief Dunham sent me. May I come in?'

'Of course.' Mary stepped back and opened the door wider.

Emma paused when she saw Tommy seated on the sofa, his mother on one side of him and the dog pushed up close on his other side. 'Oh. I'm glad to see you. We've all been wondering where you were.'

Tommy picked his head up to stare at her, brushed at his eyes with one hand then dropped it back on the dog's head. Ranger leaned against Tommy's knee.

'I was in Santa Barbara. I heard about it on my way home. I went to the shop but couldn't get near either store. Finally I found Gary. He told me my mother was with Mrs McGill so I came here.'

'Gary?' Emma cocked one eyebrow.

'One of Dan's guys. Gary Baker, just made sergeant. Good man.' It was the first time Ellen had said anything in a while and Mary looked at her sharply. Ellen had been watching both Marlene and Tommy closely and now that included Emma. What was going on in her head? Something was. 'Dan sent you to talk to Marlene?'

'He sent me over to see how she was. We will need whatever she can tell us but he wants to see how she's doing before we start bombarding her with questions.' The look she gave Tommy seemed to say she had no such reservations about questioning him. She turned to him. 'Would you mind if I sat beside your mother? She may be able to talk to me a little if I'm not standing over her.'

He didn't say a word, but he pushed himself up off the sofa and looked around the room. There weren't many choices for chairs left. Mary immediately got up, much to Millie's surprise, and motioned toward Tommy.

'Sit here. Ellen and I are going to get us all some iced tea. Your mother will feel much better if she has a little something cool to drink.' She motioned to Ellen and walked toward the kitchen, Millie close on her heels.

'What was all that about?' Ellen was taking glasses out of the cupboard but she managed to hiss at her aunt. 'I wanted to hear what Emma is going to say to Marlene.'

'I want to know why you've been studying them both like they're some kind of bugs under a microscope. You're thinking something. What is it?'

Ellen set the glasses on the counter then turned and leaned against it. 'Something's been going on at that shop for a while. I told you Marlene wasn't happy with Jerry. She called Tommy back from London for some reason and then he and Jerry got into it. I don't know what Jerry was doing but it was something that had Marlene worried sick. I'm sorry, but I can't help but wonder if there's powder residue on her fingers right now. Or maybe on Tommy's.'

Mary held the iced tea pitcher with both hands, pushed the refrigerator door closed with her hip and set the pitcher on the counter next to the glasses. 'You think one of them shot him?'

There wasn't very much shock or surprise in her question but there was a lot of sorrow.

'I don't know. I don't have any idea what happened but Marlene was there and we only have Tommy's word for it he was in Santa Barbara. Or if he was, that he just arrived home. That isn't a happy household and I don't think we can discount either of them.'

'Do you think Dan agrees with you?'

Ellen didn't say anything. She turned, opened the freezer, pulled out the ice tray and put a couple of ice cubes in each glass then returned the tray to the freezer, empty. A cardinal sin in Mary's household. She didn't look at Mary as she started to fill glasses. 'We've wondered what was going on with them. Obviously something wasn't right but we certainly never dreamed it would end in murder. And, of course, it could be someone else entirely. It would seem there has to be a connection to Miller's murder but I don't see how either Marlene or Jerry can be connected to it.'

Mary nodded, turned and almost tripped over Millie. 'One of these days you're going to kill us both,' she told the dog with more than a little irritation in her tone.

Millie ignored it and went to stand by her empty bowl.

Mary sighed. 'She wants to eat and she won't let me alone until she does. It's already past her dinnertime. I'll feed them all. You take in the tea, but Ellen . . .'

Ellen paused, a trace of a smile on her face. 'I know. I'm to tell you every last thing that happens that you missed. I will.' She picked up the three glasses and went back into the living room. Mary picked up Millie's dish, got two visiting dog dishes out of the cupboard and started ladling out dog food.

All it took was the rustle of the dog food bag and all three dogs were lined up in front of her. Evidently the lure of dinner had pried Ranger from Tommy's side but probably not for long.

The opening of her front door and the addition of a voice in the living room increased the rate at which she filled them. She returned to the living room to find Dan seated beside Marlene, speaking to her in a low tone of voice, addressing a question to Emma who had moved to a dining-room chair drawn up next to the side of the sofa where Marlene sat, then turned back to Marlene.

He raised his voice slightly to include Tommy. 'You were in Santa Barbara all day? What were you doing there?'

'Taking my résumé to some of the jewelry stores. I'm trying to get some of them to carry the pieces I make. I left this morning around ten and started home just after four. I heard about the shooting when I was somewhere around Santa Maria.' He paused, looked at his mother and swallowed. 'I didn't realize at first who . . . then when they said the We Buy Gold shop . . . Was it a robbery?'

'We're going to take Heath through the store as soon as . . .' he looked at Marlene then turned back to Tommy, '. . . the crime scene is cleared out. But it doesn't look like it. The cash register is closed and there's no sign someone tried to open it. The counters don't look as if anyone's moved anything. Nothing looks as if it's been searched but we'll see what Heath says. He keeps saying there is a shipment ready to go to Los Angeles to the smelter. Do you know anything about that?'

Tommy's eyes narrowed and his lips compressed into a straight line. 'I know nothing about the gold shop. I didn't even know the Gradys owned it until recently. Neither my mother nor I had anything to do with running it.'

Dan stiffened at that last remark. His head jerked up as he stared at Tommy, then over at Marlene. She gave no sign she'd heard the exchange but a light flush ran up Tommy's neck. Anger Dan seemed to doubt him or something else?

'You never helped out in the gold shop?'

Tommy shook his head. 'Crystal goes over there when Dad needs – needed – to be somewhere else, but neither my mother nor I had anything to do with it. He wanted it that way and, frankly, it suited me fine. He'd almost stopped designing but we had a lot of orders. I had plenty to do without adding whatever went on in that shop.'

There was something in Tommy's tone that struck Mary as wrong. A bitterness. But why? That his father had cut his mother and him out of the second business? Only he hadn't owned it. Or was that why? That he'd kept the real ownership a secret from them? Mary wondered what else Jerry had kept from his family. Was Tommy wondering the same thing?

Dan glanced at Mary and raised his eyebrows a little as if asking if she'd caught that bitterness as well. She barely nodded and he transferred his gaze to Emma. Only she wasn't looking at Dan. She was watching Marlene, studying her, waiting . . . For what, Mary didn't know. Marlene simply sat, looking into her other world. Mary wasn't sure she'd heard a word that had been said.

Dan turned back to her and took one of her hands in his. She let it lie as if she didn't realize he held it.

He called her name softly. 'Marlene, when did you see Jerry last? Did you meet for lunch?'

She turned her head toward him and blinked. 'What?'

'Jerry. When did you see him before you went over—'

She didn't let him finish. 'He's dead, isn't he? I saw him. All that blood.' She took her hand out of Dan's, wrapped her arms around herself and started to shake.

Tommy was on his feet, trying to get to her.

Before he could reach his mother, Emma was there, making shooing motions at Dan. 'Let me.'

Mary wasn't sure she'd ever seen a more grateful look on anyone's face than on Dan's as he abandoned his seat on the sofa to her.

Emma put her arms around Marlene and let her lean against her shoulder. She didn't say anything, just held her until the shaking eased. Tommy watched but said nothing.

'Can you tell us what happened now?' Emma's voice was low and gentle. 'Only if you can. But I think it will help.'

Marlene raised her head, looked at Emma and straightened up. Mary could almost see her will the shaking to stop. She glanced at Tommy with a faint look of surprise then around the room, almost as if she wasn't sure where she was or how she'd gotten here. But she turned back to Emma. 'I don't know what happened. I told someone . . . I think I did . . . Jerry didn't come back to the store at closing time. So I went looking for him. He was lying there, covered with blood. I think I screamed but I don't remember much after that.'

'Can you tell us when you saw him last?' Emma removed her arm from around Marlene but kept hold of her hand.

Marlene looked down but didn't remove it. 'At lunch. I'd made sandwiches. He came over, got his and went back to We Buy Gold.'

'Did he say anything? Seem upset? Worried?'

A ghost of a smile came and went on Marlene's face. 'Say anything? No. I had a customer. He poked his head out of the back, waved his sandwich at me and disappeared. He didn't seem any more worried than usual. He's been upset about something for months but he'd never talk about it. Just tell me I was imagining things, that he was fine and to get off his back.'

Ellen, who had taken the chair next to Mary, made a little noise in her throat and looked at her aunt with an 'I told you so' look.

Dan glanced at her but his attention was on Tommy, who had fallen back into Mary's big chair. Ranger was back by his side.

'That right, Tommy? Your father was worried about something? Did he ever mention anything about it to you?'

Tommy gave a snort of what might have been laughter. 'Mother's right. There was something bothering him but I'd have been the last person he would have confided in. My father and I . . . we weren't close.'

Mary thought that was one of the best understatements she'd heard in a long time, but lots of fathers and sons didn't get along. That didn't make Tommy a murderer.

'Right.' Dan switched his attention back to Marlene, who seemed to be coming out of the shock-induced fog. 'Did you notice the front door? Was it locked? Shop closed or open?'

She stared at him for a moment then shut her eyes. Trying to shut out the reality of what had happened? No. Trying to picture what she'd seen. 'The shop was dim. So the blinds on the front door must have been closed. That means it must have been locked. There's only one window and there's no blind on that. He was lying in the shop. I had to walk through the storeroom into the store to see him. I remember knocking something over when I ran out the back, screaming. Someone was right outside the back door and caught me. He must have called the police. I didn't.'

An intense look had taken over Dan's face. 'Do you remember who caught you?'

Marlene looked at Dan for a second, as if she couldn't quite, but then she nodded. 'Mo Black. He was right outside the back door.'

'Mo Black,' Tommy practically sputtered. 'What was he doing there? His store doesn't back onto that part of the alley. Besides, Dad told him to keep away . . .' His voice trailed away under Dan's interested gaze.

'Your dad and Mo didn't get along?'

'No.' There was reluctance in that one word. 'Mo's a good guy but for some reason he and my dad butted heads. But then, my dad's butted heads with a bunch of people lately.'

'OK.' Dan got to his feet and looked around the room. 'Marlene, I'll need to talk to you again but, for now, I think it might be a good idea if Tommy took you home. Do you want Emma to come with you? She's pretty good company, even if she is a Baxter.'

Marlene didn't look as if she got the rather weak joke, nor did Tommy, who looked puzzled. Marlene shook her head. 'No. We'll be all right. I just have to . . . we need to talk. There's going to be so much . . . I don't even know what to think or where to begin.'

Tommy got up and went to his mother, taking her arm and helping her up. 'We don't need to decide anything right now. You need to rest.'

'How I'll do that, I don't know.' But she let him pull her to her feet and started toward the door.

'Wait.'

Marlene turned to face Mary, a question on her face.

'Would you like Les – Reverend McIntyre – to come over? He probably will anyway, as soon as he hears, and Ysabel can deflect all the food donations people are going to start offering and answer the phone. Most people mean well but you don't need to be faced with all that right now. I'll call him for you.'

Tommy looked a little stunned at the thought of the phone ringing off the hook, but Emma grimly smiled.

'Mrs McGill is right. People aren't sure what to do at a time like this but they want to help so they bring food and sympathy. That can wait until tomorrow. If it's OK with Dan, I'll offer my services as official phone answerer. If, of course, that's all right with you two.'

Tommy looked at her as if he couldn't quite understand what she'd said but Marlene had no trouble answering. 'Oh, would you? I don't think I could bear to talk to anyone tonight, even Reverend McIntyre. I feel . . . I don't know how I feel.'

Mary knew she was right. She needed to be left alone, to absorb the shock, to talk to her son, to break down and cry. Emma would be a good barrier to all those who wanted to express their sympathy, which Marlene was in no state to receive, and would be an invincible one to those that simply wanted to know what Jerry Lowell had done to get himself shot dead.

The only one Tommy Lowell said goodbye to as they went toward the door was Ranger. That the dog wanted to go with him was obvious.

'Tommy, wait.' Ellen called to him. 'Do you want to take Ranger? He wants to go with you.'

The pain, the uncertainty, the shock faded and, for the first time, Tommy looked hopeful. 'You don't mind?'

'Not at all. Do we, Dan?'

'No. Take the dog. I may be over later tonight. I'll see how it goes but I'll talk to you no later than in the morning. And, Tommy, I'll need more details about where you were today, just for the record.'

Shock was back, then resignation. He snapped the leash on Ranger and followed his mother and Emma out the door.

Ellen, Dan and Mary sat silent for a moment, then Dan pulled his cell out of his pocket. 'Well, well.' He scrolled down, reading his texts. 'It seems Wilson's finally turned up and he's got his teeth into Mo Black. Damn the man.' He typed something, clicked it off and returned it to his pocket. 'I've got to go. They've finally moved Jerry's body and want to take Heath through the store to see if anything's missing. I don't want to have Wilson take care of that one. He and Heath would be at each other's throats in seconds and that won't help us one bit. I'd love to know where that . . . where he was today. He was supposed to be back last night.'

'Dan.'

He paused, looked at Mary and waited.

'Mr Wilson was having breakfast at The Yum Yum early this morning. John and Glen saw him as they were leaving.'

Mary didn't think she'd ever seen anyone who could stand so silent and still express what he was thinking, and it wasn't good.

'Thanks.' He gave her a hug and Ellen a quick kiss on the cheek. 'Don't wait up.' He was gone.

Mary collapsed into her big chair and Millie immediately jumped up beside her. Ellen picked up her almost untouched glass of tea, looked at it and headed for the kitchen.

'Where are you going?' Mary thought she knew, or at least she hoped that Ellen was going to get what she had been thinking about. She was. In no time at all, Ellen returned with a full wine glass in each hand.

She handed one to Mary and set the other on the coffee table before she dropped down on the sofa. 'I feel like I've been wrung through a wringer backward.'

Mary wasn't too sure how that was supposed to feel but she was sure it wasn't good. She felt wrung out herself.

'Why didn't you go home with Marlene? It's the kind of thing you usually do and you do it well. Why send Emma?' Ellen moved her legs so Morgan could lie down between the table and the sofa, picked up her glass and looked at her aunt, speculation in her eyes.

Mary picked up her own glass and took a sip. Its cool, citrusy taste felt comforting. She sighed a little as she set it back on the end table next to her chair.

'A couple of reasons. One, if there is even a grain of truth in your theory that Marlene or Tommy shot Jerry, Emma is much more qualified to determine that than I am. Second, she was good with Marlene, not pushy, very sympathetic, very quiet, but she got information out of her. If there's more to be gotten, I think she's the one to do it.' She smiled. 'Sending Ranger home with Tommy was a good idea. That young man looked distraught, to say the least. Do you suppose he was really visiting jewelry stores in Santa Barbara?'

'No idea, and we have only his word that's where he was.'

'True. But probably easily verified. If it's a lie, it was a stupid one, and Tommy isn't stupid.' Mary took another sip of her wine. Millie laid her head on Mary's knee then gently butted her free hand, hinting an ear rub would be nice. Mary set her glass down and obliged. 'I wonder where Eric Wilson was all day. I think that's more interesting than where Tommy was. There's something about that man . . .'

'Dan thinks so, too. He says he acts like he's already made up his mind who killed Miller and why, and he's spending more time looking for evidence to support his theory than trying to find out what really happened.' She paused and took another sip of her wine. 'Of course, he may be right. But Dan's not impressed with his methods.'

'He thinks it was Mo Black?'

'Seems to.'

'But why?'

'No idea.'

Mary remembered what Mo had told her but thought for a moment. 'Emma said they had a falling out, didn't she? That Wilson was unhappy Miller was working on the robbery thing without telling him about it. If they were on the outs, why would he be taking Miller's death so personally?'

Ellen considered that as she took a small sip. 'Guilt? Because he'd made a fuss about Miller investigating those robberies all alone? Not telling him anything?'

'I think there was a reason Miller investigated them alone and I wonder what it was.'

Ellen stared at her aunt, glanced at the glass she still held and took a large sip. 'Are you suggesting Wilson is somehow implicated in the robberies?'

'All I'm saying is it sounds as if Miller no longer trusted Wilson, and I wonder why.'

Neither of them spoke for a moment. Morgan started to snore and Ellen laughed.

'I don't know which one snores the loudest, Morgan or Dan.'

Mary had no interest in snoring. 'I wonder why Mo Black was in the alley this afternoon. His shop doesn't open onto it, does it?'

'Sort of. It opens onto the parking area behind the Chamber of Commerce building, just across the access road that opens onto Park Plaza. That's just across the alley.'

'But why was he behind the We Buy Gold shop?'

Ellen thought about it. 'Maybe he was outside at the back of his own shop, taking out the trash or having a cigarette or something, and heard Marlene scream. You can see the back of both the jewelry store and the gold shop from the Chamber back door. I know because I park back there a lot. I don't like to park on the street, I want to save that for clients, so I'm familiar with the backs of half the stores on that side of the park. He could have heard her.'

Mary nodded and took another sip. 'What do you know about David, his nephew?'

'Why?'

Holding her glass with both hands against her chest in case Millie decided to suddenly raise her head, Mary considered her answer. 'He knows a lot about computers. So does Mo. Those stores that were robbed – somehow their alarm systems were deactivated or whatever you call it. Anyway, they didn't ring. Someone like the Blacks might know how to do that.'

'I guess.' Ellen looked at her glass, took the final sip and stepped over Morgan. 'Because it's possible someone could do something doesn't mean they would. I think Mo Black is an honest man, and what I've seen of David, he's a nice young man. He's taking classes at Cuesta College and plans on going to Cal Poly next year and majoring in computer science. There's nothing that would suggest they're jewelry thieves.'

'Except David's parents are in jail for robbing jewelry stores.'

Ellen stared at Mary, her mouth slightly open in surprise. 'How do you know that?'

'Mo Black told me.'

'That doesn't make them thieves, either.' But this came out a little slower, with just a hint of doubt.

'Evidently it made Mr Eric Wilson think it might. According to Mo, he's been harassing them for the last few years. It seems he arrested David's parents, Mo's brother and sister-in-law, and some of the supposed stolen jewelry was never recovered.'

'Wilson thinks Mo and David have it? That they took up where Mo's brother left off? What is he using for proof?'

'I only know what Mo told me. I suppose it could be true but I admit it's hard to believe. I can't help wondering what happened to all that jewelry. I think Dan said there were twelve stores robbed, all in the same way, with the back door sawed through, in the last couple of years. That means it must be someone pretty young or at least agile, and someone who would know how to deactivate the alarm. They pretty much wiped out those stores, so that must have been a lot of jewelry. Luke from the library said he thinks they melted it down. You can do that with gold. Only, what did they do with it then?

And the diamonds and sapphires and rubies and things, what did they do with them? David and Mo could very well qualify on the first two counts but I don't know about getting rid of the jewelry. So I wondered . . .'

'You think Jerry's murder has something to do with the robberies? With getting the jewelry melted down? You think the same person shot him and Miller? Why?'

'I don't know, but Jerry has to sell the gold he buys in his shop somewhere. He doesn't keep it. I'm not sure how that works but could he have been helping whoever has been doing those robberies?'

Ellen looked stunned. 'Then you really do think Miller and Jerry Lowell were killed by the same person. That their deaths are connected and probably to the robberies as well.'

'I don't think there's much doubt the deaths are connected, and there's a good chance it's all about the robberies. Only, I'm not sure how.'

Ellen shook her head. 'I'll tell Dan. He'll want to talk to you. But I think this is a stretch. I don't think the robberies are connected to anyone in town, and poor Jerry was shot by someone trying to rob him.' She whistled to Morgan, who instantly raised his head, got to his feet and followed Ellen into the kitchen. She stuck her head back through the doorway. 'The glass is in the dishwasher. You'd better get some rest tonight. Tomorrow isn't going to be fun. I imagine there will have to be an autopsy. I've no idea when the funeral can be held but someone is going to have to help Les work through all this, and that someone will undoubtedly be you. The thought of this funeral gives me chills worse than the ones I keep getting when I think of Susannah and Neil's wedding. Every person in town will be there, half because they know Marlene and Jerry and are genuinely grieving, the other half because violent death is somehow exciting. And I hope you're wrong. I hope this is a terrible tragedy and no one in town is connected in any way. However, you may be right. You usually are. I'll talk to Dan.' She threw her aunt a kiss and was gone.

Mary heard the back door close, pushed Millie off her lap and went into the spare bedroom. She sat in front of the computer, hoping she remembered enough to do what she wanted to do, then typed in 'We Buy Gold Shop, Santa Louisa, Ca.'

Up popped the website. There was a picture of the shop, another of the park, a phone number, hours of operation and some buttons that directed you to different kinds of items the store purchased. Mary began to read.

# THIRTY-ONE

E llen was right. It had been a difficult morning. The phone rang as she poured her first cup of coffee. It was Les McIntyre, the pastor of St Mark's. He wanted to know what he should do. Marlene was a member of St Mark's and he wanted to help, but not step in before she was ready to see him. What did Mary think?

Mary thought they both needed to go over to the Lowells' this morning, but she wanted to talk to Emma first. See how Marlene had gotten through the night and see how Tommy was doing. She also wanted to talk to Dan.

Les agreed, saying to call him when she was ready to go. He didn't want to push difficult decisions on Marlene so soon but there was no telling when the body would be released and they had to be ready. Would they be using O'Dell's? Mary was sure they would. Then she called Dan.

Had the shop been robbed?

Not according to Heath. The last two weeks' buys were in the safe in the bag they used, ready to be taken to a smelter somewhere in the Los Angeles area. The cash they kept on hand was all accounted for. The diamonds they'd purchased seemed to be untouched. They were all in the safe, the diamonds in a special tray. The safe would have been open during the day and Jerry kept that inventory, but it all looked as usual. There was no sign anyone had tried to get into the cash register or the display cabinets. There wasn't much in them, anyway. The blinds on the front door were closed, the door locked and the open sign had been removed. Whoever shot Jerry must have left by the back door but no one had seen him. If it was a him. No one had heard a shot. Only Mo Black and John Lagomasino had heard Marlene's screams. They were dusting the shop for fingerprints and Dan was sure there would be plenty, but he doubted they'd be much use. There were people in and out of that shop constantly and there was no sign of a struggle. It looked, at least for the time being, as if Jerry either knew who had shot him or had been taken by surprise. Or both. But why continued to be a mystery.

Mary thought she had an idea why. 'Dan, did Heath look in the bag?'

'The bag that was due to go to the smelter? No. Why? Oh. Oh my God. No.'

'It seems possible to me there may be more in that bag than there's supposed to be.'

'Of course. I don't need Heath for that. I have the records of what Jerry turned into us up to his death. We haven't gone through his records at the shop yet, either. Actually, Wilson should be handling all that but I can't seem to get him to pay attention. He's too busy trying to find evidence the Blacks are involved.'

'Is Emma still at the Lowells'?'

'No. She came back early this morning. I took one look at her and sent her to the motel to get some sleep. I guess she was up most of the night. Marlene wasn't doing well but they finally got some sleeping pills down her and she went to bed, but Tommy wanted to talk. That was fine with me – we got a better picture of what might have been going on there from what he told her but, poor kid, she was out on her feet. I'll talk to her later.'

'What are you going to do about going through Jerry Lowell's records?'

'Call Cody Baxter. I need some accounting types and Wilson's no help.'

'Dan, do you think Wilson may be . . .' Mary knew her voice sounded worried, but she was. Wilson wasn't acting like any rational police officer she'd ever known, or heard of. She couldn't help wondering if, instead of trying to find out something, he was trying to hide something.

'Involved? The thought has occurred to me. How, I'm not sure. But there's more than one thing going on I haven't figured out, and not being the one in charge hasn't helped.' He paused and took in a long breath. 'What are you going to do?'

'I'm going over to the Lowells' to see what needs doing. Les wants to go with me.'

'Good.' Dan sounded distracted.

She could hear voices in the background. Someone had come in, someone he probably needed to talk to, but she had one last question. Hurriedly, she got it in.

'What about the funeral? Les will bring it up. Tommy needs to start thinking about it. I'm not sure Marlene will be up to it. What should we tell them?'

'I don't know. His body is at the San Luis Obispo morgue and they'll be doing the autopsy. I have no idea when. Tell them . . . I don't know.' Dan sounded frustrated and rushed. 'Tell them at least two weeks. It takes a while to get the autopsy done and for the coroner's office to release the body. They could hold a memorial service if they want and have the graveside service later. Mary, I've got to go. I'll talk to you later.'

She hung the phone up with a little more force than necessary. Dan wasn't the only one who felt frustrated. Funerals, like most things, required planning, and it was never too early to start. She was painfully aware she and Les would be doing a large share of it, having been in this position before. Most people weren't at their best when it was time to plan a funeral, and that was when they needed people from the church most. Luckily, Joy – wonderful, morose, efficient Joy – had stepped in when she'd needed to make decisions about Samuel's. All of her sisters had moved away and neither Dan nor Ellen had returned to Santa Louisa yet. She couldn't have gotten through it without Joy, Les and the members of St Mark's. She'd reciprocated more than once but she'd never helped plan one for a murder victim. She hadn't thought it would be easy. Dan had reinforced that fear.

Les was waiting in his car in front of the Lowells' house when she arrived with Millie in the passenger seat, looking around with what seemed to be great interest. This wasn't a part of town they frequented. Santa Louisa lay on each side of the Salinas River on land that, on the east side, was either flat or softly rolling. The town limits on the west side didn't extend very far. They quickly gave way to large parcels filled with almond trees, vineyards, olive groves and steep hillsides dotted with lavender. The Lowells' house was on one of the streets

that bordered the line between the city and county. A low
ranch-style home, it seemed to ramble aimlessly across the
top of the rise, a large plate-glass window taking up much of
the front. The double front door was painted green, the house
a beige stucco. The path that led from the street to the door
was brick, as was the long, narrow porch. There was a black
decorative light pole where the path began and black wrought-
iron lanterns on the porch. Mary was sure they were needed.
There were no streetlights on this road and no sidewalks.

She and Les stood for a moment, looking at the house, then
Mary sighed.

'I guess we'd better go in.'

Les nodded. 'This is the only part of my job I dread. I
should be a comfort to people going through this time, but I
never feel I am, that I can do enough. And a death like this
one . . . the only thing worse is when someone loses a child.'

A small chill ran up the back of Mary's neck, one she hadn't
felt in some time. She knew how grief felt and imagined the
loss of a child would be every bit as great, maybe greater, but
so was the pain of never being able to conceive, of never
having the child you so desperately wanted. She had come to
terms with that grief a long time ago, though. Now it was time
to face someone else's. She resolutely squared her shoulders
and tightened Millie's leash.

'We'll do the best we can.' She started up the walk, Les
beside her.

Tommy answered the door before they could ring the bell.
'Come in. Do you have any news?'

'Not much. Mostly we came to see how both of you are
doing and what we can do to help.'

Tommy grimaced and opened the door wide. 'I don't know
what you can do but come in. Right now, I don't even
know what there is to do.'

He led the way into a large, comfortable living room. Two
ivory sofas heavily strewn with a variety of brightly covered
pillows made an L-shape facing a flagstone fireplace with a
hearth raised high enough to form a wide seating area. Today
it was littered with newspapers. A low square table sat in front
of the sofas, covered with more newspapers, a couple of empty

coffee cups, a plate liberally coated with what looked like toast crumbs and an empty yogurt carton. Two moss-green wingback chairs were positioned in front of the large front window, a pie-crust table between them. An easy chair, covered in a floral slip cover, was in the corner, and an overstuffed chair in front of it. A cheerful, welcoming room, but not today. The only thing in the room that didn't look tired or depressed was the dog. Ranger was immediately on his feet, tail wagging, greeting Millie.

Tommy waved vaguely at the furniture then seated himself in the overstuffed chair. 'Do you know what's going on? Do they still have the jewelry store cordoned off? I keep thinking I need to go down there. Make sure everything's all right, but I don't want to leave Mom. She had a rough night.'

'I imagine she did,' Mary murmured. She seated herself on one of the sofas. 'Is she asleep?'

Les dropped down on the other.

Tommy nodded. 'We got some pills into her around two and she finally dropped off. She's in shock. So am I. It all seems so . . . unreal. I can't get my head around it, but then I didn't see him. Mom did. She's not having an easy time with that.'

Les leaned forward, his hands resting on his knees. He looked as if he was searching for words that didn't seem to be coming easily. Mary could hardly blame him. The only things that came to her mind were meaningless platitudes. She, of all people, should have ideas of what would be comforting but her mind seemed to have gone blank.

Finally Les spoke. 'I know this is hard to accept and it's even harder to have to make some practical decisions, but there are a couple of things. I really don't want to talk to your mom about this so . . . are you able to talk about some necessary details?'

'Do you mean funerals and that kind of thing?' Bitterness rang strong in Tommy's voice. Grief was absent but anger present. His father had just been brutally murdered and might have been involved in a crime. It would be hard to feel much else. Grief would come later.

Les nodded. 'I'm sorry to bring it up but we need to have

a mortuary on notice. We usually use O'Dell's, and if that's all right with you and your mother, I can give them a call. If that's what you want.'

Tommy looked a little sick. 'Yes. She'll want . . . I don't think they had any arrangements, any cemetery plots or anything like that, but I suppose . . . I have no idea how any of this works. I don't remember ever having been to a funeral. Even my grandparents'.'

'Right now, that will be enough. I'll put them on notice. We'll need to talk to Dan, see when . . . They'll have to have an autopsy. It's standard in these kinds of events. So we have a little time.' Les was doing a good job of keeping his voice low and matter-of-fact, kind but not overly sympathetic.

She wanted to get up and give Tommy a huge hug but maybe now wasn't the time. She thought he was hanging on by a very slender thread and a hug might shake him loose. He needed to keep himself together, if only for his mother's sake.

'Is there anything we can do for you right now?' Les went on, his tone seeming to calm Tommy.

Some of the tension went out of his shoulders; the rigid lines that ran down his neck seemed to relax slightly.

'Actually, there is. I really want to get down to the store and I want to talk to Dan. Chief Dunham. He was here last night but it seems all I did was answer questions. I have some of my own but I don't have any answers. Could one of you stay here for about an hour while I see if I can get into the store and make sure everything there is all right? I've called Crystal, told her not to think about opening today, but I'd like to go through it, make sure everything is locked up properly.'

'I'll stay.'

Both men looked at Mary, Les as if he'd expected her to volunteer and Tommy with a little surprise and a lot of gratitude.

'I'll drive you down and bring you back.' Les started to get to his feet. 'I don't think you need to be driving right now.' He turned toward Mary. 'You'll be all right here by yourself?'

'I'll be fine. Besides, I have Millie and Ranger to keep me company.'

Tommy also got to his feet. So did Ranger. 'I guess I should return him to the Dunhams.' There was uncertainty in his voice and reluctance. 'It was nice of them to let me take him last night. He helped.'

'There's no need to return him right now. Unless you want to, that is. No one's claimed the dog and he seems happy to be with you.'

Tommy looked hopeful for the first time. He let his hand drop down on the dog's head. Ranger leaned against his leg a little.

'All right. I'll leave him here.' He turned toward Les. 'I don't want to take up your time. I'm fine to drive. I won't be very long and I have my cell so I can keep in touch with Mrs McGill.' He paused, and a wave of some emotion Mary couldn't read passed over his face. 'But I would appreciate it if you could come back later this afternoon when Mom wakes up. She's going to need some help and I'm not sure I can give it.'

Les was only too glad to agree and they left together. Ranger followed Tommy to the door, obviously expecting to go with him, and sat staring at it when he realized he wasn't included. For some reason Mary didn't understand, it brought tears to her eyes that Jerry's death hadn't. Why she felt more sympathy for a dog . . . but it wasn't that. She sighed, looked around the room and started to collect empty coffee cups.

# THIRTY-TWO

'**M**ary. What are you doing here? Where's Tommy?' The start Mary gave at the sound of Marlene's voice almost sent the paper she was reading across the kitchen table onto the floor.

'Oh. You're up.' What an inane remark. Of course she was up. She was standing in the kitchen.

But Marlene didn't look as if being up agreed with her. Her face was blotchy, her hair tangled. She hadn't changed into her nightclothes and the slacks and knit top she'd had on yesterday were rumpled. At least whoever had gotten her into bed had removed her shoes. Her feet were bare.

'Tommy has gone down to the store to make sure everything is all right. He wants to talk to Dan as well. See if there's any new information.'

Marlene stared at her. 'Information.' She shuddered and looked vaguely around the kitchen. 'I think I'd like some coffee. Is there any?'

'I just made some. Sit down. I'll get it.'

Marlene did as instructed. She accepted the mug Mary slid in front of her without comment. Mary had no idea how Marlene took her coffee but she'd liberally laced it with cream and sugar, thinking she needed the extra energy they might provide. Marlene didn't seem to notice.

'Why are you here?' She quickly went on, as if she'd heard herself and realized how rude that might sound, 'Not that I don't want you. But . . .'

Mary refilled her mug, paused to open the back door and let in both dogs then sat back down facing Marlene. 'Tommy didn't want you to wake up and find no one here. He'll be back pretty soon.'

Marlene nodded, but not as if she cared very much. 'Did he call Crystal?'

'Yes. The shop will remain closed today. You can talk about what you want to do later.'

They sat in silence, each sipping their coffee. Mary was anxiously watching Marlene, who seemed to be staring into space. Mary was afraid to think what she was seeing.

Finally Marlene broke the silence. 'Was he shot?'

Startled, Mary nodded.

Marlene looked up. 'I don't mean was he shot by a gun. I know he was. I mean, did someone shoot him? Someone else?'

The jolt that went through Mary was hard enough to make her hands shake. She set her mug back on the table and leaned forward a little. 'You thought Jerry might have shot himself?'

Marlene answered with a shuddery sigh. 'That's what I thought when I found him. He's been so . . . different lately, so unhappy and upset. I thought he might have.' She paused, stared into her mug and set it back down. 'I don't know which is worse.'

'That someone killed him or he killed himself?'

She stared at Mary but without seeing her. 'That means I was right. Something had Jerry scared. I was married to that man for over twenty-five years. I knew what he was like. He was never very cheerful, always kind of a loner, but I didn't mind. I'm not very social either. He never questioned me about how I ran the shop. I grew up in a jewelry store. My father owned one and he taught me. I never questioned him about how he ran his design business. Only it never did very well. It was after he bought the We Buy Gold shop that he began to change. He seemed depressed, irritable, almost fearful. I never understood it. That shop made money.'

Mary wasn't sure she was following Marlene. That the gold shop made money she understood, but she thought . . . 'I thought Heath and Gabe Grady own We Buy Gold.'

Marlene shook her head. 'They were Jerry's partners but had nothing to do with running it. They own a couple more of these kinds of stores down the coast and Heath ran the stuff to the smelter, but that's about all. Jerry did everything else. Kept the books, registered all the purchases with the local police, made out the inventory list for the smelter, that kind of thing. It was just an investment for the Gradys. They didn't have to do anything else because they knew they could rely on Jerry. He wasn't very social but he was honest. Honest to a fault. So, who was he afraid of and why did someone kill him?'

That wasn't a question Mary could answer. She added it to the other ones running around in her head that she had no answers to either. However, there was one thing she did know. She had to get Marlene going again, and she couldn't do it in the condition she was in right that moment.

'Marlene, why don't you get in the shower and put on some clean clothes? It's amazing how much better you'll feel. I'm going to make you something to eat, and by the time you get cleaned up and eat something, Tommy will probably be back. Maybe he'll have some news for us.'

Maybe he wouldn't but, either way, a shower and food would be progress toward Marlene coping.

For a moment, she didn't think Marlene was going to move, but the words seemed to sink in and slowly she nodded her head. She pushed back her chair, stepped over Ranger without seeming to notice him and walked back in the direction of her bedroom. Mary waited a few minutes then quietly followed. When she heard the water start, she went back to the kitchen. What she was going to feed her, she didn't know, but there must be something in the pantry. If all else failed she knew there was toast.

Tommy came in as his mother was pushing scrambled eggs, fresh peaches and toast around on a plate. She looked up expectantly but soundless tears started down her cheeks when he shook his head. He knelt on the floor beside her chair, taking her in his arms, patting her back as if she were a small child he needed to comfort. Finally he took the napkin Mary handed him, gave it to his mother and got to his feet.

'The shop is also under investigation. They're looking for evidence there as well as at the gold shop. What that may be, I have no idea, but it looks as if we're going to be closed for at least two more days. Maybe that's just as well. I couldn't work right now and I'm sure Mother couldn't face a customer, let alone the store. I'm not sure what we'll do, but if Les comes later this afternoon, that will help.' He looked at his mother, dressed now in clean shorts and a T-shirt, her hair still damp, and almost smiled. 'We'll make it through this but it's going to be a bitch.'

Mary blinked once or twice at his use of words but decided it expressed the situation very well. 'Tommy, there are some messages on the phone table. People offering help, food, sympathy . . . I told them all thank you but you both needed a day or so. Ellen called. She says to keep Ranger as long as you want, but if he becomes a burden, let her know. And can she help in any way?'

Tommy smiled. 'Small towns can be really nice, but right now I don't know what anyone can do, except maybe help the police find out who did this. Ranger won't be a burden. He's been a real help to both of us. I'd like him to stay.'

'In that case, I need to get going. Can I bring you back dinner?'

'No, but thank you anyway. I stopped by The Yum Yum. Ruthie is sending over something. I don't think either of us wants to eat much but we need to have something.'

Mary nodded. 'I'll call you in the morning.' She snapped the leash on a reluctant Millie and, with a final pat on the shoulder for Marlene, she and Millie walked out to her car. She was anxious to get home but she had one more stop she wanted to make before that happened.

# THIRTY-THREE

The library was quiet, except for the children's section. It was packed with boys and girls around six years old, all sitting on the floor listening to Mae, the children's librarian, reading aloud. Their teacher and a woman Mary didn't know, but assumed was a mother volunteer, stood at the back of the group, beaming at the scene. Luke stood a little behind them, leaning up against the wall, listening. He turned when Mary tapped him on the shoulder. He smiled at her and motioned for her to follow him back into the main library, where they could talk and where the sight of Millie wouldn't distract the children or collect frowns from someone who might want the 'no dogs allowed' rule to be followed. They went into Luke's office and closed the door.

'I'm glad to see you. Do you know anything?' He motioned to a chair in front of his desk and dropped down into his own.

Mary assumed that wasn't a general question but he wanted information on Jerry Lowell's murder and on Marlene and Tommy. She took the chair he'd indicated and shook her head. 'Not much.'

Luke looked dubious but he didn't press her. 'Have you seen Marlene or Tommy?'

She nodded. 'Yes. Just came from there.'

'How are they?'

'Marlene's in shock. She barely knows what she's doing. Tommy seems to be coping a little better but it's not an easy time.'

'No.' Luke drew in a deep breath. 'Not easy for any of us. I can't believe something like that could happen in our little town – that someone could just walk into a shop and shoot the owner. Why? There had to be a reason. Do you think he was trying to rob Jerry? I hear those gold-buying shops keep a lot of cash on hand.'

Mary thought back to the stack of cash Jerry had held as

he peeled off the small amount of money her mother's ring had brought. He hadn't seemed concerned, just gave her the money and the receipt and put the money back in the cash register. Is that where he always kept large sums? They had a safe. Did he keep most of it there?

'I guess they must,' she answered but that wasn't why she was here. 'Luke, my sisters and I want to make a donation to the library in our mother's name. We want to purchase some books – fiction – and wondered if we can do a memorial of some kind. You know, to commemorate the donation in her name.'

The abrupt change of subject made Luke blink, but the thought of new books made him smile. 'What a lovely idea. Of course we can. I can make a book plate with her name on it, saying they were a gift to the library in memory of her. Would that do?'

It would do very well. Mary thanked him and they started to discuss the details. Did Mary and her sisters want to pick out the books or would they leave that to the selection committee? They could leave it to the committee but she had a couple of stipulations. Her mother loved mysteries and was always on the lookout for new authors. Could they find a mystery author new to the library? It would be a pleasure was his answer. Details worked out, Mary pushed back her chair.

But Luke wasn't quite ready to let her go. 'Mary, this is going to sound selfish, but I have to ask.'

She waited, wondering what Luke thought she could answer.

'Our wedding, Pam's and mine, is in two months. Lowell's is making the rings. Do you think Tommy will be able to do that? I know I shouldn't be thinking of myself right now, but I don't want to get right down to the wire and find we don't have rings.'

It might be selfish of Luke but it was also a natural reaction. Unfortunately, Mary had no idea how to answer. 'Why don't you give it a couple of days? Let's see what Dan comes up with and how Tommy seems. You've got a little time. He's doing Susannah and Neil's as well, but they've got a year. The engagement ring can wait. Let's see what happens.'

Luke nodded slowly. 'I guess. I can't help thinking . . . You know, I walked by the We Buy Gold shop yesterday afternoon. It must have been right about the time it happened. The paper said he'd been dead about two hours when Marlene found him. Is that right?'

'I think so. You walked by the shop? Did you notice anything? Were the blinds closed?'

Luke's face went blank. 'I don't remember. I wasn't thinking about that shop. I'd just dropped off Pam's laptop at Black's as it wasn't holding a charge, and was thinking about getting back to the library. I only had one volunteer and . . . There is one thing I remember, though.'

Hope surged through Mary. A clue? Something that might help? 'What? What do you remember?'

'A paneled van drove out of the alley parking lot onto Parkview. I remember because I didn't recognize it. I know most people who park back there.'

'A paneled van.' That didn't sound very hopeful. The world was full of them. 'What kind of van? Was it delivering something?'

'Not that I could see. Delivery vans usually have the name of the company on the side, maybe a phone number. This was a plain white-paneled van that looked like it was overdue a trip through the car wash.'

A white-paneled van. Where had she heard . . . 'Did you tell Dan?'

'No. There's nothing to tell. I didn't see anyone or anything out of place when I went by the shop and it was just a paneled van I didn't recognize.'

'Could you see who was driving?'

Luke sighed. 'Mary, I didn't look.'

She didn't suppose he had. She probably wouldn't have, either. 'If you don't mind, I'll mention it to Dan tonight. It probably isn't important, but if he thinks it is he'll come talk to you.'

Luke didn't mind. She gave him the money for the books and he gave her a receipt, telling her that when he'd worked up a design for the bookplate, he'd call her. It wasn't until she'd unlocked the car, standing beside the open door to let it cool a little before she and Millie got in, that she remembered where she'd heard about a white-paneled van. One had been spotted near at least two of the robbed jewelry stores. A slightly dirty van with no markings. Hope surged liberally mixed with confusion. Could it be the same van? If so, who was driving? Could it have any connection with Jerry's death? Could the person driving be the killer? Could that same person have killed Ian Miller as well? If so, who was that person? She didn't know anyone who drove a plain white-paneled van. But she had a lot to tell Dan tonight. Marlene's suspicion Jerry might have committed suicide, his increasing nervousness about something over the last year and now the van. There had to be a connection somewhere. Didn't there?

# THIRTY-FOUR

Mary woke to the sun happily beaming in her bedroom window. The sky was a clear blue, even for seven in the morning, and there wasn't a hint of a cloud. There wasn't a flutter of a breeze, either. She pushed back the sheet and sat up. It was going to be another hot day.

She thought about last night as she ladled Millie's breakfast into her bowl. Mostly they'd talked about the wedding. Susannah had brought a copy of every wedding magazine published, Mary was sure, and they'd poured through them all. Wedding dresses were discussed, ideas for bridesmaids proposed and discarded, location for the reception hotly debated. Sabrina Tortelli, Susannah's cousin and the manager of Silver Springs Winery, had suggested it for the reception. She would close the tasting room and they could hold the receiving line on their patio, which was huge. She thought a buffet dinner would work best – the winery had plenty of tables, chairs and linens and the wine would, without a doubt, flow freely. There was room for a band and dancing.

Susannah seemed to favor the idea but Ellen looked a little frazzled when buffet dinners were mentioned. If she thought they would get away with cake and punch in the church hall, she was fantasizing.

She hadn't been able to capture Dan by himself until it was almost time to go home. He seemed startled when she told him Marlene had at first suspected suicide and interested when she mentioned the white-paneled van. However, he'd cautioned her against jumping to conclusions. Especially about the van. White was probably the color of choice for paneled vans and there were thousands of them. He volunteered one piece of information – if it could be called information. Tommy's alibi had been corroborated. He had been in Santa Barbara. He'd visited three high-end jewelry stores yesterday, taking along pictures of jewelry he'd designed and one demonstration finished piece, trying to get the stores interested in carrying his custom pieces. According to Dan, he had planned to take the necklace that had been in the window. It was the best piece he'd made since he'd been back and he'd planned on using it for that purpose. But his mother had sold it out from under him. He'd laughed a little when he said it, but Dan had gotten the impression he hadn't been pleased.

Tommy might not be pleased but Mary was. At least they knew what happened to the necklace. And they knew something else. Tommy had made it explicitly as a demonstration piece to advertise his expertise as a designer of fine jewelry.

Mary wondered about that as she waited for the coffeepot to finish dripping. The day she and Susannah had been at the jewelry store, the day they'd met Tommy at the dog park, he'd gone almost running back to the store the minute they'd mentioned his mother was showing the necklace to a prospective buyer. At the time, she'd thought it was because his mother was alone in the store. Maybe not. Maybe he didn't want the necklace sold, at least not right then. Maybe it was because it was his signature piece. Or was it something else? Something she didn't understand very well. Could stones, valuable ones, be recognized? She looked at her engagement ring. Really looked. She'd worn that ring for over fifty years; not taken it off since the day Samuel had slipped it on her finger. If there was anything someone should be able to recognize . . . only she didn't think she could. If it was lying on one of those black velvet mats jewelers used, along with several other diamonds of about the same size, she wasn't sure she'd know it. She wouldn't know her mother's, either.

People kept talking about cuts – modern ones, old style – and maybe if all of them were different cuts from hers she might be able to pick it out but she couldn't even be sure of that. So, was there a way to identify individual diamonds? Big, very famous ones, probably. But your average engagement ring? What was it Mr Miller had said? The diamonds were rose-cut and old. They hadn't looked especially old to her but she supposed diamonds didn't show their age like a dress would. Or a woman. She looked at her hand again and sighed.

She needed to eat and then get dressed. She wanted to get

some meals organized for Marlene and Tommy and she also wanted to practice some more on the computer. Mr Black would be back . . . today or tomorrow, she'd have to check . . . to give her another lesson and she wanted to be prepared.

She let Millie in and watched for a moment as she headed for her dish like a laser that had locked onto its target. The Blacks. Mo Black seemed like a nice man. Very businesslike, no small talk, but pleasant and good at explaining things. She didn't recall ever speaking to his nephew. David, wasn't it? Did they have a paneled van? She hadn't noticed when he was here what he drove. Could he possibly . . . He was outside when Marlene ran out of the store, screaming. That proved nothing. This wasn't getting anything done. She picked up her coffee and walked toward her bedroom. She'd be home most of the day and it was hot. She decided Mr Black wouldn't care if she wore shorts and a baggy T-shirt. Millie certainly wouldn't. With another glance at her ring, she entered the bathroom.

# THIRTY-FIVE

The doorbell rang exactly at ten. A young man stood there, his dark hair pulled back into a ponytail, a diamond stud in one ear and thick, plastic-rimmed glasses covering what looked like gray eyes. He had on jeans and a T-shirt advertising a rock band Mary had never heard of. His appearance made the bulging traditional leather brief-case he held look slightly ridiculous. He seemed vaguely familiar but Mary couldn't quite place him. Millie's snarling bark didn't help matters. She managed to pick up the dog and smiled, a little uncertainly, at the man.

'I'm David Black. My uncle couldn't come so he sent me. I hope that's all right.' His smile was a little unsure and he kept his eyes on a still-threatening Millie.

Mary heaved a sigh of relief. Of course. David. She'd never really met him before, just caught a glimpse, but he looked a lot like his uncle. She should have known. 'Please, come in.'

She held the door open for him while she held onto a squirming Millie. 'Come over and meet this noisy thing so she knows I approve of you being in the house.' She closed the door with her foot and held onto Millie while she sniffed David's fingers. When her barks had settled down to a low rumbling, Mary set her down and watched as she sniffed David's shoes then, satisfied they weren't under attack, walked away.

David grinned. 'I guess she's decided I'm not a threat.'

'Next time she'll greet you like a long-lost friend.' Mary smiled. 'Nice to finally meet you. I hope I didn't put you out, coming today. The last few days have been hectic, to say the least.'

David nodded. 'Our shop is still closed. Why, I don't know, but I don't have anything else to do so I might as well come here.'

Mary blinked. She hoped he hadn't meant that statement quite like it sounded.

Before she could respond, he went on: 'It hasn't been much
fun. Hard to believe anyone could have walked in and shot
him like that. Or why. Jerry was . . . irascible but not a bad
guy. I can't imagine someone shooting him because he was
grumpy. It must have been an attempted robbery.'

When she'd said 'hectic' she'd meant Jerry's murder, but
David's response wasn't quite what she'd expected. What had
she expected? She didn't know. 'Where's your uncle? Is he
all right?'

David nodded. 'He's talking to the police. Again. Wilson
never gives up.' He looked around the living room. 'I have
some lesson plans for us to go over. Where are you set up?'

Mary could take a hint. The subjects of Jerry Lowell and
certainly of Special Agent Wilson were now closed. 'In here.'

He followed her and Millie into the bedroom, now office.
The briefcase went on the day bed and out came a sheaf of
papers. They began.

Toward the end of the hour, sweat stood out on her forehead.
She'd learned a lot from Mo and thought he'd worked her
hard. Compared to what David expected Mo had been incred-
ibly kind. But when she logged out for the last time, she
smiled. So did David.

'You're doing really well.' He stuffed the papers back in
the case. 'Here.' He laid a pile beside the computer tower.
'These are the class sheets from today. These others are sched-
ules for the classes we hold at the shop. You might be interested
when we finish our last lesson next week.' He looked at her
and nodded. 'You know, most people your age don't do nearly
as well. Most of them can hardly pull up Google yet and have
no idea how to send an email. You're doing great.'

Mary very much doubted that was true but was happy for
the praise. It made her sore neck and tired brain a little more
bearable. 'Will you be coming back or will your uncle? I think
we should probably schedule it today. It won't be long before
my calendar starts to fill up again.'

'Have you learned how to post things on your calendar
online?'

Mary thought so. She brought it up, they agreed on a date
and she entered it.

David smiled. 'I guess I'd better get going. If you get stuck, call.' He snapped the case shut and started to pick it up but paused. 'Mrs McGill, have you . . . ah . . . seen Tommy? Or Mrs Lowell? I've been kind of . . . ah . . . worried about them. They're nice people.'

Suddenly the expert computer operator, the accomplished teacher, the confident man was gone. A young and uncertain person stood in front of her.

Mary smiled and nodded. 'About as good as you can expect.' She sounded like a hospital nurse. She could do a little better than that. 'Marlene is really having a hard time. Tommy is trying to hold everything together for her.'

'He's a great guy. He asked me to help him computerize his inventory. That's how I got to know him. I learned a lot about gems and gold and silver from him.'

Computerize the inventory? What inventory? Feeling she was missing something was beginning to become a habit. 'What inventory? The store's?'

'No. Marlene has a program for that. Although I could come up with a better and easier one for her to use. Tommy wanted an easy way to catalog the gemstones he uses in his jewelry. You know, like the diamonds he's got.'

Mary didn't know. 'How can you do that? They all look alike to me.'

'You can tell a lot by the cut and the weight. If you had six diamonds all with the same cut and about the same weight, you probably couldn't tell one from the other but at least you'd know how many of a certain category you had. He wanted to set up something like that. Say he had four diamonds on hand that were between three to four karats, two were modern-cut and less than four karats, one was also modern and a full four karats, one was rose-cut and three karats. That kind of thing.'

'Rose-cut. That's an old cut?'

'Georgian.' Saying the word seemed to fill David with pride. 'There aren't too many of them anymore.'

Mary's brain was spinning. 'Is this the same inventory Jerry worked with to make his jewelry?'

'Oh, no.' The statement and David's shake of his head were emphatic. 'After the fuss Jerry made when Tommy used "his" gems for that necklace, Tommy swore he'd never use his dad's stuff again.'

Mary wasn't surprised. Even though Jerry had indicated he'd been pleased his son had used those stones, she'd suspected that wasn't true. 'Where did Tommy get his supplies?'

'From wholesalers, like most jewelers. The shop bought some but mostly he bought what he wanted, made his pieces and sold them to his mother. Same arrangement as Jerry had. But the gems were his. I always thought that was another reason he wanted the inventory. So his father could never say he was taking his.'

'But the diamonds and the sapphire he put in the necklace that was in the window – those he got from Jerry?'

David nodded. 'I guess all hell broke loose when ol' Jerry saw what he'd done. He and Marlene had a big fight about it. Tommy told me that's when he decided he was going to keep everything he did separate from his father and from the shop. He didn't want to put his mother in that position ever again.' He paused and shifted his weight; his eyes fastened on the wall behind Mary's head. 'He thinks a lot of his mother.' His eyes dropped to his briefcase and his voice was hardly audible.

Mary had to strain to hear his next words.

'Like I feel about Mo, probably.'

'Your uncle?'

'Yeah.' He looked straight at her, a trace of defiance in his speech and eyes. 'He's a great guy. He's treated me better than anyone else in my whole life. I graduated high school with honors because of him. My folks never cared if I even went to school. I'm taking classes at Cuesta and will start Cal Poly next quarter in computer science. I've got a good life ahead of me and it's all because of him.'

Mary wasn't sure what to say, or even if she should say anything. But he seemed to need to have her acknowledge his statement. 'Yes. He told me about your parents . . .'

'Occupation?' His eyes blazed with what could only be resentment. 'They thought they were so smart. Turns out they had no idea what they were doing. They ruined their own lives and did their damnedest to ruin mine. If it hadn't been for my

uncle . . . There's a man who knows how to do things smart.'
He smiled. 'And for their finale, they tried to rob Lowell's.
They deserved to get caught.'

It wasn't the bitterness that shocked Mary, it was the mention
of Lowell's. 'What are you talking about? Lowell's was never
robbed. We've never had a jewelry store robbery in this town.'

'Oh, not here.' The smile on David's face reminded Mary
of a wolf she'd seen in a documentary one time. 'In their old
store. The one in Sacramento. It was a much bigger store and
much better alarmed. My parents never had a chance. That's
where Mo met the Lowells. He was working on robbery then
and was one of the responding officers. He took himself off
the case when he discovered who the thieves were. Wilson
used my parents to force him out of his job.' The bitterness
melted away as fast as it had come. The smile David turned
on Mary was sunny and bright. His voice light and satisfied.
'But things have a way of turning out right sometimes. We
ended up here.' He picked up his briefcase, leaned down and
gave Millie a pat on the head, nodded to Mary and was gone.

Mary sat where she was for some time. Her legs felt weak,
somehow incapable of lifting her or holding her if she managed
to get up. David had certainly spilled over with emotions –
resentment at his parent's treatment of him and admiration for
his uncle and for Tommy. He was almost defensive about
Tommy. Did he identify Jerry with his own parents, his treatment of Tommy similar to what he'd experienced? Almost
certainly. She doubted Tommy needed a defender, though.
Under that mild front he was tough. Tough and determined.
And smart. That was what David said about his uncle, too.
He was smart. Smart because he built a new life for them or
smart because his parents got caught stealing and his uncle
didn't?

She gasped. What had brought that thought into her mind?
A lot of things. Absently, she bent over to help Millie onto
her lap. The dog sighed and stretched out over her knees. Mary
started to run her fingers through Millie's coat and scratch
behind her ears. Mo Black and Jerry Lowell knew each other
because Mo's brother robbed Jerry's store. Somehow Eric
Wilson was able to push Mo Black off the police force. Why?

Mo said Wilson always believed he had something to do with his brother but he'd never mentioned Lowell's. The Blacks and the Lowells had relocated to Santa Louisa within a short time of each other. Coincidence? Mary didn't believe in coincidences. At least not this kind. There was a connection there, but what kind? And was it connected somehow to the current robberies? And to Miller's death? This was getting much too confusing. She needed information, lots of it. Only how . . .

She pushed Millie off her lap, pulled her chair back up to the desk and logged back into the computer. She typed in Lowell's Jewelry, Sacramento, Ca, and waited to see what would happen.

# THIRTY-SIX

'**M**arlene is the third generation to own Lowell's Jewelry. It used to be Capitol Jewelry but she changed the name to Lowell's after she married Jerry and her parents passed away. It was one of the oldest and most successful stores in California. Why would she move to a small town like Santa Louisa to start over?'

Mary, Dan and Ellen sat around the glass table on the Dunhams' covered patio, watching Millie and Morgan lie on the grass, panting and happy after a spirited game of chase. It was only early afternoon but Ellen had no more appointments and declared she was working from home for the rest of the day. Dan had come home for lunch because Mary wanted to talk to him. It was easier to eat lunch and talk at home, he'd said. The remains of The Yum Yum sandwiches lay in front of them.

'Don't know.' Dan set his Coke can on the table, leaned forward so his arms rested on it and stared at Mary. 'You've got something on your mind. What is it?'

Mary held her glass of iced tea, twisting it a little as she watched the ice rock back and forth. She was having a hard time putting her bits and pieces of thoughts into words. Words that made some sense. 'Lots of things that have happened seem to tie together only I can't understand how. The newspaper article said the Blacks were caught in the store before they were able to actually get away with anything. But Jerry Lowell claimed a lot of jewelry was missing. He said they had an accomplice. Only one never showed up. Wilson was certain Mo Black was implicated somehow and managed to get him removed from the special forces even though there was no evidence connecting him to the robbery.'

'Wait a minute.' Dan sat up straight and stared at Mary. He set the Coke he'd just reclaimed back on the table. 'Mo Black was with the California Bureau Special Forces? Are you sure?'

'Positive. David told me and it was in the newspaper articles I found online this afternoon.'

'Are you saying he might have been his brother's accomplice?'

Mary shook her head vigorously. 'No. I'm not sure there was any missing jewelry. Marlene keeps saying Jerry was such an honest man, but what if he wasn't? What if he either claimed jewelry that never existed or, more likely, stole his own jewelry and blamed it on Mo Black? He'd know how to melt down the pieces and what to do with the gemstones. He'd also know what to do with the items from this latest string of jewelry store robberies. He buys gold then takes it to a smelter, or rather Heath Grady does. Maybe he had a deal worked out with Mo and David Black. Maybe they do the robberies. They'd sure know how to turn off the alarms, then he turned the jewelry into cash. Maybe Marlene suspected something and that's why she was so upset and called Tommy home.' Mary stopped fiddling with her glass and looked directly at Dan. 'Did you get a chance to look at the jewelry Jerry Lowell had ready for Heath to take to the smelter?'

Dan had a look on his face Mary had seen before. 'How you do it is . . . No. They're sending someone down from Sacramento to go through all Jerry's receipts, all the jewelry in that bag and our records, and I'm not to touch it. Neither is Heath. Which has made Mr Grady a tad testy, to say the least.'

Mary laughed. She imagined Heath was furious with the police but mostly with Jerry. If Jerry had been cheating him, Heath would be boiling mad for a couple of reasons. He wasn't a man who would tolerate being made a fool of.

Ellen hadn't said a word. She stared at her aunt, her iced tea glass in her hand, her mouth slightly open, then shook her head. 'You think Jerry Lowell was receiving stolen jewelry, mixing it with his legally purchased stock and taking it to the smelter?'

'I think it's possible.'

'Then who killed Jerry?'

'I don't know but he was acting scared. Maybe he thought he was about to be found out. Marlene said he was increasingly nervous – distraught, actually. She really did think he might have committed suicide.'

Ellen blinked then took a quick sip. 'OK. That might make sense. It also might account for Miller. If he'd found out something that connected Black and Lowell . . .'

Dan set his Coke back on the table with a bang. 'You two are forgetting something. First, it wasn't Ian Miller hounding Mo Black all these years. According to Emma, that was Eric Wilson.'

'True,' Mary acknowledged, 'but Wilson and Miller were partners. Miller must have known all about Mo Black's brother and about Mo losing his position with the Bureau. He'd know why. There had to be a reason other than whatever Wilson said.'

Dan started to say something but Mary put up her hand. 'One other thing. David said he helped Tommy set up an inventory.'

'An inventory of what?' The puzzled look on Ellen's face was nothing compared to the incredulity in her voice.

'An inventory of the jewels, or gemstones he had in stock. His father had some but they didn't include those, or I don't think they did.'

'How do you inventory a bunch of loose stones you can't identify?' Dan sounded as incredulous as Ellen. 'That doesn't make any sense.'

'Actually, it does. Sort of.' Mary couldn't keep from smiling at the unbelieving looks they both gave her. This did make a funny kind of sense. Now if only she could explain it. 'They might not be able to identify every individual gem but they can classify them. For instance, three diamonds, standard cut, between one and two karats. Four diamonds, between three to four karats and one some other kind of cut.'

'Or perhaps two rose-cut diamonds, each two karats?'

Mary beamed at him. 'Exactly. I have no idea what kind of gemstones are on Tommy's inventory but it does show that weight and especially cut could get someone's attention.'

'Especially if that someone was an expert in the retrieval of stolen jewelry.' Dan sat back, picked up what remained of his Coke and stared at his aunt. 'Why I pay detectives . . . '

'You mean if Mr Miller knew there were old rose-cut

diamonds of about the size, or weight, as ones listed as stolen it would have attracted his interest in the necklace Tommy made when he saw it in the window.' Ellen stared from Dan to her aunt and looked for a second as if things were at last starting to make sense. Then puzzlement settled back on her face and she threw herself back against the sofa cushions. 'It still doesn't tell us who killed Ian Miller. Tommy? I doubt it. Mo Black? Why? Jerry Lowell? Maybe. If he thought Miller could identify stolen gems. But he couldn't. The best he could do is wonder. Besides, didn't Jerry have a receipt of some kind for those diamonds? The sapphire, too?'

'If they came from jewelry he bought through the We Buy Gold shop, he did.'

'Oh? How do you know that?' Ellen cocked her head to one side as she turned toward her husband. There was a trace of a smile on her face but doubt in her voice.

'Because by California state law he has to give a receipt with a description of every piece he buys to the seller and keep that receipt for three years. He also has to get the seller to sign a declaration of ownership and give proof of who they are – drivers' license or something – and he has to take a fingerprint. Then a copy of that goes to us and another copy goes to the state. He's not a licensed diamond dealer, just a licensed second-hand shop, so he'd buy the gems and describe where he got them and from who.'

'He would?' She was looking at Dan as if she wasn't quite sure what he'd just said.

Mary had an easier time following. 'I had to give him my fingerprint when I sold him mother's ring. He wanted it on four forms. He said he'd fill them in later but I had to sign two of them.'

'What were the other two for?' Ellen turned her attention to her aunt. Forms she understood.

'I have no idea. I think he said one was for his records and he had to keep it for I don't know how long. What the other one was for, I don't know.' She turned her attention to Dan. 'One of those went to you? Or your office. Did he have to do that for all his sales?'

Dan nodded. 'There has to be some way to prove ownership of the jewelry and other things people sell. That diamond ring could be your great aunt Judy's but it also could be stolen from the house down the street. Most people don't have any proof of ownership for a lot of things. Who can find a receipt of purchase for your grandmother's sterling silver set for twelve? So the law was designed to build in some accountability, in both the seller and the shopkeeper who buys them. We check the lists of stolen items we have, then if there is nothing that looks like a match, we just file it. After thirty days the shop owner is free to do whatever he wants with it. Resell it, send it to the smelter, take it apart, whatever.'

Mary had been following this with interest. What Jerry had her do had seemed excessive for one small ring. Besides, he knew her. But she could understand the need for the rather elaborate procedure. However, there was one thing she didn't know. 'What happens when the shop owner takes the jewelry to the smelter? Does he have to show them paperwork on each piece of jewelry?'

Dan folded his fingers together to make a tent and looked at Mary over the top of them. 'That's a very good question. I have no idea. We comply with the law at our end but have never had any need to go further. The We Buy Gold shop is the only one in town that is a licensed second-hand shop dealing with items that fall under the law and we've never come up with a single piece they've sent us a description of that was suspicious. It's almost become one of those routine tasks you have to do but don't pay much attention to. The state tells us they're working on an electronic filing system to handle all this but it isn't up and running yet and none of us care much. Debbie Turner comes in a couple of afternoons a week, does all the filing and inputs what we need into the computer that's not an arrest or crime report. The Lowell stuff is included in that and we never hear any more about it. As I said, we've never had a match.'

'Agnes doesn't do your filing?' There was a very broad smile on Ellen's face and a lot of fake innocence in her voice. She got a snort for an answer and laughed. 'Why do you keep Agnes if she can't do much of anything?'

'I wish I knew.' Dan's sigh was long and heavy. 'She's been there a long time, for one thing. Since before I came back to town to take this job. But she's kind. Great with the kids who get dragged in for whatever reason, good with parents whose kids are missing or worse, not one bit intimidated when we bring in a belligerent drunk, and she can take accurate messages. Besides, we all like her. God knows why, but we do.'

Ellen laughed hard enough that Morgan picked up his head. Evidently satisfied all was well, he dropped it again.

Their little exchange barely registered on Mary. Her mind was still on the stolen jewelry. 'Dan, do you have a list of the pieces stolen from the string of robberies?'

He shook his head. 'Just the local ones. We might get some from other parts of the state but not always. Out of state, almost never. We wouldn't have known anything about Miller's investigation if he hadn't come to town, told me what he was doing and then gotten himself killed.'

Mary shuddered a little at that. 'Do you have a list of the robberies, the dates, where they were located, that kind of thing?'

'No. Same reason.' His eyes narrowed as he examined her. He leaned forward. 'What are you getting at? You're on to something. What is it?'

Mary shook her head. 'No. I'm not. It's just that all kinds of things are running through my head. It's like a puzzle where nothing fits. It should but nothing seems to.'

'When something does, you come tell me, hear? The last thing I need is you going off half-cocked and getting yourself into trouble.'

'Why ever would you think I'd do a thing like that?' Mary did her best to look innocent but it didn't seem to work.

'Past events, that's why.'

'You have nothing to worry about. I'm clutching at straws, same as you.' She paused. 'Even if Jerry was guilty of receiving stolen jewelry, we're still left with one big question, aren't we?'

The smile Dan gave her was rueful. 'Yes, we are. Who committed the robberies?'

Finally Mary asked the question that had been most on her mind. 'You don't think Mo Black and his nephew are responsible?'

'Mary, right now I don't have any evidence to suppose they are. I also don't have anything that says they're not. That goes for just about everyone involved in all this.'

No one said anything for a moment, then Mary set her glass on the table beside Dan's Coke and got to her feet. 'Millie and I had better get going. Thanks for the tea and for listening to me. I'll see you both tomorrow?'

'Of course.' Ellen looked at her aunt speculatively. 'What are you going to do now?'

'I took a lasagna out of the freezer this morning. I told Marlene and Tommy I'd bring dinner. I'm sure they're still in no mood to cook anything but they have to eat. I have some French rolls, too, and some things to make a salad. That should hold them for a day or so.'

'You're giving them my lasagna?' Dan looked like a little boy who'd just lost his ice cream.

Mary laughed. 'I'll make you another one. Besides, this is a small one. Just enough for two meals for two not-very-hungry people.' She leaned down to snap the leash on Millie, who had appeared beside Mary before she had completely gotten to her feet. She straightened and looked around for her purse.

'Let us know how Marlene is doing, will you?'

Mary nodded at the concern in Ellen's voice but turned toward Dan. 'Did Tommy ever get to talk to you? He wanted to know how long the shop needs to stay closed, among other things. If you have a message for him, I'll deliver it.'

'We should be finished there by tomorrow. He already knows that. But you might tell him that Heath wants the We Buy Gold shop back in business asap. He wants to talk to Tommy. He asked if I knew where he was, if he'd come back to the jewelry store yet.'

Ellen gasped. 'He wants Tommy to open that shop where his father was killed? Isn't that a bit insensitive?'

'He didn't say he wanted Tommy to do it, just that he needed to talk to him.' He turned to face Mary. 'If he's there, could you tell him?'

Mary didn't say anything for a minute. The very idea that Tommy would try to take his father's place in that shop made her skin crawl. But maybe that wasn't what Heath wanted. Maybe they were jumping to conclusions. She nodded. 'Of course.'

# THIRTY-SEVEN

There were two cars in the driveway – a blue Toyota Camry with magnetic signs on the side advertising Jerry Lowell, Custom Jewelry, and a small, brown, somewhat elderly pickup. Mary wondered if the Camry belonged to Jerry or Tommy. She didn't recognize the pickup.

Tommy answered the doorbell. 'Hey, Mrs McGill. Thanks for coming.' His eyes looked narrowed, his mouth repressed with what seemed like anger. The smile he gave her was forced but he held his hands out for her box. 'Here. Let me take that.'

He took the flat cardboard box Mary used to carry the food and stood back to let her and Millie enter. Ranger appeared from behind him to greet Millie.

'This all looks wonderful. I'll take it into the kitchen. Everyone else is in the living room.'

Mary hesitated as she watched his retreating back. What was the matter with him? The look on his face . . . that wasn't grief. It looked more like barely suppressed fury. Wondering what had happened to make him so upset and who he meant by 'everyone else,' Mary walked into the living room and stopped in surprise. She opened her mouth slightly as she stared at the occupants of the room but she couldn't help it. That Emma Baxter was here was no surprise but she hadn't expected to see Mo Black. However, there he was, sitting next to Marlene on the sofa, a glass of what looked like iced tea in his hand and a faint flush of red decorating the tips of his ears.

Emma sat in one of the red chairs that faced the plate-glass window. She jumped to her feet to greet Mary, guiding her over to the other chair like an honored guest. Marlene and Mo said nothing. Marlene looked a lot better. Clean, well-brushed hair, a fresh T-shirt and cotton slacks, sandals on her feet and a flush of color on her cheeks. Blush? Somehow Mary didn't think so. She let Emma help her into the chair, Millie right beside her knee. She didn't know what to say. The room had the feeling of a conversation interrupted – a conversation she wasn't going to be invited to take part in. What that might be, or even if there had been one, she didn't know, but the mood in the room was tense, as if she'd interrupted an argument. She had no idea what to do next. Not a common occurrence for her. She decided to start with the obvious.

'You're looking better, Marlene, but I don't imagine you feel much like cooking. I brought lasagna. All you have to do is put it in the oven. It will keep for a couple of days in the refrigerator if you don't want it tonight.'

'Oh, I'm sure we'll have it tonight. You're right. I don't feel like getting a meal. People have been offering to do so much but I don't feel like seeing anybody, either. I'm glad you came, though.' She smiled at Mary, not an especially bright one but a smile nonetheless.

Mo's face showed nothing but a faint look of anxiety. Mary waited for someone to say something, to explain why Mo was there, but no one said anything. Ranger plopped down beside Emma, Millie put her head on Mary's foot and the silence went on.

Finally Mary had had enough. 'Have you talked to Les? Reverend McIntyre?'

Marlene looked up from examining her hands, seemingly surprised. 'About what?'

A jolt of irritation ran through Mary but she damped it down before answering. 'I thought he was coming over last night to offer whatever comfort he could and to discuss your wishes if you were ready.'

'Oh.' Marlene looked confused, as if she was trying to remember. 'Yes. He came. But we didn't . . . I couldn't . . .'

'We were talking about that right before you came.' Emma's tone seemed carefully moderated.

'Have you come to any decision?' Mary saw Mo plainly from where she sat.

His back was rigid, his hands folded tightly around the glass he clutched in his lap. He kept his eyes straight ahead, not looking at Marlene, not looking at any of them. She thought the pink had spread to his whole ear.

'Marlene thinks they should have a memorial right away and then a graveside service later just for the family.' Emma spoke in the same detached tone but her eyes were on Mo.

Mary was trying to sort this out. Why was Mo here? Why was he so uncomfortable? Marlene was, too. Tommy had looked like he wanted to hit someone and Emma seemed to be refereeing something but Mary wasn't sure what. 'What does Tommy think?'

'Tommy thinks it's too soon to make any decisions. Right now the very thought of a memorial makes me sick to my stomach.' Tommy walked into the room carrying two glasses of what appeared to be iced tea.

From the color, Mary was certain it was instant. He handed her one and the other to Emma. 'I put lemon in both of them. If you want sugar, I'll get some.' His tone said plainly he couldn't care less if they wanted sugar. It was only some remembered semblance of politeness that made the offer. He offered nothing to his mother.

Mary took a sip. It was instant. The lemon helped. Sugar wouldn't have. 'You don't ever have to have a memorial service if you don't want to. A small graveside service when the authorities . . .' She didn't want to say 'release the body' but couldn't come up with an alternative.

Tommy saved her the trouble. 'When they release the body?' Bitterness and anger were ripe in his voice. His eyes dug into Mo Black like knives. 'I think that might be the most appropriate plan.' The gaze he turned on his mother was only a little less intense. 'What do you think, Mother? Shall we skip the memorial?'

Misery was written all over Marlene's face; misery that hadn't been there a few minutes before. She seemed to tremble slightly as she looked at her son and Mary could have sworn her eyes misted over. 'I think that's a good idea. I'm not sure . . .'

'That you'd want to revisit some of your memories? I have some I don't want to, either.'

Ranger left Emma's side and walked over to where Tommy stood towering over all of them, closing and opening his fists, blinking rapidly. He pushed up against Tommy's side and

whined softly. Some of the anger, the tenseness that kept him
stood so stiffly seemed to fade as his hand dropped on the
dog's head. He started to rub Ranger's ears and sighed. 'It's
O'Dell's Funeral Home, isn't it? They're the one you notified?'
He seemed to address Mary.

'Yes. They do most of Saint Mark's funerals. They're very
kind and helpful.'

He sighed again, this time deeply and with what sounded
like resignation. 'Could you call them? Tell them I'll bring
my mother in tomorrow to start making arrangements. I'll call
Reverend McIntyre in the morning and tell him we're only
going to have a graveside service. I guess I'll have to do
something about a grave, too.' He gave a short laugh then
looked around as if for a chair.

Mo Black immediately got up. 'I think I'd better go. I only
thought . . . I wanted to make sure you were all right.' He
stared at Marlene but immediately turned to include Tommy.

He extended his hand to Marlene, who slowly reached out
and took it. That he held it a little too close and for a little
too long was hard to miss. Gently, he released it. She let it
drop in her lap, stared at him for a moment then dropped her
eyes.

'I'm so sorry,' he almost whispered.

'Yes. I know you are.' Her words sounded monotone, an
acceptance of something that had been discussed before.

Tommy took the hand Mo extended but his rigid stance
didn't soften. Neither did the look on his face. 'You did what
you had to.' His eyes shifted to his mother. The anger seemed
to fade from his face but not the anguish.

Emma got to her feet, the expression on her face a mixture
of emotions, not one of which Mary could read. 'Tommy, let's
postpone our walk. I think your mother needs you with her
right now. Maybe tomorrow morning?'

Tommy looked startled and not too pleased but his mother
settled the matter.

'Thank you, Emma, for everything. Yes, I do think Tommy
and I need to talk.' There was a set to Marlene's jaw that made
Mary think their talk might not be too pleasant. She wished
she knew what was going on, but that it wasn't something

more than Jerry's murder, she was sure. What had Tommy meant about memories? Whose memories? What had Jerry done that they didn't want to remember? What had Mo done? In the meantime . . . 'Emma, I'm also leaving. Can I give you a ride back into town?'

Mo broke in. 'I'm going right by the police station. No trouble to drop you off.'

Mo sounded a little anxious, as if he wanted to talk to Emma badly, but so did Mary.

She had some questions for her and they didn't all have to do with the little scene playing out here. 'That's nice of you, Mo, but I have information about the Baxter family Emma wanted. We can talk about that on the way back.'

A quick flash of displeasure passed over Mo's face, almost too fast to be noticed if you weren't watching, but he only nodded, said one more goodbye all around and was gone. Mary watched through the plate-glass window as he climbed into the front seat of the brown pickup. The door slammed behind him a little too hard and the engine roared a little too loud as he took off down the street. Mo Black was either furious or badly upset about something. She stared at the empty street for a moment then turned to pick up her purse. She took Millie's leash out of it and managed to snap it onto the squirming dog. 'Emma, if you're ready?'

Emma had a red and blue striped tote bag already slung over one shoulder. She nodded.

Mary walked over to Marlene, leaned over and gave her a squeeze. 'If you need anything . . . anything at all, please call. I'll do whatever I can to help you both.'

'You can find whoever it was who shot my father.' Tommy tried to insert a small laugh but it fell flat.

Mary smiled back to show she knew that wasn't something he expected.

What he couldn't know was she planned to do exactly that. Find out who had killed both Ian Miller and Jerry Lowell, and why.

# THIRTY-EIGHT

Neither of them said anything until they were almost in the center of town.

Finally Mary broke the silence. 'I felt as if I interrupted something back there. Is everything . . .'

'All right? Aside from Jerry Lowell being murdered, Marlene dropped a little bombshell on Tommy. She told him she'd asked Jerry for a divorce the day before he was shot.'

Mary jammed on the brakes so fast that Millie flew off the backseat and ended on the floor with a loud yelp of protest. Mary barely heard her. 'She did what? Why?'

Emma sat back up and loosened her seat belt a little. 'Why don't you pull into the police station parking lot and I'll tell you? This man behind almost rear-ended us and I don't think he's too happy.'

Mary glanced in her rearview mirror at the glaring man behind her and did as Emma suggested. 'All right. Tell me.'

Emma undid her seat belt, rubbed her breastbone lightly and took a deep breath, let it out slowly and turned toward Mary. 'It came up while we were talking about the funeral. Marlene didn't seem able to deal with any of it but Tommy said they had to think about it. They didn't even have plots. Did she want a memorial service? That's when she broke down.'

'Was this before or after Mo got there?'

'Before. She said she couldn't take it anymore. Jerry had changed over the years. He used to be such a good guy but he wasn't anymore. He'd tried to cheat the insurance company when Lowell's was robbed and blame it on Mo Black. He'd lifted money from the store when they were in Sacramento, thinking she'd never find out, but she did. She sold the store, which was her heritage, thinking they needed a fresh start. When they came here, she told him he was to have nothing to do with the store, only his custom jewelry business. That's when he opened the We Buy Gold shop. She said she became sure something was going on there but she didn't know what. She'd finally decided she didn't want to and didn't want any association with it, or with Jerry. He wasn't the man she'd married and she wanted out.' Emma sighed deeply. 'When she found him, she thought maybe it was her fault. That she'd pushed him over the edge. But Jerry didn't commit suicide. He was murdered and it had something to do with that shop.'

Mary couldn't seem to do anything but stare at Emma. That Jerry wasn't the paragon of honesty Marlene had claimed wasn't a surprise but that Marlene had been driven to getting a divorce was. Mo Black. He'd tried to blame Mo and it had somehow cost him his job. Why, then, were they on speaking terms? Maybe they weren't. Or . . . something that had been a half-formed thought in the middle of the night returned. This had all started with Miller. Why had he come to Santa Louisa? Because he had a lead on who was robbing jewelry stores or a lead on what happened to the jewelry. Maybe . . .

'Emma, do you have access to the files on those robberies?'

'The files . . . no, that's not my case, but I can get them. What are you thinking?'

'I'm not sure, but can you get me the location of each one of those stores and the dates they were robbed?'

'You have an idea.' It wasn't a question.

'It's not an idea as much as a possible line of inquiry. Ian Miller had to have a reason for showing up here. There's a connection somewhere between Santa Louisa and those robberies. I'm not sure what it is but I may have an idea where to look.'

Emma stared at Mary for what seemed like a long time. Long enough for Millie to get bored with the backseat of a car that wasn't moving. She started to climb between the seats in an effort to get to Mary. Almost abstractedly, Emma picked her up and set her in Mary's lap. 'All right, I'll get you that information on one condition.'

'What's that?'

'If anything, anything at all comes of this, you'll tell me immediately. Promise?'

'Of course.' She smiled at Emma, who didn't smile back.

'Dan's told me you're good at solving puzzles but it's gotten you in trouble before. Remember. You promised.' She started to open the door but slammed it shut again and slid down in the seat. 'Blast and damn.'

'What's the matter?' Mary looked over the top of Emma's head at the man leaving the police department. Cowboy hat worn low over his forehead, tight jeans and cowboy boots, he didn't even glance Mary's way. Gabe Grady. She looked at Emma, who had one arm up blocking her face. Gabe had been trying his charms on the female population again.

'Gabe came on to you?'

'More than that. He invited me out to the ranch. Thought I might like to see where my grandparents had lived. He'd show me around. Just him and me. Sure. He knew exactly who I was, knew I was a cop. He thought the whole thing was one big joke.' She sat up and watched the old pickup Gabe drove leave the parking lot. 'I wasn't nearly as amused.' She opened the door but paused. 'Give me your email address. I'll send you the information as soon as I get it. And don't forget: you don't go detecting anything outside of your own house.'

Mary smiled, watched as Emma typed her email address in her phone and headed for home.

She really wished people would quit worrying about her. She wasn't going to do anything dangerous. Only look something up on the Internet. And try to put some pieces of this puzzle together. Dan was more than capable of doing this but she thought he might be handicapped by the state police. They didn't seem to share information too readily, and she doubted Eric Wilson was any help. He seemed almost determined not to share information. Not so Emma. Her only goal seemed to be finding the killer. What a delight she was. Tommy seemed to think so as well. She wondered if . . . no. She was getting way ahead of herself there. Besides, she needed to think about all that had happened. Sort out what she actually knew from what she suspected and that was going to take some doing. Maybe, when she and Millie got home, she'd pour herself some iced tea and make a list. She'd done that before and it hadn't helped much, but this time she'd do it on the computer.

She laughed out loud. Millie, who had moved to the front seat, cocked her head as if to ask, *What?*

'We're about to put that expensive black box to good use, Millie, my dear. Right after you have your dinner.'

# THIRTY-NINE

Mary pushed her chair back from her desk and gave a snort of disgust. It was obvious she had a long way to go before she'd mastered the black beast.

Or maybe there wasn't much information on Eric Wilson. There was virtually none about the ten-year-old robbery at Lowell's Jewelry. She'd found one old newspaper clipping but it didn't tell her any more than she already knew. Evidently the interrupted robbery had not been of much interest to anyone but those involved.

There was a little more about Eric Wilson, none of it interesting. He'd been with the California Bureau of Investigation for over twenty years, hadn't risen very high in rank and seemingly had no specialty like his partner had. The biography mentioned a couple of high-profile cases he'd been involved with, along with Ian Miller, but that was all. No mention of any family or outside interests. It was absolutely no help.

Eric Wilson was one of the arresting officers at the Lowell robbery. Maybe the press had forgotten it but he hadn't. He had continued to hound Mo Black, determined to prove him guilty of something after all these years. She hadn't found anything about Black's dismissal from the Bureau on the Internet, either. There had to be a connection. All of those people couldn't just show up at the same place ten years later and there be no reason. What it might be, however, she was no nearer discovering.

Mo said you could look up anybody. Maybe so, but you couldn't always find much. Perhaps she didn't know where to look. People in the books she read, and in the movies she sometimes saw on TV, seemed to be able to access any kind of information they wanted. Maybe she was doing something wrong. She'd look up herself, see if she was there.

She was. It didn't say much, just a list of a lot of committees she'd chaired. It did say retired teacher but nothing about home economics, which was just as well. It gave the town but not her private information. That also was good. Nothing about Millie. That was too bad. Who else? She looked up John Lagomasino then Karl Bennington and Luke from the library. Bare bones information about each. Some of the photos they had posted for John were clearly not him, but they did have one good one of him in the pet shop. There was more about Karl and his veterinary work but almost nothing about Luke. She sighed and glanced at the clock. Almost five. Time to start thinking about dinner. She had accomplished nothing this afternoon but guessed she'd made some progress on finding her way around the Internet. She started to close the lid but paused. Maybe she'd search for one last person. She typed in Heath Grady. Up popped a picture of Heath in his cowboy hat, boots and tight jeans, a scowl on his face. Heath seemed to scowl a lot. There was a little more about him. She began to read. Heath, or G&H Enterprises, of which he was president, owned several businesses. The pyrotechnic company, of course, and more than one gold-buying shop. Three of them, in fact. The one in Santa Louisa was the only one of its kind in the county. The other two were in Santa Maria and Santa Barbara. The licenses for all three shops were in the name of G&H Enterprises. He had a BA in accounting from the University of Long Beach. Mary would never have guessed that. Somehow, accounting didn't seem something that would interest Heath. There was nothing else about Heath and nothing about Gabe. She logged off and went to start dinner.

The doorbell rang about eight. *Masterpiece Mystery* had just started and Mary had settled in, Millie beside her, to relax and enjoy. Who this could be, she had no idea, but the doorbell couldn't be ignored, especially as Millie was already at the front door, barking her most fierce warning bark.

It was Emma. She stood in the doorway, a slightly worried smile on her face and a notebook clutched to her breast. 'I hope it's not too late but I have the information you wanted. I have some other information, too.'

Holding onto Millie's collar, Mary opened the door wider and ushered her in. Millie seemed to recognize Emma as a friend as she soon quit barking and started wagging her stump of a tail. Mary let her go, making sure the door was securely closed, and motioned Emma into the living room.

She clicked the TV off and pointed toward the dining-room table. 'That was quick. You got both lists?'

Emma nodded, took the chair Mary indicated and set the notebook on the table. 'My uncle gets things done when he wants to. He got these sent out to me right away.' She grinned at Mary. 'He said if you wanted them there was a reason and it probably was a good one. His only stipulation was if you came up with anything, you needed to share it with me right away and I was to let him know immediately.'

Mary nodded and smiled but, inwardly, she seethed. If one more person told her she was to share information . . . why would they think she wouldn't? Did they think she was going to go after a murderer armed with nothing but Millie?

Emma pushed the folder across the table toward Mary. 'Here are the names and locations of all the stores and the dates of the break-ins. I also had him send us descriptions of the jewelry missing. It's long but mostly says the same thing. Fifteen gold wedding bands, eighteen gold-link bracelets, that kind of thing. It's only the larger, more important pieces that have any detailed description. Like the estate jewelry pieces.'

There was a peculiar look on Emma's face and a certain tone in her voice that brought Mary's head up to stare at her.

'Estate pieces? The kind that would have rose-cut diamonds?'

Emma nodded. 'One brooch had two matching rose-cut diamonds. Another piece, from another store, had a large and very beautiful sapphire. The pendant it was in was over a hundred years old.'

Mary formed a soft, 'Oh.' That was about all she could say as she stared at Emma. 'So how . . .'

'I don't know. But my uncle told me one thing. Mo Black called Ian Miller a couple of months ago. They had kept in touch all these years. They weren't close friends but evidently Ian thought Mo had gotten a raw deal, that Eric Wilson had had it in for him and used the robbery of Lowell's store to get him. That's what started the rift between Wilson and Miller. Anyway, Mo called Miller, told him he had reason to believe someone in our town was receiving stolen jewelry and asked if they'd had any recent large jewelry thefts. Miller wanted details but Mo was vague. Just said he thought there was something going on in a business here that smelled to high heaven and he thought Miller should take a look. According to my uncle, Miller came to him. Wanted to know if he should follow up. He believed Mo, said he'd been a good agent and if he had a lead on something it was probably worth following. My uncle agreed. They also agreed not to say anything. They really didn't know much. Mo hadn't said what business or what exactly he suspected. Miller came over here just before the Fourth to talk to him, to find out more. We figure he found out a lot more and ended up dead.'

Thoughts, things people had said and done, rushed at Mary, filling her head. Mo had apologized to Marlene and said he was sorry. She'd known what he was talking about. Had she also known Mo was going to call in the cops? Maybe. She'd decided to divorce Jerry. He had a history of being dishonest. Petty things – trying to cheat the insurance company, pilfering things from their . . . her . . . jewelry shop. But things hadn't got better. Jerry had got involved with . . . what? Liquidating stolen jewelry? How much had Marlene known or suspected?

Emma's voice cut through the thoughts bombarding her. 'Everyone is in an uproar. Our auditor confirms there was a whole lot of jewelry in that bag Jerry had put aside for Heath to take to the smelter. About half of it wasn't on the list he'd given to the police. If any of it matches the list of stolen pieces, well, it's pretty certain Jerry was dealing in stolen jewelry. Wilson is on his way down to LA to talk to the smelter. He's sure Mo and David committed the robberies and Jerry was turning it into cash. Or gold bars or coins. Dan's out at Marlene's right now, talking to her. My uncle's been on the phone with Mo and I think he wants him to come to Sacramento. Or he might send someone down here. He sure doesn't want Wilson talking to him. I think we need to explore the Gradys.'

Mary started. The Gradys. Could they . . . she didn't see how. They traveled, that much was true. They owned the We Buy Gold shop but they had nothing to do with running it.

From what she'd heard, the only thing Heath did was pick up the jewelry that went to the smelter. Did he check the books? He must have. Heath wasn't the kind of person to trust someone else. Had Jerry set up some kind of false bookkeeping system? One good enough to fool Heath? Mary knew nothing about bookkeeping. She kept her checkbook balanced to the penny but someone else did her taxes and that was all she required. What kind of books a shop like We Buy Gold had she couldn't imagine.

It was almost as if Emma had read her mind. 'Heath Grady is already screaming and yelling. Dan called him in about an hour ago. He wants to go through the shop's books, their records. Heath can't stop him. Their business license states they have to turn over their receipts to the police if asked. Hasn't stopped Heath from calling Jerry every name in the book. Says his reputation is on the line and if that SOB was cheating, if he had anything to do with stolen goods, he'll dig him up and beat him to a pulp.'

She stopped and a shadow of a grin appeared. 'He sounds like he means it. But something was going on in that shop. My uncle is sending down a whole team of accountant types to go through the records and see if they can come up with something.'

Mary nodded. 'Sounds like Heath. He can be as explosive as one of their fireworks.' She thought about fireworks. About the Fourth of July. About the Gradys getting ready to load their equipment into their paneled van, about the painted firework displays all over that van. 'What does Dan think?'

'About what? The Gradys?'

Mary nodded.

'Nothing.'

'Has he mentioned the white-paneled van?'

'The one that was evidently spotted at a couple of the robberies? No. Those vans are a dime a dozen. There's nothing to say it was the same van or that it had anything to do with either robbery.'

'There was a white-paneled van coming out of the alley right about the time Jerry was shot. They may be all over but I don't know anyone in town who has one, or at least an unmarked one.'

Emma stared at her for a moment. 'How do you know that?'

'Luke was walking by and he saw it. He remembered because he doesn't know anyone who owns an unmarked one either and wondered whose it was.'

'Who's Luke?' Puzzlement showed on Emma's face. So did interest.

'He's the head librarian. He'd walked over to Mo's to drop off his fiancée's laptop and was going back to the library.' She almost smiled at the look of incredulity on Emma's face. 'He didn't see who was driving it and says he didn't notice if the gold shop's closed sign was up or not. He didn't hear Marlene scream, didn't know anything had happened until he heard the sirens and all the police showed up.'

Emma started to shake her head, first slowly, then a little faster. 'I didn't believe him, but he was right. He doesn't need a detective on staff. How do you do it?'

'Do what?'

Emma pushed back her chair and stood. She smiled and shook her head once more. 'Never mind. I'll deliver this little piece of information to Dan and then I think I'll have a talk with Luke. Who else should I talk to?'

Mary thought. 'Well, Glen Manning, at the bank, might be able to tell you something about Jerry's finances.'

'We'll need a court order, but the accountant types will handle that. What else?'

'Have you found out anything about why Wilson was in town several weeks ago and never mentioned it?'

'No.'

That was a reflective no, Mary thought.

'I told my uncle and asked if I should push the issue. He said he'd take care of it. But what I think . . .' Emma paused.

Mary waited, hoping she'd go on.

She did. 'I think he somehow found out about Mo's phone call to Ian Miller. There may have been an email. The computer geeks are trying to break into his computer right now. It's Miller's personal computer, not one of ours, and it's proving harder than they thought. I think Wilson might have managed, though. I wouldn't put it past him to snoop through Miller's desk and eavesdrop on his cell calls. They had adjoining desks.

Finding out Ian's passwords wouldn't have been that hard. Wilson's been jealous of Miller for years and would have liked nothing better than to solve the mysterious jewelry store robberies before Miller could. If he could have gotten the arrest it would have made him a happy man. He's staring retirement in the face and his hasn't been a notable career. Collaring whoever is doing this and finding the jewelry would have sent him out with a high profile. He'd have loved that.'

Mary's breath caught in her throat. 'You really believe Eric Wilson would do something like that? To his partner?' But even as she said it, she could believe it, too.

'It would explain what he was doing in town.'

'Trying to find out what was going on at the We Buy Gold shop?'

'Trying to find out what store in town Miller was investigating. It wasn't much of a leap to connect either We Buy Gold or Lowell's Jewelry. He was probably also looking to see if he could hang anything on Mo Black. Wilson holds a grudge and he never quite forgave Mo for not being guilty of helping to rob the Sacramento Lowell's store.'

'He's not going to find anything on him this time either. If Mo Black was in league with Jerry Lowell to rob jewelry stores and liquidate what they stole, he wouldn't have called Ian Miller and alerted him to the fact.'

Emma nodded. 'I thought about that and so did Dan. But try to convince Wilson. We can only do our best to keep him away from Mo Black until we figure out who actually killed both Miller and Lowell.'

Mary thought about that. 'Do you think anything he did could have contributed to Miller's death?'

Emma shrugged. Her eyes glistened suspiciously and there was a catch in her breath. 'I don't know but he could have stirred the pot.'

She turned to go but Mary stopped her with one more question. 'Emma, if Mo Black isn't responsible for the robberies and the Gradys aren't and Jerry Lowell isn't, who is? And who else would want to murder either Ian Miller or Jerry Lowell?'

'I don't know who committed the robberies. Whoever they

are, they're clever and certainly professional. But we don't know they're the ones who killed Miller and Lowell.'

'What other reason would anyone else have?'

'Oh, I can think of a couple.' Emma's voice sounded tired and unhappy.

With, Mary thought as she listened, good reason.

'Jerry wasn't an honest man. Marlene was sick of it and worried what his continued pilfering, or worse, would do to her reputation and the reputation of her store. She knew he was into something again and this time she was worried that he was in over his head. Shooting him may have been a solution.'

'But she was going to divorce him.' Mary's stomach twisted. She didn't want to think Marlene could be capable of such a thing.

'Divorce would have been messy. It could have exposed whatever Jerry was mixed up in.' She stopped for a moment and her voice was even sadder when she went on: 'Or Tommy could have discovered what his father was doing. He could have uncovered where the gems he used in that necklace really came from and why his father had a fit when he used them. He might have thought both he and his mother were better off if his father was dead.'

'But why shoot Miller?'

'Miller was getting too close to what Jerry was doing. You heard Mo Black. That apology could very well have been because he started this whole chain by calling Miller and alerting him that something wasn't right.'

The knot in Mary's stomach tightened. She couldn't believe either of those two would . . . but she didn't really know them. However . . . 'Then who robbed the stores?'

'I have no idea. And, Mary, I didn't say either Tommy or his mother did do this. Just that we can't rule them out. Like we can't rule out the driver of the white-paneled van, whoever he is. We can't even rule out Mo. Right now, we can't rule out anyone. So . . .' Her smile was more like a grimace but her shoulders straightened and she slung her bag over her shoulder with obvious purpose and resumed her usual brisk attitude. 'I'll go find Luke, see what he has to say and keep poking around. If your vague idea bears fruit, let me know. See you later.'

Somehow *Masterpiece Mystery* had lost all of its appeal. Mary had her own mystery and solving it wasn't proving to be fun. The thought of Tommy Lowell shooting Ian Miller in the back was almost more than she could bear. Or Marlene, for that matter. She thought about it. Not only could she not bear to think about it, she couldn't picture it. Although she'd never seen Marlene lose her temper, she might have with Jerry and hit him with something. It didn't seem likely, but not impossible. Shoot him, though?

Although it hadn't been proven conclusively, she was certain whoever shot Jerry had also shot Miller. The motive for either Marlene or Tommy killing Miller sounded thin to her, but shooting him in the back sounded farfetched. She couldn't prove that either. At least, not yet. She didn't think Mo Black or his nephew were guilty. She was certain whoever was robbing those jewelry stores killed both men, only who was robbing the stores?

She looked at the clock. Eleven. How had it gotten so late? She got up, stretched and looked around. Where was Millie? She called her name but no small black body appeared. Had she let her out and not let her back in? She walked into the kitchen, half expecting to hear scratching at the back door but all was quiet. The light over the back door showed an empty yard. Starting to feel anxious, Mary walked back through the living room, searching every corner. No Millie. Could she be asleep under her desk? A brief glance into what was now her office showed no sign of the dog. Her bedroom door was slightly ajar. She pushed it open and turned on the light. There was Millie in the middle of her bed, curled up in a ball and snoring lightly. Mary grinned, partly in relief. It was past their bedtime and Millie had evidently got tired of waiting for her. The dog had better sense than she had. She was solving nothing by sitting in her chair, trying to solve a puzzle that was quite obviously missing some of its pieces. Maybe she could find some of them, but not tonight. She, too, was going to bed.

# FORTY

**M**ary pushed back her chair and stretched. She'd been on the computer for over two hours and her back was killing her. If she was going to do this often, she would have to get a proper desk chair. This straight-backed kitchen chair was going to be the death of her.

'Are you in here?'

The voice was familiar. Millie was on her feet, heading for the living room, her whole rear end wagging.

'Morgan didn't come, Millie. Sorry. Next time.' Ellen walked into the office and stopped in the doorway. 'I've seen you in lots of strange outfits but this one is an all-time low. What have you been doing?'

'Trying to find a link between these robberies. There has to be a pattern somewhere but I sure can't find it. I think Ian Miller found it, though.' Mary looked at herself. What was Ellen talking about? She didn't look so strange. Perhaps the bright yellow gauze pants were a little . . . but she'd gotten them for a quarter at the rummage sale. The red and green floral sleeveless cotton shirt was a few sizes too big but the orange and purple sandals were cool and comfortable. They'd only been a dime.

'Why do you think Miller found a connection?' Ellen abandoned her aunt's choice of clothing, at least for the moment.

'He was shot.'

'You want to get shot, too?' Ellen leaned against the door frame and peered at her.

'Of course not.' Mary knew her tone was a little snappish but that was a silly question. 'There has to be a connection somewhere and I hoped, if I could find something, it might give us some idea as to who committed those robberies.'

'Some idea as to who shot poor Ian Miller and Jerry Lowell as well. Leave that up to Dan and the rest of the police, will you? You wouldn't look good with a bullet hole in you.'

'I guess I'll have to. On TV they can find almost anything in one of these.' She gestured toward her waiting computer which showed nothing but a sea coast someplace unidentifiable. 'Just a few key strokes and you've got all the information you need. I can't make this blasted thing give me the weather report.'

Ellen laughed and straightened up. 'It takes a while. I came to get you for lunch. We're meeting Dan at The Yum Yum. He says he needs sustenance if he's going to be able to continue to deal with all these people.'

'What people?'

'The suspects he has and the state police who are questioning them. The poor man is tearing out his hair. Go change into something a little . . .' Ellen stopped, looked Mary up and down and smiled, '. . . less bright and we'll go.'

Mary looked at the computer then back at Ellen. She should probably stay here and continue to . . . do what? She was getting nowhere and she suddenly realized she was hungry. A plate of Ruthie's tuna salad would revitalize her.

'Ten minutes,' she told Ellen.

The Yum Yum was, of course, packed. Someone stood and waved to them from the large back booth. Susannah. Neil was there. So were Pat and Karl and, of course, Dan.

'We've been waiting for you.' Pat moved over.

Mary slid in beside her, with Ellen next to Dan. 'Have you ordered?'

'We thought we'd wait until you got here. It's a good thing you came when you did. Ruthie was starting to glare at us.' Susannah blew her aunt a kiss then moved a little closer to Neil.

Mary sniffed the air and was glad they were sitting a few spaces from her. They both gave off a faint but definite odor of horse.

'You two been doing horse calls this morning?'

Susannah grinned at her. 'How can you tell?'

Ruthie appeared with a tray of glasses and started handing them around. 'You're all getting unsweetened tea. If you want it sweet, sugar's on the table. Lemon slices are on this dish.'

She indicated a small dish she sat in the middle of the table. 'Chef salad is the special. You ready?'

They were. Ruthie trotted off with their orders and they all began to bombard Dan with questions.

'I see Heath's van is outside the We Buy Gold shop. Have you let him back in?' Karl had to lean forward a little to make himself heard.

'That is the most garish van I think I've ever seen,' Pat remarked before Dan could answer.

'It's great advertising, though,' Ellen put in. 'You can't miss it.'

Dan grinned and leaned around Ellen to answer Karl. 'He's over there right now, going through the latest collection that was supposed to go to LA to the smelter. Seems there's a whole bunch of jewelry with paperwork that never made it to us. Heath is trying to explain how that happened.'

Karl usually didn't show much surprise. Mary supposed he'd learned that calm demeanor dealing with animal emergencies. He looked pretty surprised now. 'You think Jerry really was dealing in stolen jewelry?'

'I don't know if what he had was stolen but it certainly wasn't anything we ever saw paperwork for. Where he got it is something we need to find out.'

Dan had everyone's attention.

'Does that mean you think Heath might know something about it?'

'It doesn't appear that way. He says every time he's come to pick up a bag of jewelry to take to the smelter, all of the paperwork seemed absolutely in order. He has two other shops and is certainly familiar with the California state laws and what he needs to see. Jerry always had everything ready, showed him copies of all of the receipts with descriptions on them and copies of the verification by the sellers with required ID. He claims he never had a problem and never had any cause to be suspicious anything was wrong.'

The table fell silent.

Finally Ellen spoke. 'You believe him?'

'I have no reason not to.'

The expression on Karl's face was now more puzzlement

than disbelief. 'Who was Jerry Lowell working with? I doubt he did those robberies.'

There was caution in Dan's voice. 'Don't forget, we don't know the extra jewelry was from that string of robberies. We don't know whether the gems in the necklace Wilson was so interested in were from the stolen jewelry, either. Jerry could have been buying jewelry he wasn't sure about and didn't want to run it through the system.'

'Isn't there a lot of it? That's the way you made it sound.' Ellen broke off as Tina, one of Ruthie's new waitresses appeared, both arms loaded.

No one said anything as she distributed plates, smiled at them and left.

'This doesn't look like a chef salad.' The plate in front of Ellen held fish and chips.

'That's mine.' Karl frowned at his plate then looked around. 'Who ordered tuna?'

'I did.' Mary pushed her plate toward Dan. Pot roast and mashed potatoes couldn't belong to anyone else. It wasn't until they got all the plates in front of the right people that the conversation continued.

'Is that likely?' Neil took a bite of his fish taco and looked at Dan.

'That Jerry just wasn't claiming everything? It's not unlikely. Have I ruled out that he might have been liquidating jewelry from those robberies? No. I haven't. But I'm not coming up with a suspect, either.' He loaded his fork, took a bite and smiled before he went on. 'If Jerry was working with whoever did those robberies, I'm no closer to knowing who they are than I was before Miller came to town. It could be anyone.'

'Not really.' Neil laid down his fork and seemed to consider. 'It almost has to be either someone from around here or someone who comes frequently. The wineries bring in a lot of people but they don't usually come every couple of weeks.'

Dan nodded. 'True. But those robberies have been pretty spaced out and there's nothing to say whoever did them brought everything to Jerry at one time. The We Buy Gold shop is the only one of its kind in the county. Lots of people travel some distance to get here. No one would notice a stranger going in that shop.'

Mary took another forkful of tuna, wondering briefly what Ruthie put in it that made it better than hers. 'Luke noticed a white-paneled van leaving the day Jerry was shot.'

'Mom and Dan were talking about that last night. Dan said there was no real reason to connect them. White-paneled vans are as common as dirt.' Susannah picked up her last fish taco and put it on Neil's plate. He smiled.

'You don't think it's significant?' Mary twisted to get a better look at Dan's face.

He shrugged. 'We have no evidence to prove otherwise. We have no license plate, no identification on the van, no description of the driver, no reason to suppose the van that left when Jerry was killed was the same van someone saw in Arizona. Nothing except no one recognized it and we all think we know every car in town. We don't.'

'I don't know anyone who drives one.' Mary looked around at everyone, feeling a little defensive. She was certain that van was somehow connected. 'Do any of you?'

'Sure.' Neil wiped the last of Susannah's taco off his mouth. 'Tommy Lowell has one.'

It got quiet around the table as everyone stared at Neil.

Finally Dan spoke. The deliberate and soft tone of his voice said he had slipped back into police mode. 'Can you describe it?'

Neil seemed to find the sudden attention unnerving. His eyes got wide and any interest in what remained on his plate disappeared. 'It's a white-paneled van. Big front window and front side-passenger windows. No windows any place else. Fairly new – not the real tall ones, more the size of one of the large SUVs. Why?'

Dan didn't answer. 'How do you know he has one?'

Neil had gone from surprised to a little unnerved. 'He was in it the afternoon Jerry was killed.'

'Coming from where?'

'The south. He got off the freeway at the south end of town. Susannah and I were getting off at about the same time. We were coming from Murphy's Miniature Horse Farm. Remember, Sus? We commented on it.'

Susannah nodded. 'That was right before we saw all the commotion around the park and the police cars.'

'Did he see you? Wave at you, acknowledge you in any way?'

Neil and Susannah both shook their heads. 'I don't think he saw us, and frankly after we saw all that was going on I don't think either of us ever thought about him again.' Neil looked to Susannah for corroboration. She nodded.

The sinking feeling Mary had before was back. She couldn't believe Tommy Lowell was responsible for killing his father, nor did she think he had robbed anybody. She also didn't think that owning a paneled van proved anything. Dan had already said so. But it wouldn't hurt to remind him.

'Dan, you said yourself the world is full of white-paneled vans. That Tommy Lowell has one doesn't prove a thing.'

Pat, who had been largely silent on the question of murder and Tommy Lowell, chimed in. 'Ellen, didn't you say Tommy claimed to have been in Santa Barbara that day? That he got back in town to find his father already dead and the police all over the place? Doesn't the fact that Neil and Susannah saw him drive into town prove he was telling the truth?'

Dan dropped his napkin on the table and pushed back his chair. He looked around the table, his face troubled. 'Mary is right. That Tommy has a paneled van proves nothing, but that Neil and Susannah saw him come into town doesn't let him off the hook, either. He could easily have driven out a short way and driven back, making sure he saw someone he knew. All this does is earn him another visit from me.'

The tight way Dan held his shoulders and the distaste on his face spoke louder than any words that he didn't like what he was about to do. The thought that Tommy Lowell might have shot his father, and probably Ian Miller, destroyed what was left of any of their appetites. Plates were pushed away, the check collected and paid and, largely in silence, they went their separate ways.

# FORTY-ONE

'**W**hat's the matter with you?' John Lagomasino grabbed Millie as she was about to throw herself on Mary, whining and crying a greeting. 'You look like you just lost your best friend.'

'Not quite.' She sank down in the office chair behind the counter and let Millie crawl up in her lap, trying to protect her face from wet slobbery kisses. 'I was only gone an hour, you silly dog. Besides, you got to stay here with all your lizard friends.'

John laughed. 'I don't think the lizards are especially fond of her but the new batch of kittens we have seem to be. Curious, at least. Want to see them?'

'Not right now.' Somehow kittens, cute as they might be, weren't going to cure the depression that had settled over her.

'What's the matter?' John pulled a stool up in front of her and took both her hands. 'What's happened?'

'Tommy Lowell has a white-paneled van, that's what's happened.'

John dropped her hands, sat back a little and stared at her. His look plainly said he thought she'd gone crazy.

'What are you two doing?' Glen Manning set two white sandwich boxes on the counter next to the cash register and examined Mary with a worried look. 'What's happened?'

She must look worse than she thought. She'd changed into her blue seersucker pants and a fresh white cotton tunic before she went to lunch so she shouldn't look that bad. It was the worry over Tommy. That must be it. 'Tommy Lowell has a white-paneled van, that's what's the matter.'

Glen looked a little startled but not as if she'd gone crazy. 'Yes, I know. The bank carries the note for him.'

'It does?' Somehow that fact startled her out of her depression. 'How long has he had it?'

'I don't know. Almost since he came back from London but

he doesn't use it much. Drives that little Toyota of Marlene's mostly.'

'Why?' Mary wasn't sure why she felt a little better. The fact that Tommy didn't drive his paneled van much wasn't necessarily a good thing. Was it?

Glen shrugged. 'Why does it matter what Tommy Lowell drives?'

Mary took a deep breath and let it out slowly. She'd been taught that in her Silver Sneakers Yoga class. It lowered your blood pressure, which she was sure was at record highs, and steadied your nerves. If ever nerves needed steadying . . . 'I'm not sure it does. However, the only thing that seems to connect the jewelry store robberies and the murders, or at least the murder of Jerry Lowell, is the sighting of a white-paneled van.'

John gave a little gasp. Glen glanced at him then turned to Mary, guarded curiosity the only expression on his face. 'Go on.'

'There's not much to tell. Only that twice a white-paneled van was seen either parked near or right by the robbed stores and at about the time the robberies took place. But that was in two different states and there were no signs or any distinguishing marks on either van. Then Luke saw a white van leave the alley in back of Jerry Lowell's store the afternoon he was shot. Again, no identification on it and he didn't see the driver. But that's three times and that makes you wonder.'

'You mean it makes Dan wonder.' Glen looked around the store, which was empty, and sat on the counter.

'I'd wonder, too.' John got up, picked up Millie out of Mary's lap and set her on the floor. 'Go play with the kittens. You're going to put poor Mary's leg to sleep, lying on her that way.' He perched back on his stool and wiggled his fingers at Glen, who handed him a sandwich box. He opened it, picked up a half, took a bite and swallowed before going on. 'All these vans may or may not be connected but it's not too surprising they don't have any identifying signs or lettering. Most don't get painted any more. They buy those magnetic signs.'

Magnetic signs. Ellen had one. She didn't use it much,

just when she was showing property. Said she loved it because when she wanted a little privacy she could take it off. It was great advertising but there were times when she didn't want to advertise. When she and Dan were going someplace, for instance. Of course, most people who lived here knew her car, but it made her feel more private.

'Do the Lowells have a magnetic sign?' She knew the answer before either of the men spoke. She'd seen one on one of the cars in the Lowells' driveway the day after Jerry died. The day she'd taken them the lasagna. What had it said? Lowell's Custom Jewelry. It could be taken off and put on another car or just left in the garage. It could be put on a paneled van when you were trying to sell your custom jewelry and taken off when you didn't want anyone to know who you were. That thought made her a little sick.

'Who else in town has magnetic signs?'

John and Glen looked at each other. Glen shrugged.

John seemed to be thinking. 'Most of the realtors. Reliable Plumbing, a couple of the electricians, Perkins Appliance Store – a lot of people.'

'How do you know all this?' That John did know, she never doubted.

He also knew everyone in town and, unlike her, he was almost as bad a gossip as Agnes, and a lot more factual.

He smiled. 'One of the people who makes those signs is in our social group. We get together almost every weekend, unless we have a dog show or one of our bitches is ready to whelp. He told us about some of them. He's the one who did the Gradys' van. That was a very special custom job. You'd never know it wasn't painted, would you?'

For a moment, Mary thought she'd forgotten how to breathe. The Grady van wasn't painted. All those fireworks were magnetic signs. That meant they could come off. What else did it mean? Anything? Again, half the businesses in town used those signs. It didn't mean a thing. Except that, when they were off, the Gradys drove a white-paneled van.

'The Gradys' van? All those fireworks are signs? They can come off?'

John nodded. 'He did a great job, don't you think?'

Mary had to admit, whoever 'he' was, he'd done an outstanding job. 'Does Dan know this?'

Puzzled, John shook his head. 'I have no idea. He's probably never thought about it. You really can't tell the difference unless you're up close and . . . why?'

'Mary, you aren't thinking that the Gradys . . . Heath Grady is a reputable businessman. He works hard and keeps meticulous records. He's not a thief and he's certainly not a murderer. Why, that's . . . half the country drives white-paneled vans. It proves nothing.' Glen sounded not only defensive but almost angry.

Maybe he was right. He knew Heath a lot better than she did and, she had to admit, the few dealings she'd had with him had been excellent. He read his contract, abided by the terms and delivered what he said he would. She couldn't have asked for more. None of that sounded like someone who would rob jewelry stores. Or did it? Those robberies had been carefully planned and the disposal of the jewelry had been also. Would Heath really not have known Jerry Lowell was falsifying records and inserting stolen goods with legally bought gold? She didn't know. What she did know was a headache was coming on and she wanted to go home, take some Tylenol and put her feet up.

'I'm sure you're right,' she told Glen. 'I don't think Heath robbed or murdered anyone either. I have no idea what's going on but I'm glad Dan's looking into it. He'll figure it all out. In the meantime, I think Millie and I will go home. Thank you again for letting her stay.'

With repeated claims that Millie was welcome any time Mary wanted to drop her off, she started for home, but not to sit in her reading chair, sip tea and read. The computer was waiting for her, and the vague idea she'd had when she asked Emma for a list of stores and dates had crystalized. She had a date with her computer.

# FORTY-TWO

An hour later, she was convinced she knew who had committed the robberies, and if she was right, who had murdered both Ian Miller and Jerry Lowell. But she wasn't sure the evidence she could produce would convince the police. She thought Ian Miller had probably discovered the same pattern she had and had also wondered what to do. It was suggestive but by no means enough to convict someone. No more so than the fact someone owned a white-paneled van. But the suggestions were mounting up. She groaned aloud, leaned back and stared at the computer. What should she do now? Call Dan, of course. See what he thought. But the idea that she might be casting a shadow of doubt on someone who wasn't guilty hung over her. Should she look for more evidence before talking to Dan? No. That wasn't only silly but possibly dangerous. Someone had shot both Miller and Lowell. She didn't want to be the third corpse. Besides, where else could she look? No, she'd tell Dan what she'd learned and then it would be up to him.

Only Dan wasn't in. Agnes said so in a tone that seemed to end the subject.

'Agnes, where is he? I need to talk to him.'

'I have no idea. You know as well as I do, Mary McGill, that man never tells me anything. He and that rude policeman from Sacramento took off about an hour ago. I don't know where they went or when they're coming back.'

Agnes must mean he was with Eric Wilson. Were they questioning Marlene? Tommy? Talking to Mo Black? Or had something new come up? Frustrated, she tried to think what she should do next. Leave a message with someone? Not Agnes. She'd give Dan the message but she'd spend the next ten minutes trying to get information out of Mary about why she wanted to talk to Dan so badly. However . . .

'Agnes, who is there? Gary? Ricker? Who?'

'That cute Emma Baxter's here. She just got off the phone. You can talk to her if you want. Mary, I never thought I'd see the day when I'd say nice things about any Baxter, but this girl seems to have some sense. Her grandfather never did and her poor mother was so worn down she couldn't say boo to a goose. Why, one time . . .'

Emma. She'd talk to Emma. She managed to cut Agnes off when she paused briefly for a breath. 'Let me speak to Emma.'

With a sniff, but blessedly no more comments, Agnes transferred her.

'Emma Baxter.'

'Emma, this is Mary McGill. I've been talking to John and Glen at the pet store and they told me something, then I got on the computer and I think . . . I've maybe . . .' She was stumbling all over but she wasn't sure what to tell Emma. She wasn't sure she had anything real to tell her, but if she did . . . 'Can you come over?'

There was silence on the other end. 'You can't tell me on the phone?'

'I'd rather not. I need to show you. I'm not sure. Maybe I'm jumping to conclusions but I think I may have found what Ian Miller found. Can you come?'

There was no pause now. 'I'll be right there. I need to find a car.'

Mary didn't pause either. 'Millie and I will pick you up. We'll come now.'

Mary could hear a soft laugh. 'You must really think you've got something. I'll be waiting outside for you. Oh. I have Ranger. Is that all right?'

'Of course. Millie will be thrilled. Where's Tommy?'

'He had a meeting. Ranger wasn't invited.'

The phone went dead. Mary stood up, headed for her purse and car keys then stopped. Millie was rolled up in a ball, under her desk, sound asleep. 'We're going to get Ranger. Aren't you coming?'

Millie raised her head, saw the purse in Mary's hand and raced for the door.

# FORTY-THREE

'See what I mean? Every one of these robberies took place in a town where they were and within no less than two months of a performance. That can't be coincidence. Can it?'

Emma Baxter sat in Mary's chair, staring at the Grady Pyrotechnics website. She kept looking from the calendar of events on their site to the list of stores robbed. It showed the location and the date of each break-in. Everyone but one was within two months of a Grady Pyrotechnics show. That one was within three months.

'The Gradys should update their schedule more often. This list of past performances goes back over two years.'

Mary nodded. 'I imagine they want people to know how many they do or maybe so they can get references or something. The list of current bookings doesn't seem too heavy.'

Emma scrolled the calendar sideways to look at the dates blocked off. 'This goes up to the end of this year. They don't seem to be booked much. I wonder why. They put on a great show.'

'Maybe they don't need to.'

Emma's face had changed from interested to anxious. She ran her finger down the list of stores once again, compared the dates of the robberies with the dates the Gradys had been in that particular town and groaned. 'John was sure about the magnetic signs? Those aren't paintings on the Gradys' paneled van?'

'He's positive. He knows the man who did them.'

She looked almost sick. 'Then, Mary, we have a problem.'

Mary knew that but she began to wonder if they had another one she didn't know about. 'I know we do. Do you know where Dan went? I think we need to talk to him, don't you?'

'I don't know where they went and he's not answering his cell. We need to do something. Mary, Tommy is on his way to the Grady ranch right now. Heath Grady asked him to come out. He wanted to talk about the We Buy Gold shop.'

'Tommy went? Why?' Anxiety started to build. This didn't sound one bit good.

'He wanted to know if his father owned any of the shop or was just an employee. Jerry always acted as if he owned it and Tommy wanted to know where he and his mother stood. Heath sent Gabe to get him, saying they'd work it all out. I'd like to know what he means by that but I don't think it's anything good.'

'You think Tommy might be in danger?' Mary struggled with that. Why would Heath and Gabe want to hurt Tommy? He didn't have any more idea than they did what was going on. In fact, he didn't have as much.

Emma began slowly, as if she were trying to work out something in her mind. 'If Heath and Gabe really have been robbing those stores, and it sure looks likely, then they were the ones adding the stolen jewelry to the legitimate pieces. They had to falsify the records in some way, adding it to the inventory checked by the police department. I don't know how they did it but Heath knows Tommy has access to his father's bank account and to all the records in the jewelry store. If he thinks Tommy may come across something that can incriminate him . . .'

'Or he may try to offer Tommy the same deal he offered his father, whatever that was. If Tommy turns him down . . .'

'Not good either way. Let me try Tommy's cell. See where he is and try to warn him.'

'How are you going to do that with Heath and Gabe right there?'

'No idea, but I'll try.'

Mary watched while Emma tried to contact Tommy.

'He's not picking up.' Her worried expression intensified.

'Call Dan,' Mary instructed. It seemed to be the thing she always thought to do in an emergency. She wasn't sure this was one but she was sure they needed to talk to him.

Only Dan wasn't answering either.

She was so absorbed in wondering what to do next that she didn't notice someone had come in her back door until Morgan stood in the doorway, wagging his tail in greeting. Ranger was on his feet and so was Millie.

'What's Ranger doing here?' Ellen appeared behind Morgan, a smile on her face that died stillborn. She looked from Mary to Emma, then back. 'What's wrong?'

'We can't find Dan.'

'He and Wilson went someplace. Not sure where. Why? You both look stricken. What's happened?'

'We're not sure, but Tommy has gone out to the Grady place and we're worried about him.'

'Why would you . . . Oh, oh. What have you found out?'

'It may be nothing . . .' Mary broke off as Emma took over.

'It's definitely something. It won't stand up in court, at least not yet, but it's more than enough to take a hard second look at the Grady brothers and, if we're right, more than enough to be worried about Tommy.'

Ellen sat on the edge of the day bed in what was now Mary's office, her face a few shades paler than when she walked in. 'Tell me.'

They did. They showed her what Mary had found on the computer, the dates of the robberies compared to the visits the Gradys had made to the same towns, the magnetic signs and the fact they owned the We Buy Gold shop and had access to the inventory that went to the smelter.

'It isn't concrete proof,' Emma said, 'but it's enough to start looking at these guys a lot harder.'

'There's no time to look harder. Tommy is out there right now and we don't know why or what might happen. Dan's still not answering his cell?'

Emma shook her head. 'I left him a message. Told him to call me right away. Agnes doesn't know where they've gone either.'

'How about one of the other policemen? Weren't there some other special forces down here?' Ellen sounded more cautious than alarmed.

Not so Emma. 'I am the police. The only one left and I've made up my mind. I'm going after him.'

Mary sucked in her breath and Ellen let out a gasp. 'You can't do that.'

'Why not? I'm a sworn officer of the law and I feel a citizen might be in danger. It's my duty to do something.'

Mary and Ellen looked at each other. Put like that . . .

'You don't have a car.' Mary gulped a little as she spoke. Emma couldn't go alone and, from the look on her face, she was going, one way or another. 'You don't know where you're going either. I'll drive. They won't dare do anything if I'm there.'

'No. I don't think it's safe and I can't protect you and Tommy. I'll take Ranger and . . . maybe I can get a Santa Louisa police car.'

'Santa Louisa doesn't have that many cars and they're almost all black and whites.' Ellen looked at Mary with an almost helpless expression.

The set of Emma's jaw said she was going.

'Taking Ranger is a great idea but you still don't know where that ranch is. I do. I was on that ranch many times during the time we had it for sale. I'll go get Tommy.'

'No, you won't. Not only am I a police officer, that creep Gabe invited me out to the ranch. I'll just tell them I accepted his invitation and, while I'm there, I might as well give Tommy a lift back to town.'

Mary snorted. 'They'll believe that one, all right. No. We'll all go. They can't shoot us all and Tommy. We'll leave a message for Dan, tell him where we are, and then when we get back we'll give him all our information and see what he wants to do.' She turned to Emma. 'Do you have a badge and all that if we need it?'

Emma grinned. 'I have a badge, a small spray can of mace and a gun.'

Ellen swirled around to look her up and down. 'You have a gun? Where?'

Emma had on a pair of baggy khaki shorts, running shoes and an oversized T-shirt with UCLA Bruins and the bruin bear, the university mascot, emblazoned across the front. She barely seemed to move when a gun appeared in her hand. She grinned at the astonishment on both Mary and Ellen's faces. It disappeared again under her shirt. 'Women get special holsters and training in how to get to our guns fast. Let's just hope I don't need to use it.'

It was a hope Mary fervently shared. 'Ellen, call Dan and leave that message. I'm going to feel like an absolute fool if we get out there and find they've finished a nice friendly meeting and Gabe is on his way back to town with Tommy.'

'Maybe so but, for the first time in my life, I'd be delighted to feel like a fool.' Emma snapped the leash on Ranger.

Mary managed to get Millie's snapped on her harness then picked up her cell and slipped it into her purse.

'Morgan's leash is in the car.' Ellen watched her aunt and shook her head. 'Are you sure you want to take Millie?'

Mary reddened slightly but kept her voice neutral. 'Ranger and Morgan are going and I'm not going without her.' She half expected Ellen to suggest they both stay home and was ready to challenge that.

Ellen shrugged and led the way to her car.

# FORTY-FOUR

I t's beautiful out here.' Emma craned her neck, looking out of one window then another. Not an easy task as she sat in the middle of the back seat, Ranger sitting upright on one side and Morgan on the other.

'It is. All these beautiful oaks and pines. Right now it's dry. We haven't had rain in I don't know how long. I feel sorry for the cows. They don't have much grass left.' Mary had twisted a little in her seat to see Emma.

'It's still beautiful but it's a long way out of town. This is where my father and my uncles grew up?'

'Right down this road.' Ellen turned onto the dirt road by the old red barn. Right ahead of them was the gate that led into the Grady property. The gate was open.

'They must be here. This place is locked up tighter than a fortress when they're gone.'

'Should we close it?' Emma's voice sounded tight, as if suddenly she was on guard. The relaxed, interested quality had disappeared and the policewoman awareness had taken its place.

It was that, more than anything else, that tightened the knot in Mary's stomach. Why were they doing this? If she was right, Heath and Gabe Grady were dangerous. They could . . . but they wouldn't. That was why they'd all come. Safety in numbers and, in this case, that was true. The Gradys were nothing if not smart, and it wouldn't be smart to kill three women, one a policewoman, one the wife of the chief of police, and an old woman. They'd have to get rid of Tommy as well and the three dogs. They might get rid of them all but it wouldn't be anything more than ushering them off the property. That would be fine with Mary. She clutched Millie tighter.

The driveway, if you could call it that, made a slight turn and came out between two oaks onto the dirt-packed yard

Mary had visited before. The barn was on one side of the yard, the house straight ahead.

There was a sharp intake of breath from the backseat. 'Is that where my father grew up?'

Horror and shock were in Emma's voice. 'It's a shack. How could . . .'

'Not a shack.' Ellen brought the car to a stop and they all stared at the house. 'It's a house. It has bedrooms and . . . everything.' Her voice faded away as she looked through the driver's window at the empty front porch.

The screen door still hung by one hinge, the screen in shreds, keeping out nothing. The front door was pushed open, barely visible in the dim interior. There was no sign of life anywhere.

'It's just a little rundown, that's all.'

'A little? One push and the whole thing would fall down.'

Still clutching a wiggling Millie, Mary looked around. The pickup she'd seen the other day was parked under the lean-to that bordered the barn. The paneled van was nowhere to be seen. Where were the Gradys? Where was Tommy?

'We might as well get out.' Ellen opened her door then walked around to the back and let Morgan out. She held onto his leash tightly, keeping him closely by her side. For protection or because of his obvious interest in the ground squirrels that darted freely around the yard, Mary didn't know.

She also got out, making sure Millie was close beside her.

Emma slid over and exited by the other door. She let Ranger out but left her side door open. Ranger looked around and sniffed the air. The hair on the back of his neck stood up. A low rumble started in his throat. He seemed oblivious to the ground squirrels. Instead, his attention was glued on the barn door.

'What's the matter with Ranger?' Ellen looked at the dog, took a step back and pulled Morgan even closer to her side. She looked at the barn then at the house.

Mary thought she looked poised for flight.

'Ellen.' Emma didn't look any more relaxed and Ranger looked downright dangerous. 'Can you get cell phone service out here? I didn't realize how isolated this was.'

Ellen nodded. 'They put in a new tower about a year ago.'

The fact they weren't entirely cut off from the rest of the world didn't seem to make Emma feel better. 'I don't like this. Where is everybody? They must have heard us drive up.'

As if on cue, Gabe Grady strolled out of the barn, cowboy hat pushed back on his head, cigarette hanging out one side of his mouth. He looked them all over, especially Emma, and smiled. The smiled died as the rumble in Ranger's throat escalated.

'Well, this is a pleasant surprise. What brings you lovely ladies way out here?' He took the cigarette out of his mouth and flicked it away, never taking his eyes off the dog. 'What's the matter with him?' The smooth as butter tone in his voice hardened as he stared at the dog.

'He doesn't like hats.' Emma smiled, a little stiffly, Mary thought, but still, a smile. 'You invited me out to see where my father had lived and, since Ellen was coming out to . . .' she glanced at Ellen out of the corner of her eye, '. . . look at a piece of property, I thought I'd tag along.' She looked around, holding tightly to Ranger's leash. 'Tommy said you were bringing him out here so we thought we'd pick him up while we were here – save you a trip back to town.'

Gabe pushed his hat farther back on his head, keeping his eyes on Ranger, whose hair was standing straight up. 'That dog doesn't seem to like me much.'

'I told you. It's the hat.'

'Well, I'm not taking it off for some damn dog. Why don't you put him back in the car?'

It wasn't a question, nor was it a request. It was an order. Mary's breath caught in her throat. She didn't know Gabe very well but he'd always been pleasant, breezy and funny. This was a side she'd never seen and she didn't like it. Her grasp on Millie's leash tightened.

'He'll bark.' There was steel in Emma's voice. 'Where's Tommy?'

'In the barn with Heath. In our office. They're having a meeting and they're not done yet.' He smiled at them. At least, Mary thought he tried to but it looked more condescending than friendly. 'Why don't you ladies run along? I've got some business in town so I don't mind bringing ol' Tommy back one bit.'

'Why don't we ask Tommy before we leave? See if he's finished?' Ellen used her sweetest voice but her knuckles were white as she clutched Morgan's leash. She didn't really have to hang onto him that hard. He sat by her side calmly, unlike Ranger, who looked like he was ready to go on attack any minute. Millie paid no attention to any of them. Her total concentration was on a ground squirrel who got closer to the Gradys' front porch with every hop.

'You can't go in there.' Gabe took a step back and spread his legs, as if he could guard the barn door from them. Why? What was in the barn that he didn't want them to see? Or did he not want them to get to Tommy? Gabe took out another cigarette, lit it and threw the match on the ground. Ellen took a step to the left. Morgan got to his feet. Emma took a step to the right, Ranger tight beside her.

'Tommy. We're out here. Do you want a ride home?' Emma's voice rang out loudly in the otherwise still country air. She tried again. 'Tommy?'

One of the sliding doors of the barn was pushed back. Tommy appeared. 'Hey.' He shielded his eyes from the setting sun with his hand. 'What are you doing out here?' He took a better look. 'All of you. Mrs McGill, Mrs Dunham. I sure didn't expect to see . . . Hey, Ranger.'

Ranger's head came up, his ears pricked forward and, with a joyous yelp, he lunged toward Tommy, almost yanking Emma off her feet. At the same time, Millie evidently decided the ground squirrel was too close to the house and she, too, lunged but not at Tommy. She yanked the leash out of Mary's hand and ran toward the squirrel. Startled, the squirrel bypassed the van, leapt on the porch and headed for what it probably thought was safety. It ran through the loose screen into the Grady house, Millie hot on its heels, her leash flying after her, barking and yelping at full throttle.

'Millie, no!' Mary started after her at what she thought was a brisk trot.

Tommy was way ahead of her. He crossed the yard in a full gallop, Ranger happily running beside him and Emma still holding onto Ranger's leash, trying to keep up.

Tommy slowed down at the stairs, trying to avoid the cracked and broken steps. Ranger didn't bother with the stairs. He gave a gigantic leap, landed on the porch and crashed through what was left of the screen door. Emma, who'd let go of the leash, paused at the foot of the stairs, watching as Tommy disappeared behind the dog.

Ellen, Morgan and Mary all arrived at the same time, Morgan tugging at his leash, determined to catch up with Ranger. Or maybe he wanted his turn chasing the squirrel. Mary wasn't sure but she was sure she needed to retrieve Millie. She took hold of the railing and, careful of where she set her feet, started up the stairs.

'Shall we?' Ellen murmured to Emma.

'We'll never get a better chance.' Emma grabbed Mary's arm and almost lifted her up the last two stairs. 'Get in the house.'

Mary didn't pause to wonder why the urgency. She pushed what was left of the door aside and ran in, Ellen right behind her, trying to keep Morgan in control.

'You can't go in there!' Gabe sounded somewhere between fury and fright as he screamed at them. 'Keep out of my house.'

'What the hell is going on out there?' The voice roared louder than a lion with a thorn in its paw.

It was Heath. Mary could see the doorway to the barn through the front window of the house. He'd pushed both barn doors open and stood directly in front of the paneled van, his legs apart and hat pushed back, as Gabe had. The difference was he carried a long-barreled rifle. Mary had only enough time to see the scope on the barrel and wonder if it was the gun Dan was looking for when she felt someone grab her and pull her back.

'Why were you standing there? That idiot has a rifle. You could have been shot.'

Ellen looked more shaken than Mary could ever remember seeing her, and no wonder.

Heath had lifted the rifle to his shoulder, ready to shoot someone, and now Gabe came thundering into the room, shouting and waving his arms. 'Get out, get out!'

'So Heath can shoot us? I don't think so.' Emma had her own gun out and shoved it in Gabe's face. He was up against the wall before he knew what happened, Ranger in front of him, lips drawn back, ears flat, just waiting for someone to give him the OK to attack.

'Do you greet all your guests like this?' Emma's voice was filled with anger. 'Yelling, screaming and trying to shoot them? Or just the ones you think might arrest you for grand larceny and murder?'

Gabe looked from her to the dog and grew several shades whiter. 'I never murdered no one. I don't know what you're talking about. This is our property. No one invited you. Come on here with a gun and vicious dogs, a man's got a right to protect himself.' His voice had developed a little belligerence but he hadn't moved away from the wall.

'That's one of the dumbest arguments I've ever heard. We're here at your invitation. What do you have to hide, Gabe? What are you and Heath up to?'

Ranger still stood in front of Gabe, the hair on his back standing at attention, his lips pulled back to expose formidable-looking teeth. The rumble in his throat intensified. Gabe never took his eyes off him as he sputtered more protests at Emma.

Morgan and Millie ignored the little drama going on close to them. They had the ground squirrel cornered. It was as flat against the wall as Gabe and trembling almost as badly. Mary tore her attention away from Gabe and Ranger when Millie gave one sharp, threatening bark. She was crouched down, ready to attack.

Mary had never seen her dog look like that and was horrified. 'Millie, don't you dare!'

Gabe, Ranger and everything else momentarily forgotten, she grabbed Millie by the collar and picked her up. 'Oh, the poor thing.'

The squirrel saw his chance and ran. He might not have made it around Morgan but just then Tommy yelled out, 'Look at that!'

They all did.

Mary had taken no notice of the room. Things were happening so fast there hadn't been time. Now, she did. There was little furniture in what she supposed was intended to be the living room. Instead, it was full of electronic equipment. Computers, screens, copiers, fax machines and a whole lot of other things she didn't recognize. Except for one wall. It was taken up by a large commercial safe. It stuck out into the room, its weight making the already uncertain floor bow. It might not have taken up so much room when the door was closed but today it stood open, giving them all a clear view of its contents. Gold bars. A tray of gold coins. And another one piled high with gold jewelry. The contents of a smaller, shallower tray sparkled even in the dim light. Diamonds. A latticed crate, stuffed with shredded paper, sat on the floor, half filled with gold bars. The crate's top was clearly labeled, Fireworks. The Gradys were getting rid of the evidence.

Everyone stared at the safe.

*All that gold*, Ellen mouthed.

'From the robberies.' Emma's gun dropped from Gabe's head as she stared at the contents of the safe, then at the crate.

'I've seen a lot of gold,' Tommy said almost reverently, 'but never that much.'

Mary couldn't say a word. She just looked, her mouth slightly open.

Even the dogs looked. Millie had given up trying to escape Mary's arms when the squirrel disappeared and Morgan and Ranger seemed to be trying to figure out what held the humans so transfixed. No one noticed Gabe until he made a dash for the front door. He was down the front steps, yelling for Heath not to shoot, when they all turned to see nothing but an empty flapping screen.

'Damn and blast.' Emma ran for the door and was out on the porch as Gabe reached the van. He was in and the door slammed before Emma could yell, 'Stop or I'll shoot.'

The only response she got was the roar of the engine. The brake released with a jerk and Gabe headed for the barn. 'Get in the van!' he yelled at Heath, skidding to a halt.

The back of the van fishtailed on the packed dirt. Heath raised the rifle to his shoulder and got off a shot at the house. Emma, who was on the porch, threw herself back into the room, almost landing on Tommy, who was hanging onto Ranger. The dog was straining at the leash, determined to go after Gabe.

'For God's sake, don't go out there again. You'll get killed.'

'Not if I can help it.' Emma's voice was grim, her jaw rigid. 'Who has a cell phone? Call nine-one-one. Make sure your GPS is on so they can find us. Tell them to watch out for that van and hurry. Be sure to tell them the fireworks signs are gone. They're looking for a plain white-paneled van and a man armed with a rifle.'

Mary crept up to the window, standing to one side as she clutched a now-quiet Millie. The van, motor running, still sat in front of the barn. Emma was right. No firework images decorated the van's sides. When had they taken them off? Why was obvious. Wherever they were going, they didn't want to be noticed. She barely had time to wonder where that was when Heath came running out of the barn, still carrying the rifle and also a brown briefcase. He opened the cab door, threw in the case then turned and did something Mary couldn't see. The next thing she knew, the van was roaring through the yard and a ball of red fire was flying through the barn doors. She barely heard the pop over the louder ones from Emma's gun.

'What are you doing?' Tommy sounded breathless and terrified. 'You're going to get killed and then what will I do?'

'I'm trying to shoot out their tires but I missed.' She turned to Tommy and smiled. 'I may have gotten their gas tank, though. They won't like that much.'

'We won't like what Heath threw in that barn, either.' Ellen's voice was shaky and scared. 'I think it was a lit firework and now the barn's on fire.'

# FORTY-FIVE

They all stood on the front porch of the Grady house, staring at the barn. Ellen was right. It was on fire. At first, it was just a faint crackling, but within minutes – seconds – it took hold. Old grease, dried-out straw, wooden pallets that held piles of cardboard and plywood boxes, hundred-year-old boards that were the siding for the barn all made a perfect storm. Flames flickered then burst into life as they climbed up walls and embraced the boxes of fireworks.

'We've got to get out of here. That barn is going to go up any minute and there's not one thing to keep the house from going next. Everyone, get in the car.'

Ellen and Morgan were halfway down the steps. She looked back over her shoulder. 'I'll call nine-one-one again, but the rest of you, hurry up. Mary, where are you going?'

Mary was going back in the house to shut the safe door. Everyone was yelling at her but she'd heard safes were fireproof and if they could save any of the contents, well, that had to be a good thing. Some of the stolen jewelry was in that safe, she was sure, and that meant it was evidence. She shut the door with her hip, keeping a now-frantic Millie close to her chest, but swinging the wheel lock proved more difficult.

'I'll do that. Get yourself and Millie into the car, and hurry. Those fireworks are going to catch any minute and then we're going to have the biggest fireworks show this county has ever seen.'

Mary slid out of Tommy's way and headed for the front porch. She held Millie under one arm while trying to navigate the steps without putting her foot through one of the boards. Suddenly Millie was gone. Panic filled her, but once again, it was Tommy. He held Millie under one arm, had Mary by the other and they were on the ground. A loud whistle and popping noise stopped them. The sky lit up with a red and white blaze of color. Then another, this time blue and green. A loud groaning noise sounded through the increasing roar of the flames. One side of the new metal roof tilted.

'The rafters are on fire. They won't be able to hold that roof up much longer, then there'll be fireworks everywhere.' Tommy paused, staring open-mouthed at the barn.

Another groan announced one end of the metal roof had collapsed, the old struts burned through. Flames shot up through the empty space, followed by more fireworks. Rockets were shooting into the air, whistles and explosions preceding more bursts of fiery color. A blast of heat seemed to sear them and smoke was all around. Mary coughed, reached for the rear door of the car and almost fell as she was propelled from the back and pulled from the front. Millie landed in her lap and the door closed. The front door opened and the back of Tommy's head appeared. 'Drive.'

Ellen did.

Mary looked back in time to see one of the rockets, its nose still in flames, land on the roof of the house. Then another. Then a piece of one of the huge fireworks, its core still burning. The roof was ablaze before they'd cleared the gate.

Ellen had her cell phone pressed to her ear as she drove. She must have been talking to Dan. 'We're all fine. All the dogs are fine. We're heading back to town. The Gradys are someplace ahead of us. I don't think they'd try to get out the back way – the roads are too unpredictable. But the house and barn are in flames. Are the firetrucks on their way? There's a barley field next door to them that's been cut and is dry . . . Well, tell them to hurry. Yes. Aunt Mary was right, as usual. The Gradys had a safe full of gold bars and a lot of jewelry. I'll bet you anything some of it is going to match that stolen stuff.' There was a pause.

Mary could just hear a faint murmuring on the other end. Ellen held the phone away from her ear. The murmuring got louder.

'I'll tell you why we were out here later. Right now, I just want to hear sirens. Lots of them. Never mind. I hear them. What do you mean, you hope the GPS works? They don't need it. All they have to do is look up and follow the fireworks. And, Dan . . . oh my God.'

Ellen broke off and stared at the sky ahead of them. It, too, had suddenly erupted into flames. Bright red and blue flames, and the explosion that went with them rocked the car.

Ellen seemed to be battling the steering wheel to keep their car on the road but finally she got it under control, pulled over to the side and stopped. She sat, staring ahead, her hands still glued on the wheel. Then she gave a shaky little laugh. 'That must be the Gradys. Emma was right. She did hit their gas tank.'

# FORTY-SIX

They got there sooner than any of the emergency vehicles. Sirens sounded, but in the distance. The scene in front of them was eerily quiet. Just a white-paneled van wrapped around a telephone pole, the only sound that of the flames consuming it.

A man lay on the other side of the road, partially propped up by a fence post, bleeding from his head. His left arm had an unnatural bend in it and he seemed to be holding it in his lap. He barely focused on them when they approached.

'Gabe, are you all right? Are you burned? You don't look burned. But your arm . . .' Emma knelt next to him but he didn't seem aware of her.

His eyes stared out across the field but focused on nothing.

'There's almost no gas around here.' Tommy approached the car slowly, cautiously. It had gone up in flames but they seemed to be dying down. 'I think they lost most of their gas before they crashed. Good thing. There wouldn't have been much left of any of them if they'd had a full tank.'

'Where's Heath?' Ellen had a good grasp on Morgan's leash but he wasn't giving any evidence of wanting to do anything but get back in the car.

The smell of smoke, gasoline and blood were doing strange things to his sensitive nose and he wasn't happy. Ranger stood by Emma, seemingly oblivious to all the alien smells. Instead, he surveyed the surrounding countryside.

Millie trembled in Mary's arms.

Mary was doing a little trembling of her own. 'Is he all right? How badly is he hurt?'

'Don't know. His arm's broken but I'm not sure what else.' She also looked around. 'Has anyone seen Heath? He's not in the van, is he?'

Ellen was close enough now to see into the van's window. 'No. Thank goodness. I really wouldn't want to try to get too near this thing. The door's not closed all the way on this side. He must have been thrown out.'

'Or jumped out.' Mary thought Heath Grady's feeling of self-preservation was strong. If he'd seen an accident about to happen, or had noticed something wrong with the van, she was sure his first instinct would be to save himself. But he wasn't in sight. 'Can you see if Heath's rifle is still in there?'

'Mary, I can't tell and I really don't want to get closer. But if it's in there it will never fire another bullet. It looks as if everything in the cab is fried.'

Sirens were closer now. The first engine rounded the bend, saw them, slowed, waved and kept going. Then a second passed. The sirens screamed and so did Millie. Mary thought her head would explode from noise, anxiety and fear. Heath was around here somewhere, and if he was alive, and not too severely injured, probably dangerous. Why were all those engines passing them by? They needed help. They needed a firetruck and an ambulance.

They got both. A small tanker pulled over, turned off its siren but not the flashing lights and men began jumping off – men with foam canisters in their hands. They began spraying the van, the weeds it sat on and the telephone pole.

One of the EMTs knelt beside Gabe. 'Compound fracture – bad one. Almost certain concussion. Don't know what else, yet.' He slit the sleeve of Gabe's shirt on his good arm and put on a blood pressure cup. Gabe didn't seem to notice. 'We're going to have to give him something before we can move him. That arm's going to hurt like a—' He glanced at Mary and broke off.

She stood back, trying to keep out of the way, but stared from Gabe to the now-smoldering car, wondering where Heath was. She was in no doubt he was the dangerous one. He had been in the passenger seat when they left. Had he been thrown from the van somewhere back down the road?

A Highway Patrol car pulled up. Two patrolmen got out, two Mary had never seen before. She wondered how they had even found them. It was usually the sheriffs that patrolled this remote area.

'Only one person in the car?' The question was general, addressed to them all.

Emma reached into her pocket, pulled out her wallet and flipped to show her badge. 'The victim is a suspect in a series of robberies we've been investigating. His brother was in the van with him when they left. They're responsible for that.'

She pointed back toward the way they'd come. The sky that had been alive with color was filled with smoke. Bursts of fireworks still exploded but they seemed lower and almost without color against the gray smoke. As they watched, the first plumes of white smoke appeared. The firemen had found the well. Mary wondered if the house had gone up as well as the barn. It could hardly have escaped at least some damage. If they could keep the fire from spreading into the neighbor's barley field . . . She'd let the firemen worry about that. She was worried about something else. The sun was starting to set. If Heath was hiding in the underbrush lining the road, and there was plenty of it, he'd be able to cross one of the fields around here and possibly get away. If he had that rifle with him . . . She didn't want to think about that.

'Where's the brother?' One of the patrolmen looked at the van with a slightly sick expression on his face.

'Not in there.' Tommy was beside them. 'I managed to get close enough to see the cab was empty. The passenger door was open, though. I don't know where he is.'

The patrolmen looked at each other, evidently wondering what to do next, when a car came careening around the bend, came to an abrupt stop behind the firetruck and a familiar figure jumped out of the driver's side. Agent Wilson climbed out of the other.

'Hey, you can't . . .' The patrolman's sentence died away as he recognized the man now embracing one of the women.

Morgan wagged his tail, waiting impatiently for his turn to be hugged. He didn't have to wait long.

Then Dan got down to business. 'That's Gabe Grady. He's a suspect in a murder case. Make sure they know that when you get him to the ER. How is he?' This was addressed to the EMTs who now had Gabe on a gurney and were ready to lift him into the ambulance.

'Hey, Chief,' the older one said and grinned. 'He'll live. Not very comfortably for a while but he'll make it. We'll call ahead and have someone from our office meet us at the hospital.'

Dan nodded. 'Where's Heath?'

'No one knows,' Emma answered. 'We need to get a search party out here.'

'Now, listen here, Baxter. You can't be ordering up search parties, especially when you don't even know if these Grady boys are responsible for anything more serious than reckless driving.'

Eric Wilson stood a little away from Dan, who had one arm around Ellen and his other hand resting on Morgan's head. He looked at them with distaste and at Emma with even more.

Her response evidently wasn't what he'd expected. 'It's about time you got over your grudge against Mo Black, Eric. The Grady brothers are almost certainly the ones who robbed all those jewelry stores and killed both Ian Miller and Jerry Lowell. Miller was your partner. I'd think you'd want to capture the one who shot him.'

Wilson hissed in his breath but before he had a chance to respond the ambulance driver interrupted. 'We're ready to pull out. Can you people move to the side of the road?'

The van fire seemed to be out as well and the firemen were mopping up, putting their canisters back on their truck. With Wilson and Emma still glaring at each other, they moved over behind the ambulance. Slowly, it started to pull away. Mary thought she and Millie were the only ones watching it. Everyone else was busy arguing or watching the argument. Millie barked. Mary stiffened. A man was hiding in the grass on the other side of the board fence. She could clearly see him inching his way farther into the field. So could Millie. She growled. Mary gasped. Heath. Crawling on his belly, dragging a brown case and the long rifle.

'There he is!'

The words escaped Mary before she had time to think. Heath stiffened at the sound of her voice, got to his feet and began to run. A large stand of oaks stood in the middle of the field. So did a herd of cows. Their heads went up to watch the running man.

'Stop.' Dan's voice rang out and the ambulance jerked to a halt. The firemen looked around, startled, and caught sight of the fleeing man.

'Hey,' one of them called. 'What's that guy doing?'

'Trying to get away,' Dan shouted back. He turned to the two troopers who stood, staring at Heath's rapidly disappearing back. 'Go after him.'

One of them drew his gun.

'Not like that. Run.'

'He's too far away.' Emma reached down and unsnapped the leash from Ranger's collar. The dog hadn't taken his eyes off Heath since he'd started to run and every muscle in the dog's frame was ready to move. 'Take him.'

That was all Ranger needed. With one bound, he was over the fence and after Heath. The cows watched with seeming amazement as the dog closed in on their man, but not as much as Mary.

'He's just like Rin Tin Tin,' she told Millie.

Heath looked over his shoulder and hesitated. The dog was rapidly closing ground. Emma had sprung over the fence and was outdistancing the patrolmen. Heath stopped and raised his rifle.

Mary held her breath. So did everyone else. She thought she heard a soft groan from Tommy but was too busy praying Heath wouldn't shoot to be sure.

'Do something,' Ellen implored Dan. 'Shoot him.'

'He's too far away.'

Heath's eye was glued to the scope and the rifle was aimed directly at the dog roaring toward him. Without conscious thought or planning, Mary screamed, 'Heath, look out behind you!'

Heath didn't look behind him but that one second of hesitation made the difference. Ranger gave a huge leap, landed squarely on Heath's chest and sent the gun flying. They both hit the ground with a huge wallop. Mary didn't know if he was unconscious or just winded but, either way, he wasn't getting up. Ranger stood on his chest, his snarling jaw just inches from Heath's throat. Emma paused only long enough to kick the rifle farther from Heath then pulled Ranger off, rolled Heath over and knelt down, putting her own gun to his head. The state troopers arrived, out of breath but with handcuffs, and it was over. They started to pull Heath to his feet but the ambulance crew was already halfway across the field with a stretcher and their gear. They examined a subdued and staggering Heath and pronounced him fit to walk, then they all started back across the field, watched carefully by the wary cows.

They weren't the only ones. Emma seemed almost as wary of them as she carried Heath's rifle suspended from a small branch she'd picked up and inserted through the trigger grip. Mary wondered if that was safe, but since the gun was evidence she assumed Emma had to do the best she could not to compromise it.

'That girl thinks on her feet,' Dan said.

'She's some woman.' Ellen sounded almost reverent.

'She doesn't follow orders.' The scowl on Wilson's face would have made the Grinch proud.

'What orders?' Dan's voice was mild but, from the look in his eyes, Mary knew he was fuming.

'I told her not to call in a search team.'

'She didn't. Instead she risked her life, and that of the dog, taking down a suspected murderer. I have every intention of arresting Heath Grady for the murders of Ian Miller and Jerry Lowell, as well as grand theft. Mo Black had nothing to do with it or the robberies and I'll make that clear to Casey Baxter when I talk to him, which will be soon. And I think Emma Baxter should get a commendation. So should Ranger.' He glared at Wilson then turned to Mary, who still clutched Mille. 'Arrange something.'

The anger in his voice shook her. 'Arrange what?'

'A ceremony of some kind. Give them the keys to the city.'

Emma smiled – the first Mary had seen in a long time. 'That won't be necessary but I do hope you'll say some nice things about me to my uncle.'

'Done.' Dan smiled as well but it didn't last long. He turned to the two highway patrol officers. 'Take him into town and deposit him at the station. They'll be expecting him. I'll be right behind you.'

'We can't do that,' one protested. 'We're still on duty here and . . .' His voice faded under Dan's glare.

'I'll clear it with your superior. Get moving.'

They did. Heath, the expression on his face every bit as furious as Dan's, was deposited in the back of their black and white car. They all watched as it drove off, the ambulance right behind it. The firemen quickly followed, but not before telling Dan a tow truck was on its way. They'd been in communication with the units dispatched to the Grady ranch and that fire was also almost out. The barn was a total loss, and the house wasn't much better, but the barley field had been saved. They waved as they drove away.

'Wilson and I are going back to the station. I want Emma to ride with us. Ellen, can you take Mary and the dogs all to our house? I have some questions for them but we don't need to do it at the station. It's almost dark, so follow me closely. I don't need you lost out here.'

Silently, Emma and Wilson got in Dan's car. Mary looked at the sky as she got into Ellen's, still holding Millie. Dan was right. It was dark. The sky no longer glowed with fireworks but a thin layer of smoke hung over the trees. You could smell it more than see it. There was still a faint glow back where the Grady ranch had been. The firetrucks that had put out the fire hadn't returned but the worst was over. She settled down in the passenger seat, Millie on her lap, and let her head rest on the back of the seat. Relief and exhaustion seemed to overwhelm her but something distracted her. Movement. She caught it out of the corner of her eye. The cows. What were they doing? She sat up straight and rolled down her window. They were standing in a circle, staring at something – she couldn't make out what. Suddenly one grabbed whatever it was and tossed it in the air. The cows all watched as it fell back to earth. Another picked it up with a toss of her head and flung it back up. Heath's cowboy hat. The cows were playing toss with his hat. She started to laugh as the car rolled down the road toward home.

# FORTY-SEVEN

The Dunhams' backyard seemed full of people. At least, it seemed that way to Mary. She sat in a chair with cushions, Millie on her lap, trying to balance a paper plate with a huge slab of pizza on it. She gave up, set it on the small table next to her and picked up her glass of wine. She was so tired that the wine threatened to put her to sleep before Dan could get here, but she'd take that chance. She didn't remember a time when she'd felt so exhausted.

Evidently everyone felt the same. Ranger and Morgan lay on the grass, watching the humans who weren't doing much moving either. Ellen had ordered pizza shortly after they'd arrived back, had set out a variety of drinks and paper plates and cups and told everyone to help themselves. People had been arriving and leaving, looking for Mary and Millie, wanting to know if they were all right and what had happened.

John, of course, knew about Gabe almost immediately upon his arrival at the hospital. He hadn't been called to scrub in on the operation scheduled to set his arm but he'd been told the details, which he was delighted to relay to the rest of them. Gabe did have a concussion, and also some second-degree burns, but nothing that wouldn't heal in time. The arm was going to be tricky. It was more smashed than broken, but with a couple of surgeries and a lot of therapy he should make a good recovery. How good his treatment would be in prison, he didn't know.

Glen wasn't with him. He was at the bank with the accountant types who had come down from Sacramento. They were going over the books for G&H Enterprises with a fine-tooth comb. Jerry Lowell's books were included. It seemed Jerry actually had been a partner in the We Buy Gold shop and had liberally mixed legal and illegal monies. Figuring it all out would take some time.

Mary listened to all this in silence. She couldn't imagine

what Tommy must be feeling. His father a willing partner in all those robberies then murdered by the Gradys. Why? Because they thought he was going to crack under the strain they might be discovered? Probably. What kind of man his father had turned out to be was a burden he'd always have to live with. Not an insurmountable one, but still . . . not easy. Thank goodness he had Ranger. She wondered what he'd do now. Stay in town? Go someplace else? What would Marlene do? Life wasn't going to be easy for either of them, not for a while.

'Tommy.'

He looked startled to hear his name but got up and came to her. 'Do you need something, Mrs McGill? Another piece of pizza? More wine?'

Mary wanted neither. She shook her head. 'Just to talk to you. Can you sit down?' She gestured toward the empty chair beside her.

Tommy pulled it out and sat. He looked guarded but showed no other emotion until Ranger came to stand beside him. His hand reached out for the dog and his knuckles showed white as he buried his fingers in the dog's fur. He waited.

Mary hesitated but only for a second. She knew Dan would ask Tommy the same question but, after all that had happened, she wasn't going to wait for the answer. 'Why did Heath want you to come out to the ranch?'

Tommy's head was turned away from her. He seemed to stare at the oak tree growing in the corner of Ellen and Dan's yard. Mary had to lean closer to him to hear his answer.

'He wanted me to buy him and Gabe out of their share of the We Buy Gold shop. He said they were getting out of the business and he'd make me a good deal.'

'Did he say they were leaving the area?'

'No. Just that they wanted to do something else and were selling all the shops.' Tommy paused and the expression on his face tightened. So did his hand on Ranger's fur. 'He said my dad cheated him and getting himself killed was the last straw. They wanted out and it was my responsibility to take it over.'

'Yes.' Sympathy for Tommy filled her. How awful to have that thrown in his face after everything else, but this wasn't the time to try to offer comfort. She needed . . . wanted . . . information. 'Did he say anything about the van? Were they loading it when you got there?'

Tommy nodded. 'The back door was open when I got there. All I saw were crates like the one that was on the floor of the house. They were marked "Fireworks." Heath mumbled something about loading up for a show then closed the doors. We went into his office and I was trying to understand what he wanted me to do when you all drove up.'

Mary wondered what would have happened if they hadn't driven out there. She didn't think Tommy had been in any real danger. He hadn't seen what was in those crates, had no reason to think they weren't fireworks and would never have been let near the house. They probably would have made some kind of deal with him and returned him safely back to town. She would never know.

The sliding door to the dining room opened. Emma walked onto the patio, Marlene and Mo Black behind her. Dan came out last, his hat in his hand. He glanced at Ranger, stepped back in the house and set the hat on the dining-room table.

'It's about time,' Ellen said. 'We were getting worried.'

Dan sighed. 'There's been a lot to sort through and we're not finished yet. Is that pizza?'

'What there is left. We've had a parade of people in and out of here for the last couple of hours all wanting to know what happened.'

'I'm glad you saved some. I'm starved. Emma, come get a piece.' He headed for the pizza box.

Emma ignored the offer and pulled a chair up next to Tommy and Ranger.

Marlene didn't bother with chairs. She went to Tommy, bent down and gave him a huge hug. 'I can't tell you how worried I've been. You could have been killed as well.'

'They didn't want to kill Tommy. They wanted money from him.' Was that remorse in Emma's voice? Had she, too, realized Tommy might have been safer if they hadn't ridden to his rescue?

Mary thought so but she said nothing.

There was no remorse in the way Emma looked at Tommy,

nor was there any in the way he looked back at her. Maybe
. . . but Dan was talking and all thoughts of a budding romance
left Mary's head.

'We've found out quite a lot.' Dan put the crust of his pizza
on a paper plate and addressed them all. 'First, Heath and
Gabe had no intention of leaving town, not until the three
musketeers here decided to ride to the rescue.' The look he
gave Mary and Millie had more resignation in it than anger
but he made it clear he still wasn't happy. 'I know all about
the ground squirrel and what you found in the house, but Heath
wouldn't have burned down the barn if you hadn't found the
open safe. The Gradys had rented a storage unit under another
name and were in the process of moving all the remaining
jewelry and gold bars into it. Miller, thanks to Mo Black, who
put him on the trail, had gotten too close and Jerry was falling
apart. They needed to remove anything that could tie them to
the robberies, and that included things like extra declaration
forms from people selling items through the We Buy Gold
shop.' He turned to Mary with just a hint of a smile. 'You put
your fingerprint on one too many forms. Heath would have
used it to create a whole inventory of items you sold to the
shop that you never laid eyes on.'

Mary gasped.

So did Marlene. 'Is that how they did it? Oh, Mary, I'm so
sorry.' She looked as if she was about to burst into tears.

Mo reached for her hand. 'It wasn't your fault. You did the
right thing. You couldn't have done anything more.'

She blinked rapidly then looked over at Tommy then back
at Mo. 'So did you. You've been blaming yourself for Ian
Miller's death but you shouldn't. You, also, did the right thing.'

'Sometimes the right thing can be painful.' Mo's words
were so low Mary had to strain to hear them.

She had to agree.

'They weren't going to a storage unit when they tore out
of that yard. Heath had some kind of briefcase with him and
he deliberately burned down that barn. Why?' Ellen had moved
her chair around so she faced Dan and the frown on her face
showed that she, at least, didn't think all the questions had
been answered.

'According to Gabe, Heath was getting worried. That's why he shot Jerry. They'd had a series of arguments with him. Jerry wanted out. Heath kept saying not quite yet. But he put together an emergency escape kit. Bank books, passports, charge cards in fake names, the key to the storage unit and a key to some-place else we haven't determined yet, all in that briefcase. That office was full of records Heath couldn't afford to have anyone see, so his last task before getting out was to burn it down.'

Quiet descended as they all thought about all that had happened. Finally, Dan asked one more question. He turned to Mary. 'How did you make the connection between the robberies and the Gradys? We looked at them but never came up with anything. Their bank account showed exactly what it should. According to recorded sales, they weren't in any of those towns when the robberies occurred that we could deter-mine . . . What made you think it was them?'

Mary thought back. 'A number of small things. The Gradys seemed to know Jerry pretty well but there didn't seem any basis for a friendship. Jerry didn't have friends.' She glanced over at Marlene then went on. 'Everyone said Gabe loved electronic devices, like cell phones, computers, that kind of thing. Whoever robbed those stores had to know how to disable the alarms. I thought Gabe probably could do that. But those were just a couple of things. The one thing that got me thinking about them was they traveled to so many places with the fireworks – places they legitimately should be. I wondered if any of the robberies were committed in the same towns or near where they had put on their shows. Turned out all of them were. The robberies were never while the boys were in town but that would have been stupid. Heath isn't stupid. But they were all within a couple of months after the Gradys had left. Twenty-six is just too great a coincidence not to be taken seriously.' She stopped, sighed and turned to Mo Black. 'I think Miller found the same thing and came to the same conclusion. He said to me the morning of the murder that he'd heard of the Gradys. I didn't think anything of it at the time but later I got to wondering: why would he? Unless he went to a lot of fireworks shows or had some reason to put one on, he probably wouldn't have. He wasn't from here so there was no reason for him to know anything about them.' She sighed deeply and shook her head. 'I had a huge advantage over him. I know them. I knew what I was looking for. I think he was looking for anything, any festival, any celebration, anything those towns had in common. Fireworks shows came up. So did the Gradys.'

'I think you're right.' Mo's voice was soft and filled with sorrow. 'The Gradys lived in a town where I suspected something was going on with a gold resale shop. Not conclusive but worth following up on. Don't know what he found out but evidently more than the Gradys felt comfortable with.'

No one said anything. Finally Millie yawned.

So did Mary. 'I think it's time to go home. I'm exhausted and so is Millie. Could I talk one of you into giving us a ride?'

'We will.' Mo stood and stretched. 'It's almost eleven. I need to get Marlene home. It's been a rough week for her. We'll drop you off. Tommy, you coming?'

Tommy stood also, reached out his hand, took Emma's and pulled her to her feet. 'Are you going back to your hotel? We can drop you off.'

'We're not done yet. Emma's coming back to the station with me. I'll drop Mary off on our way there.' There were black rings under Dan's eyes. He looked like he was more in need of a nap than going back to work but that wasn't probably going to happen any time soon.

Mo turned from helping Marlene. 'Is that where Wilson is? At your police station? Is he trying to take Heath Grady apart?'

Dan grinned but it wasn't very mirthful. 'Wilson's on his way back to Sacramento. Seems Emma's uncle wanted a few words with him. I believe "early retirement" was mentioned.'

Mo's laugh was loud and truly mirthful. 'About time. Does that mean I won't have the pleasure of his company every few months?'

Mary frowned. 'I don't know how you can laugh. Why did your department let him harass you like that? Why did they let him push you out? The newspaper accounts I read all said you had nothing to do with the Lowell store attempted robbery.'

She stopped abruptly and heat ran up her face. How could

she have let that slip? That had to be a painful subject for both Mo and Marlene.

The laughter stopped. In his softest voice, Mo said, 'Newspapers don't always get things right. No one pushed me out of the Bureau. I quit.'

'You did?' Just one more surprise in a week with way too many of them. 'Why?'

'David. He'd had a rotten life with my brother and his wife. I was his last hope. And he was mine. We were all that was left of our family. My job wasn't exactly safe. The hours weren't predictable and I'd been thinking it was time for a change. So I made one. Wilson already had it in for me and my leaving seemed to fuel his fire. Seems I'd made an arrest he wanted and he never forgave me for that. When my brother pulled that stunt, Wilson took great joy in telling everyone, especially the newspapers, that I'd been eased out because I was under suspicion. Of course, he was reprimanded but . . . Anyway, I won't miss those little visits.'

'No. I'm sure you won't.' Mary looked at Mo and then at Marlene, who didn't look one bit surprised, then at Tommy, who seemed resigned. Mo Black was a good man. Maybe things would work out . . .

Dan said, 'Tommy, I almost forgot. Emma's uncle said they haven't been able to find a home for Ranger, so if we can keep him a few more days they'll try to figure something out.'

Tommy's face collapsed, his hand resting on Ranger's head as the dog pressed himself into his knee.

'I told him not to bother. I was pretty sure we already had a home for him. Was I right?'

'You mean . . .' Tommy's voice was guarded but hope was there as well.

'Was that before or after you told him you'd offered me a job and I took it?' Emma's tone was light but she kept her eyes on Tommy. Was that hope in her voice also?

'Why, I believe it was before. Wanted to give him the good news first.'

'You're saying you're both staying? Emma is going to stay here, in this town, and I get Ranger?'

'Seems that way.' Dan looked at Mary. 'You and Millie ready to go home?'

She looked at a beaming Tommy, a shyly smiling Emma, and Ranger, who sat between them. Mo and Marlene stood close together, arms almost touching, watching the young people, smiles on both of their faces.

'Seems as good a way to close out the day as I can think of.' She also smiled. 'It's going to be an interesting year.'